A SUPERNATURAL MYSTERY

BLINDSPOTS

DAVID SAKMYSTER

CHARADE
MEDIA

Copyright © 2024 by David Sakmyster

ISBN: 979-8-9876847-9-5

Cover art and design by J. Kent Holloway

Charade Media, LLC
www.charadebooks.com

ACKNOWLEDGMENTS

I'd like to thank my early readers: Amy, of course; Dad as always, giving you something a little more exciting to read when you're up at 5 in the morning; the incomparable Bill Rader, and the incredibly swift and insightful Daz Pulsford, and the brilliant writer Jeremy Robinson. Cheers to all, and thanks especially to Kent Holloway and Charade Media for bringing new life to one of my favorite books and opening the doors to finally offering a series.

And, of course, thanks to all of you—the readers!

BOOK ONE

STRANGERS

1

I n the dark, Monica Gilman reached for the gun, moving as slowly as she dared, praying the bed wouldn't creak, at least not enough to draw the attention of the intruder downstairs.

She kept the Smith & Wesson 9mm in the bedside drawer. After a moment of fumbling around notepads and papers, the TV remote, and a small bottle of sleeping pills, the gun settled into her hand like it belonged there. It was the same magic feeling she'd had in St. Cecilia's church five years ago when Paul had slipped the wedding ring on her finger. She had never taken it off, not even once, not even to clean it. It had been perfect, just like this gun, with its stainless-steel handle, cool at first, then warming to her touch, responding to her need.

Intimately familiar with the 9mm, she often slept with it beside her when Paul wasn't there, and its simple presence calmed her during his absence.

He was away a lot lately. And she was scared enough as it was. Alone in this house.

In her condition.

Paul had bought her the gun last year, and he had taken her to the shooting range every weekend for three months until she had felt comfortable with it. Loading, aiming, holding her breath, firing. Again and again, flinching with each recoil until it felt right. The 9mm magazine held twelve rounds, more than sufficient if she lost her focus and sent a few shots wide. "You never know," he had told her, "And I'll feel better knowing you're not defenseless if something should happen."

'Something.' What he didn't say was: *Like what happened to your mother.*

She pushed the avalanche of memories aside and tried to ignore the fear gnawing at her insides. She had to focus, remain in the present, grounded.

Reality. Were the noises downstairs *really* real? A response bubbled up in her thoughts, something her mother always used to say, the way she had always concluded Monica's favorite bedtime story. "Was that Velveteen Rabbit *really* real, Mama?" *Yes, he became really real.* Monica was a girl who was at once spoiled and adored, cherished, and protected. Loved fiercely, even more so because her parents knew Monica would be their only child; she was a miracle, appearing in defiance of a squadron of doctors who had assured them it was time to seek other options.

But in the end, she had let them down when it counted. And *that* was real, as real as any childhood fable.

Another sound jolted her back to the present. Someone was downstairs, maybe several someones, in the dark, moving about in the kitchen. Now into the living room. The floorboards creaked, whimpering under stealthy feet.

The alarm's been deactivated, Monica realized. *Or the wires were cut.* How did they get in? Did she forget to arm the system? No, not possible. It was the first thing she did whenever she came home—lock the door immediately, arm the system. She kept the downstairs windows locked all year round, and only when Paul was home did she feel safe enough to let in some air. The last thing she did every night, whether Paul was there or not, was to double-check the alarm. There was no way she had forgotten.

But someone was inside. Someone who knew the code—or had stolen it or managed to disable the system from the outside. She squeezed the gun's now-sweaty grip and slowly swung her legs over the bed, disentangling herself from the heavy cotton sheets.

Her heart thundered so hard she almost couldn't hear the sounds from downstairs—sounds already competing with the November wind, roused and defensive, as it rattled the windows and tugged at the shingles.

It was happening. *This was real. Real, real...* The nearest neighbor was five hundred yards away, and only four other houses were within a mile. Privacy. Isolation. Paul had bought her this house because it was precisely what she needed, but right then, she had never felt so scared.

She took a deep breath to settle her shaking hands, released the safety on the 9mm, and set her trembling feet onto the rug. *It won't happen to me*, she thought. *Mom wasn't ready. I am.* The first step was the hardest, willing her muscles to move, to actually get out of bed and step toward the door. Toward the hall. Toward danger.

Her feet rebelled. Why not stay, lock the bedroom door, barricade herself inside and call the police? She looked to the phone next to the digital clock, the blue numbers glowing the time: 2:23 a.m. Surely if the alarm was deactivated, the phone would be dead too—they shared the same line. Maybe the intruder—or intruders—had been spying on her, knew about her, her condition. Knew that she'd never be able to identify them. They could steal, assault... rape. Anything, and she'd be powerless. Every nightmarish scenario played out in her brain's sadistic theater; there were things worse than death. At least death would be merciful. But for Paul to come back and find her assaulted and hysterical, locked in the bedroom, her mind in a panic—what would he do?

Probably what he should have done years ago. Have her committed.

She would not let that happen.

She ignored the phone. It was too late for the police. But maybe there was some small hope. If someone had cut the lines, the interruption in the alarm signal would have sent a warning pulse back to the monitoring station. Maybe the cops were coming after all. Maybe the intruders would flee if they heard the sirens.

Too many maybes. She had to act. As quietly as possible, she slipped out into the dark hallway. Inky-black shadows yawned before her, and a translucent blue light filtered up from the open space to her left, beyond the railing, looking down into the foyer and the dining room. A solid wall on her right proudly displayed framed pictures like war medals. She knew them all by heart—wedding photos, collages of their honeymoon on the deserted beach in Bermuda. Her vision quickly tugged back to the left, sensing some furtive movement below—a darker figure blending with the shadows, moving quickly toward the stairwell.

Coming upstairs.

Now it was real.

Monica steadied the gun with both hands, aiming at the top of the stairs. She inched forward, listening to muffled footfalls. *Should have bought a dog,* she thought, amused at the sudden notion of something so simple and practical, and angry with herself for not thinking of it before. If she survived the next few minutes, survived this night, that's exactly what she'd do. Tomorrow morning, in fact—get up and find the perfect watchdog, some cute but deadly furball with teeth, something to curl up with in her king-size bed, to snuggle with her—and to scare off any foolish intruders.

But if she really meant to buy one, that would mean leaving the house. Going out there. With them...

She took a step back toward the bedroom and slipped into a deeper shadow. She knew she'd now be almost invisible to whoever emerged at the top of those stairs—whoever it was that seemed to be coming toward her with deliberate knowledge, seeking her out. Confident in his steps, sure of her location.

Steadying the gun with both hands, she held her breath and waited. The darkness at the top of the stairs shifted and then parted, producing a darker, denser form.

One figure...so far. It paused on the top step as if aware of her presence. She heard breathing—shallow, rushed. Tense, perhaps scared. Or just excited by the things he was contemplating, approaching her bedroom.

The 9mm's trigger felt inviting, softly yielding to her finger. If he took just one more step...any sudden motion...she would fire. Over the roaring in her temples, the house creaked and grunted as the winds shook out a last desperate warning. She listened closer but couldn't make out any other sounds from downstairs. No creaks, no footfalls.

Hopefully, this meant the intruder was alone. Should she call out? Warn him she was armed? At best, if she surprised him and he turned and ran, that might only save her for tonight. He'd be back—whoever he was. Paul would be gone another two nights. She couldn't stay awake and alert forever. And...

And she had had enough. Enough of living in fear.

The intruder took another step. The floor groaned and sagged under his weight. He hunched his shoulders, and the darkness about his body swirled.

But the wavering blue light from downstairs avoided his face, and instead the shadows moved in and coalesced, enhancing his impenetrable mask.

Something scuffled...a hand scraping against the wall, feeling for something. Monica's finger tightened, the trigger moving halfway, the hammer pulling back. Her blood roared, seething through her veins, pounding rhythmically in her throat; her head felt airy, detached.

Something clicked. White light exploded like a supernova, and she only barely registered the figure on the stairs—a large man dressed in black sweatpants and a t-shirt. A baseball cap on backwards.

He stepped forward and, in the dazzling light, his hands looked huge, his fingers as long as talons. His mouth opened, words came out as frantic gibberish, something…

…something lost in Monica's scream.

She saw his face, or rather, the lack of one. Above his neck, nothing but a blur, a swirling mass of indescribable features, a miasma of shape and texture that defied comprehension.

She fired.

Steady, deliberate. Holding firm against the recoil.

Again.

The blasts were swallowed up by her escalating scream.

The faceless intruder jerked back after each impact, then lurched two steps ahead. Splotches of red blossomed on his chest and stomach, and still he came forward.

She fired again, just as her scream died.

And she heard him speak. A single word. Forced out in a choked exhalation before he staggered the last few steps and collapsed onto his knees right in front of her, just before she fired one last time…directly into the swirling kaleidoscope of his face.

"Monica…"

Blood and brains and bits of his skull blasted out and spurted onto the white rug. Finally, after wobbling unsteadily on his knees, the intruder collapsed onto his back. His legs straightened and continued twitching too long, far too long without a brain, or much of a head left to command them. The air smelled of sulfur and the retching pall of death.

Monica gagged, dropped the gun, and stumbled to the balcony where she vomited over the railing, a long dribbling stream that clung stubbornly to her chin. For an instant, she thought of her father, how he had left the example of an easy way out, and she thought about jumping... but then, quickly, before she could take a breath and clear her throat, she reached back down and snatched up the gun, again pointing it at the fallen intruder, expecting him to rise at any second. Then she spun and aimed at the stairs, then between bars of the railing, down into the foyer.

She listened. To the wind, to the creaking windows and the crackling trees, and then to the tomb-like silence inside her house. Returning her aim to the dead man, she backed into her bedroom and took her eyes away, only to snatch up the cordless phone with her free hand. She rushed back to the hall, hit TALK and held the shaking phone to her ear.

A dial tone chirped in her ear. At least that was something. This intruder wasn't as good as she had feared. She dialed 911.

An operator picked up on the second ring. "911 Operator. What's your emergency?"

"Hello?" She choked out the word.

"Is this... Mrs. Gilman?"

"Yes?" God bless technology and caller databases.

"You're calling from 96 Clarence Mills Drive?"

"Yes."

"Are you okay?"

She swallowed, eyeing the intruder, staring at the blood seeping into the carpet, staining the white fibers a thick, dark black. She looked at the man's face, at the unrecognizable features around the gore-streaked hole punched through his forehead, and she expected his face to suddenly revert to something familiar—like a werewolf changing back into human form after death.

"Mrs. Gilman?"

"Yes, yes. I'm okay," she whispered. "I... there was a man. A break-in." She took her eyes away and lowered the gun a few inches.

Her attention drifted to the pictures on the wall. The soothing, familiar images. Her wedding photo—those two people holding hands. Their whole lives ahead of them. Two people having found each other despite the odds, despite the obstacles —especially hers. Paul was so understanding, so noble. He was the one, the one she needed, the one she'd been searching for through so many lost years, the only one who could truly understand her. She smiled again at that picture, at those two people in love, and it calmed her, as if seeing them still on their rightful place on the wall was assurance enough that everything was going to be all right. This, what just happened, *was* real, but she had survived it. She was still here, still alive.

She looked at her hair in the picture: all pinned up and speckled with glitter, his cut short, and that cute five o'clock shadow on Paul's lip and chin. *Their faces—their faces…*

Unrecognizable. Blurry, indistinct.

A lump had lodged securely in her throat.

"Mrs. Gilman? Is the intruder still in the house?"

"Yes. But… he's dead. I shot him."

"Okay, just calm down. Is your husband home?"

"No, he's on a trip. Sacramento. Won't be back until Thursday night."

"We're sending a car. Don't move. Are you sure the intruder was alone?"

"I… I think so."

"We'll be there soon, Mrs. Gilman."

"Thank you. Stay with me, please."

"Of course. Do you know the intruder?"

Monica shook her head. She was glad the operator was still talking—it rooted her, settled her down like a cup of peppermint tea. She didn't want to be alone with her thoughts or with this corpse. "No, I don't think so. I…"

She frowned, noticing something. Just as she saw the scattered petals, and the tied stems that had been in the intruder's left hand, and she caught the scent of roses—pink, her favorite—

she saw a glint of something else. Something sparkling in the painful light.

"Mrs. Gilman?"

"Wait..." Suddenly woozy, her head spinning, she stepped forward on wobbling legs, and her eyes locked on one tiny object.

She bent down, gingerly reaching above the broken rose petals for his lifeless hand. And then she froze, choking on the abrupt fear, the certainty that he would suddenly spring to life, faking all this time until he could grasp her wrist, and then her throat.

But he didn't move. She slowly took his hand. Raised it to her face. Felt the familiar contours of his big fingers, the roughness of his palms. The tiny hairs, starting to turn gray around his knuckles. And then...

No, no, no. Don't let this be real. This can't be, it can't. Nothing can be this real.

She stared at the ring, at the unique platinum and titanium mix, at the Aztec-like design she had picked out herself. Five years ago.

Five years that had finally brought meaning to her never-ending struggle with a disorder that threatened, every day, to unravel her mind.

"No, God no..."

"Mrs. Gilman?"

The room spun in the opposite direction, then back again, and the floor started to melt away. The walls... those figures in the pictures on the walls... all those faceless men and women, scowling, snarling, laughing, mocking.

"I just killed my husband."

2

Jake Griffith fled across the dunes, flushed out of his meager hiding spot by the helicopter's relentless spotlight. The chopper dipped so low now that its whirling rotors roared in his ears, kicking up fierce sandstorms and hurling dust and twigs into his face as he scrambled from garage to shed to alleyway. Dogs barked at him, people inside their trailers shouted obscenities, and lights flickered as faces pressed to the windows.

He vaulted a rickety wooden fence, darted around another shed, and then ran for the cover of a back street lined with swaying palm trees.

Why did I run?

That question had been plaguing him for the past half hour. His only answer: he thought he had a chance. It was as simple as that. All the guards had been chatting near the bus while he and five other convicts were working the east side of I-5, picking up trash and beautifying the roads before the imminent plague of old folks arrived, descending on southern Florida like a horde of locusts.

Why did I run? Only another year and he would have been up for parole. And it wasn't as if he'd killed someone or robbed a bank or anything. He'd just been in the wrong place at the wrong time. On the beach, of all places. Selling a dime bag to someone he thought was a rich college kid on Spring Break. Instead, he had the bad luck to meet Joe Pearson of the State Police. Nice little sting operation they had going, and it nabbed poor Jake... during only his second week in the business.

Just his bad luck. Par for the course.

Why did I run? If not for that chopper, he might have had a chance, he could have been blending in with vacationers on Cocoa Beach right now, scraping together enough cash to strike out for South America—maybe Belize, which, to Jake, always seemed like a great out of the way place to start a new life. It wasn't like he'd miss the one here. And it wasn't like anyone would miss him.

He could have been well on his way, if not for that helicopter. Why the hell would they have a helicopter on hand just for a half-dozen harmless convicts out picking up trash? Probably just more of his signature luck—maybe a speed enforcement chopper that just happened to be in the neighborhood. It had found him in just under five minutes. He hadn't even had a chance to change and, in his adrenaline-fueled sprint across the poplar forests and bug-infested swamps, he had all but broadcast his position in his bright orange jumpsuit.

Like a starved bloodhound, the helicopter had picked up his scent and, for the past twenty minutes, it had tracked him mercilessly across the back roads of Cocoa Beach and now into Port Canaveral. The pilots must have called in the motorcycles as well —those Hells Angels cops capable of going anywhere he could.

Except maybe the ocean. That one thought kept him going. It was his only chance. Dive in and submerge. Then swim, swim for dear life, and let the waves and the tide and the night save his ass.

He dared a backwards glance, and in the murky, palm-shrouded twilight, three bouncing headlights danced upon the backs of hills.

All those hours in the prison gym were paying off now, but he was almost at the end of his race. Running on exhausted legs, his muscles screaming for rest, he seriously contemplated just giving himself up. *Right after this one last try,* he thought as he headed toward the crashing surf. In seconds, he cleared the brush and came upon a beach strewn with clumps of seaweed, empty Budweiser cans, and a few scraggly looking gulls feasting on a washed-up, eyeless grouper.

The bikes were still gaining, their motors howling. Ahead, the Atlantic stretched out into a violet-raspberry horizon while two freighters and a casino cruise ship lazily drifted off to sea. Toward the north stood the flickering red lights of Kennedy's launch platform, and Jake had a twinge of despair thinking of all the launches he had witnessed in the past, all the miraculous ascensions—how he loved just gazing at the rising vessels, wishing he could be among the crew, escaping the shackles of this world, escaping his bad luck and all its tragic conse-quences...

Bright headlights, bouncing from his right, stabbed at his eyes just as the helicopter's spotlight ensnared him from above. A jeep roared to a stop in front of him, skidding into the tide and blocking off his escape.

He slid, staggered, and then fell to his knees, trapped in the concentration of beams as the tide crashed into his weary legs and stung his face.

So close!

Behind him, the three bikes leapt over the dunes, bounded onto the beach and dug into the sand. He imagined laughter from under the helmets. They drove in circles around him as the tide pulled back, then cut their engines and leapt off their bikes, approaching in a semi-circle. The doors to the jeep opened and two more men in blue burst out.

Rooted in the helicopter's spotlight, Jake involuntarily raised his hands. He closed his eyes and imagined he had just set foot back on Earth, stepping off the Space Shuttle to cheers, flash-bulbs and raining confetti.

He could hear the voice yelling at him but couldn't make out the words until the chopper ascended and flew off into the night, its work done.

"…in deep shit now, son! Knew you were nothin' but a two-time loser."

Jake opened his eyes. Five guns were pointed at him. Three men still had their helmets on, and Jake focused on their shiny faceplates, the stabbing moon-like reflections beaming off their visors; he stared at those lights rather than glance at the faces of the two men from the jeeps.

"And to think, you almost made it to parole."

He recognized the voice of Officer Thomas Fenrik, his chief tormentor back at the Cocoa Community Correctional Facility. The hulking guard took immense delight in reminding Jake daily of his lot in life and acted as if it was his sacred privilege to psychologically abuse him whenever possible. Although lately, his taunts were having less than the intended effect.

"Sorry," Jake said, and paused to catch his breath. "Just thought you guys needed a little exercise."

"Oh," said Fenrik, "we'll be getting our exercise when you're back in detention. Away from the cameras, you'll wish you were never born."

Maybe I already do, Jake thought, and then winced, recalling a houseboat in the Everglades, a series of nightly beatings, abuse… and worse. *Nothing could top what I've already been through, asshole.*

The wind died down, and another surge of the Atlantic pounded his legs, almost protectively—as if trying to nudge away the men coming with handcuffs. Jake put his hands behind his back and tried not to look, but in the end, as always, he couldn't resist. Had to glimpse at each one in turn, like he did with everyone he met, every time. Search their faces, look at the out-of-focus features and try to force those obtuse elements to resolve, to associate with something, anything, from his memory.

But he failed, just like he had failed at everything in his life.

When he looked now at their faces, it was the same as every other time. There was nothing there, nothing recognizable. The bikers had taken off their helmets, and he was surrounded by faceless outsiders, strangers coming for him in the night.

3

The Daedalus Institute
Northern Vermont
November 25

D r. Gabriel Sterling was furious. For the third time in two days, Alexa Pearl had ignored his demands that she stay away from his patients. But this was the last straw. She was in with Franklin Baynes, subjecting the poor man to more of her pointless experiments.

When she had first arrived, Gabriel had humored Alexa. She was, after all, the acting head of the Daedalus Institute—a fact he still couldn't accept, even after all these years. Eight years ago, to his utter astonishment, she had shown up out of the blue. Only twenty-one years old at the time, Alexa arrived with the deed, the papers, and the key to a basement vault that had been locked before the passing of Gabriel's late father—Atticus Sterling, the initial founder of the Institute.

That she had neither prior psychological training nor degrees of any kind was not Gabriel's major problem with his new boss.

That she was blind since birth wasn't the issue. What he couldn't tolerate was her complete lack of respect for his position, for his thirty-plus years of schooling and experience, for the two decades he had struggled after his father's passing to not only maintain the Institute but to restore its badly maligned reputation.

Only to lose it all to her. A final slap in the face from a father who had never shown him an ounce of respect. Gabriel had always wondered if his father had maybe had another family somewhere and, since Alexa's arrival, he had given serious thought to the possibility that she might be his own half-sister or something. At times, it felt like the only thing that made sense.

How else did she wind up with that damned key? The vault in the basement had been sealed tight; its titanium bank-style door had defied Gabriel's every attempt at entrance, forcing him to wait and act merely as caretaker all those years until the eventual claim-holder came. Would that he had dynamited the damn thing.

Gabriel had brought up the subject when he had visited his mother in her nursing home last Christmas; but Darcy Sterling, nearly eighty now and no longer quite with it, wasn't in the mood to talk, especially about her late husband's potential infidelities. She had her own issues with Atticus, Gabriel knew. But that still left him with the mysterious Alexa Pearl.

His career, hell, his whole life, was in Alexa's dangerously inexperienced hands. Gabriel's staff didn't know what to make of her either, this blind woman and her hand-picked team of associates: three men and two women, each of them with disturbing snake tattoos on their necks—as if branded, part of a brotherhood. Her perennial favorites were Lance Critchwell, a bald man built like a tugboat, and Ursula Markoff, a blonde with the body of a showgirl and the warmth of an ice trawler; these two followed Alexa everywhere and, lately, had taken to wearing all black cotton sweaters or wool turtlenecks, black khakis and shoes—going monotone as if deferring to their boss's lack of sight.

The other staff members—the orderlies and nurses Gabriel liked to consider his own, those who had been here throughout the years—were just as baffled by Alexa; and surely felt just as betrayed.

Now, he took the central stairs two at a time, winding around above the lobby until reaching the second floor. The Daedalus Institute was a renovated nineteenth-century gothic mansion built with red sandstone blocks. Slate rooftops were adorned with pinnacles, peaks and awnings; Notre Dame-like spires reigned over each corner, towers complete with stone gargoyles. Inside, the floors were checkerboard marble, the windows crossed with wrought-iron frames, the walls and shelves made of thick African mahogany.

It was more like the House of Usher than a house of solace, nevertheless, it had become something like home for the current residents, many of them originally seeking only temporary help but finding the fresh mountain air and the scintillating views too comforting to leave. They came for therapy, to be among others like themselves, to learn new techniques for coping. On the five levels, thirty once spacious rooms had been converted into eighty-four smaller living areas, little more than monastic dorm rooms. They were comfortable, yet retained little of their previous luxury.

But the views out of every window were magnificent— white-crested peaks, dazzling seas of lush evergreen forests. In the winter, when the snow piled up, the grounds sparkled in the sun and shimmered under the star-streaked moonlight.

Gabriel rushed into a wide, sunlit central hallway. His tweed sports jacket flapped behind him as he passed a nurse's station without looking at the two orderlies. In front of the door to Franklin's room, Ursula Markoff stood, arms crossed under her firm breasts, which strained against her V-neck sweater.

Gabriel slowed. "Is Alexa still in there with him?"

"Yes," Ursula said coyly, her blue eyes refusing to blink, exuding a chill like a distant, implacable glacier. She made no move to get out of his way. "Since one-thirty."

Shit. Gabriel glanced at his watch. *Two hours.*

He hoped he wasn't too late.

Shoving Ursula aside, Gabriel barged in, making sure he banged the door hard against the inside wall.

He took in the scene in one glance, but already knew what he would find. Franklin Baynes sat hunched over in his chair, his head lolling to the side. Electrodes were hooked to the raw patches around his temples, clinging like flypaper to his skin while he mutely stared at the images projected on the white wall.

A sequence of photographs—*pictures of faces*, one after another; each remaining for about five seconds before switching to another face.

Thick curtains were drawn, the room drenched in shadows that fled as Gabriel opened the door. A monitor was hooked up to a terminal operated by Lance Critchwell, whose bulk obscured the projector and most of the patient's body. Franklin's brainwave patterns scrolled across the black monitor, violet and green lines zigzagging over the screen.

The shadows fled, then returned, as the image on the wall turned all white, before shifting to another wall-sized face.

Alexa sat in a chair on the other side of Critchwell, in front of an open laptop. Her cane lay across her lap. At first, she presented an air of frailty and sympathy but, upon further study, that gave way to the sense that a great inner strength lay coiled up inside her, like a spring waiting to be released. She wore small rectangular black glasses, too-tight cotton slacks and a nondescript gray sweater. She presented herself as someone unconcerned about her appearance, and yet Gabriel had seen her appear radiant on more than one occasion—when she needed to impress or to cater to government inspectors, health advisors and politicians.

He raised his fists. "What the hell are you doing?"

"Dr. Sterling." Alexa spoke in a subdued tone. "What do you *think* we're doing? Kindly remove yourself—or stand quietly in the corner until we're finished."

For all her apparent frailty, she still displayed an unmistakable sense of control, confidence, and power; something she exuded whenever she set foot in a room, like an exiled queen returning in triumph.

Gabriel held himself back, keenly aware of Critchwell tensing as if ready to spring to Alexa's defense; something in his eyes seemed to say: *Try it, asshole.* Regardless, Gabriel steeled himself and took another step into the room. He'd been pushed around long enough. "Mr. Baynes is my patient, and I didn't authorize more of these tests."

"I don't need your authorization, Dr. Sterling. Or did you forget who's paying your salary?"

"What's this going to accomplish? Franklin's mind is a mess. The drugs he's been on—"

"...won't interfere with this experiment." Alexa calmly nodded toward Critchwell, who wiped some perspiration off his bald head, tapped some keys, and started the pictures moving again. A face appeared for a few seconds, then another, speeding up now, switching from one to the next as Franklin stared at them, open-mouthed, without reacting. Meanwhile, Critchwell leaned forward and carefully monitored the readout of Franklin's brainwaves.

Gabriel fumed. Franklin Baynes had come to him ten years ago, a remarkable individual before his condition got the better of him. A renowned Napa Valley winemaker, Baynes was a solitary man who had quietly expanded his family's vineyards and created several award-winning blends of Pinot Noir that had become the talk of the industry. But his success had caught up with him, dragging him out of seclusion, forcing him to mingle, to accept awards, to make speeches.

It was too much for him. In 1999, on the night he won a gold medal in the West Coast Wine Competition, he looked out over the crowded hall and saw a veritable army of faceless, shifting creatures — subtle, leering monstrosities. He collapsed in a panic attack, his mind seizing up, and when concerned colleagues tried to help, he broke someone's nose and smashed a bottle over a woman's head.

Gabriel had read about Franklin's case several days later. He immediately flew out to the psychiatric hospital outside of Malibu, where he diagnosed Baynes with Type I *Prosopagnosia*, commonly called 'Face Blindness'—a condition marked by the inability to recognize faces. Prosopagnosiacs suffer a lack of facial perception and are unable to resolve varying degrees of facial details and features—regardless of how long they studied the person, and regardless of who that person is. Friends, relatives—their own parents—no one was exempt. Most patients with Franklin's level of the condition described seeing only a blur—a blur of nothingness where a person's face should have been.

Some developed Prosopagnosia after traumatic head injuries or illness, but Franklin had been afflicted with the condition since birth. The Malibu doctors were only too happy to remand Franklin into Gabriel's care, and he had been at Daedalus ever since.

But then Alexa came, and it was like she was magnetically drawn to Franklin. She never showed such a high level of interest in any of the other patients. At least, not after the first few sessions. Gabriel was always puzzled by the patients Alexa seemed to favor as worthy of her attention, the worst-case prosopagnosiacs, all of them close to her own age, as if maybe she related better to the younger patients. But whatever Alexa was searching for, she hadn't found evidence of it yet—in anyone other than Franklin.

And it was clearly frustrating her.

Watching Franklin's brainwave output, Gabriel spoke through his teeth. "There's no response. There's never been a response. You keep showing him faces of other prosopagnosiacs. Why? Why this test? His pulse, his blood pressure, all normal. You've had no hits, not a single change in these readings, not with Franklin or anyone else. Not for eight damn years!"

"Not yet," she said, turning toward him and lowering her sunglasses until her white, clouded eyes seemed to seek him out.

Gabriel refused to be intimidated. "Why are you wasting everyone's time with this bullshit? Can't we give the other treatments time to work? Let me continue with therapy. Drugs and counseling, I can bring him back, and ..."

Alexa waved her hand as if shooing off an unseen gnat. "This is more important."

"What is? Subjecting him to images we know he'll never react to? He has prosopagnosia, and, unless you've been treating him with some new drug I don't know about, this is useless. He'll never show a response to any of those faces!"

Gabriel pointed at the screen, but then realized the futility; Alexa obviously couldn't see his gestures. He had to put a stop to this, to take a stand now, as he should have done years ago... Regain control of his institute. What could Alexa do? She couldn't run this place without him.

As Gabriel started moving toward Franklin, the door opened, letting in a sea of brightness that everyone reacted to except Alexa, who only tilted her chin in the door's direction.

"What now?" she hissed. Her nose wrinkled. "Nurse Stamers, is it?"

God, she is good. If Gabriel didn't know better, he might have speculated that Alexa had just been wearing white contact lenses and faking all this time. She was so quick—just from the nurse's perfume, she could tell who had entered the room.

"Ms. Pearl," said the thin brunette in white scrubs. "There's something on the news. You told us to keep an eye out. A case in Philadelphia. We thought you... and Dr. Sterling would be interested..."

Alexa's head whipped around to Critchwell. She pointed a

bony finger. "Search the Web, find it! Nurse Stamers, what's the name?"

The nurse looked at the sheet of paper in her shaking hands. "Monica Gilman. And ..."

"That will be enough. Kindly shut the door behind you." In the regrouping shadows, Alexa stood, her hunched silhouette lurching on the wall as she moved in front of the projector bulb. "Email me the link, quickly!"

Critchwell tapped some keys, and the story appeared on the wall, replacing the latest of the faces from the slideshow. Gabriel teetered uncertainly, caught between deciding whether to rescue his patient or to wait and see where this was going.

Back at her Braille-equipped laptop, Alexa's fingers moved over a small wheel. A conversion program using ASTI code existed on most Web pages, and she had software that translated emails and documents instantly, feeding the output to a wheel-shaped device below her fingers. Her lips moved as her brain processed the translation from her fingertips. Faster and faster, her fingers trembled until they stopped and lifted off the wheel. "Find me a picture!" she ordered, jumping to her feet, and standing in the path of the projector, which thrust her shadow onto the wall.

"Put it on the screen. Now!"

Critchwell scrolled down in the story and clicked on a picture, enlarging it. A clear news photo of Monica outside a courthouse, frightened eyes, red and puffy, looking out over a sea of reporters. Franklin moaned, a thin line of drool seeping from his open mouth. His vacant eyes stared at a spot in the center of Alexa's shadow.

"Ms. Pearl," Critchwell pointed out, "you're blocking it."

Alexa cursed. She stepped out of the way and sat down precisely in her chair.

Gabriel decided now was the time to get Franklin out of this, pull off the electrodes and kick these people out of the room. *And then it's time for Ms. Pearl and me to have a long overdue talk.*

But suddenly Franklin screamed—a high-pitched, wailing howl. His brainwaves spiked, and the monitors flashed angry crimson lines and blinking numbers. Alexa's head spun sideways, her mouth open in muted surprise.

"Holy shit!" said Critchwell.

Gabriel froze. "Impossible." The word drowned in Franklin's still-trailing scream and the machine's insistent alarms. "It's got to be some kind of mistake." But then he saw Franklin—poor Franklin, who rarely seemed more animated than a dead tree—jerking in his chair, convulsing, pointing to the woman's face on the wall, to the dark, sad but magnetic eyes; the narrow chin, the haunted expression only too commonly seen within this institute's walls. Gabriel knew that face only too well. But Franklin—

Franklin *saw* it. *Saw her*. It was undeniable. The test was conclusive.

Somehow, impossibly, Franklin Baynes recognized this woman.

ALEXA PEARL LUNGED FORWARD, into the path of the projector, then stood there, arms wide in a messianic pose, facing the wall.

"This is it!" She spun around, pointing. "Dr. Sterling, get on the phone with this woman's attorney. Now! And then, take the next flight to Philadelphia and bring her back here."

"She's on trial for murder," Gabriel objected.

"Get her acquitted! Given the facts, they're probably leaning that way already. Have them release her into our custody. We'll take full responsibility."

"But—"

"Dr. Sterling! Even someone of your limited influence should be able to manage this."

Gabriel's mind was still reeling. He mumbled something as she continued talking, her monotone voice crackling. "This is your top priority, Dr. Sterling. And play it up to the cameras. Get on the news, talk up the condition—make it a grand and dramatic announcement, a chance to enlighten the world about Prosopagnosia. And to bring Daedalus to their attention."

Dizzy, spinning with a sense of unreality as if he had just stepped into a disjointed dreamscape, Gabriel stumbled for the door.

4

The arraignment began at 9:30 a.m. Monica Gilman was in the courtroom at nine, waiting, watching the clock over the empty judge's bench. Her lawyer sat at her side, trying to calm her, to assure her this was just an arraignment, that she wouldn't have to relive the incident. They were just entering the 'not guilty' plea and moving on, preparing for the trial—which, he also assured her, would not come to pass. She was a sympathetic defendant, a devastated widow.

He told her this case had already become something of a sensation. Happily married woman shoots her husband in self-defense, believing him to be an intruder. A distraught woman, in obvious hysterics over what had to be viewed, even by the prosecution, as a monumental tragedy.

Plus, she had a condition, albeit a strange and rare one. He had just heard from a specialist, and this doctor, a psychologist really, was on his way from Vermont. When he arrived, they planned to speak to the D.A. and the judge together.

Monica listened, but she didn't care; the affairs of the trial were as distant to her now as the memory of her fleeting happiness, the sense of perfect belonging she'd had with Paul. All of it gone, forever out of reach.

This, at last, was *real*.

Relive the incident? At this point, once more wouldn't matter. Her mind had been locked in cruel replay mode all week, forcing her to endure the same scene over and over, except now she noticed the obvious details: the roses, the sneakers he always wore around the house, the ring.... And yet, helplessly, she always pulled the trigger again and again, and, with each shot, her guilt struck like the bullets themselves, tearing into her heart, pulverizing it beyond recognition.

She had been pushed past the limits of anguish over what she had done, and now, as if sensing all bets were off and the floodgates open, she had gone deeper, fishing for an earlier trauma to drag out in the open.

A similar courtroom. Fifteen years old, she had been put on the stand, asked to identify her mother's killer, asked to relive another horrific trauma. Back one summer night from a double date, she had walked past the open front door without even registering that the top hinge was broken. Her boyfriend was behind her, followed by Jim and Kelly, coming to drop off Monica. And maybe they would stop in and chat with her mom over some apple pie before heading home.

They almost knocked Monica over when she stopped suddenly, two steps into her house. A body lay in a heap, and Monica couldn't make sense of where her mother's familiar paisley nightshirt ended and the torn skin began; there was so much blood, so many loose flaps of intermingled fabric and flesh. It wasn't until her friend screamed that Monica even realized where she was, what was happening. All she could think was that same phrase, her mother's words that matter-of-factly explained how anything in life could happen: that this was as *real* as could be.

That scream jolted the figure standing over Monica's mother, a black silhouette melding with the hallway's deepest shadows. He had been just standing there like an artist admiring the quality of his work. But instead of a paintbrush, a straight razor glinted in his hand, fresh blood dripping from its edge.

She saw him, and he saw her—then he saw her friends, the two big football players. He turned and bolted straight through the living room window like it was a paper wall and raced into the night.

Her three friends didn't get a good look at him; but Monica did; or at least, she had been in a position to see him. And when her father returned, minutes later, back from a well-deserved night out at a ball game, and he saw what had been done to his wife—his high-school sweetheart, the only love of his life, and he saw Monica nearly comatose from the shock—he did the only thing he could think to do: he told Monica to be a good girl and help the police catch this monster and put him away forever; and then he went upstairs, sat in the bathtub and wrapped his head in a towel. He was always thoughtful like that, careful to pick up after himself and not create an undue mess for his girls to clean up. Then he put the barrel of a Colt .38 in his mouth and pulled the trigger.

Monica had already picked her mother's killer out of a lineup —a minor triumph given that she had to guess; the five men they brought in were the same height, with the same hairstyles and body builds. She had a twenty percent chance, and she went with her gut feeling—after a prayer to her mom for help.

But while she had guessed right that time, and her selection had supported the detectives' other corroborating evidence—a bloody shoe print match near his house—the bastard got himself a good defense attorney.

One who did his homework. He had checked up on Monica's history, interviewed the right people at her school and on her track team; and then he hit pay-dirt, digging up some interesting nuggets, namely the one thing she desperately needed to keep hidden.

And so, the defense attorney put her on the stand. The defense attorney in his blue pin-striped suit and power red tie asked her only one question. But it was a doozy.

He asked if she could pick him—the attorney—out of a group of three people. Amid the chuckles from the jury, of course, she had to say yes. And she was reasonably confident. She was told to leave the room, then return. In the meantime, the attorney changed his outfit—took off his suit coat and tie, and sat in the second row. And from the side room they brought in three men, all the same complexion, body type and hair—and all wearing blue pinstripe suits and red ties.

Monica was led back to the stand and made to choose. She looked helplessly at the D.A., who only shrugged and seemed annoyed at the defense's stalling tactics. If he had been a little sharper on the uptake, he might have objected and got the trial turned around. As it was, he demurred, and Monica had to choose.

Thirty-three per cent chance this time, she had thought. Better odds than before. Surely, luck would be on her side again.

So, she made her choice. Again, went with her gut.

And knew immediately she had been tricked. The gasps from the jury, the shockwaves through the crowd, the delayed reaction from the D.A. demanding a recess.

Then, back in the judge's chambers, she had to sit and nod and admit it all, everything the defense attorney had found out.

She had Prosopagnosia. She'd been diagnosed with it many years earlier—after suffering with the condition all her life, believing into her teens that she was normal, that everyone saw the world the way she did—everyone had trouble seeing faces, making connections, recognizing anyone.

Recent studies showed that five percent of the population had some form of Prosopagnosia, the defense's expert witness explained to the jury and the stunned courtroom at the trial of her mother's killer. Five percent. But only in the most extreme cases, like Monica's, was it this severe. She couldn't recognize even her closest friends. She couldn't identify her own parents at the morgue, for God's sakes. And for damn sure, she couldn't point out her mother's killer. Not accurately.

Reasonable Doubt. No question. End of trial. Killer goes free. Smiling, grinning in that blurred-out hollow face, shifting pale eyes mocking her as he walked out of that courtroom.

Prosopagnosia.

She had coped all her life. Found methods of recognizing people. Trained her senses in other ways. Memorized hair styles, her mom's perfume, her dad's aftershave. Fashion tastes. But mostly, she relied on people's voices. Sometimes she had to wait until someone spoke before she knew who was coming toward her. But she coped. She managed.

When she met Paul, she had told him about her condition at once, believing she had to be upfront about it. And he had understood.

At least, she thought he did. But apparently, he was too much the romantic. Old habits died hard. He wanted to surprise her for their fifth anniversary, but damn it, she had warned him time after time—*don't wear hats, keep familiar, recognizable clothes and styles. Always, always announce yourself first if you think I'll be surprised.*

Of course, he had expected her to be asleep, and he had planned to sneak into bed with the flowers, wake her sweetly, and...

And now the scene shifted, and the replay began again. Gunshots and a hot blast of blood, skull, and brains.

She bit her lip and suffered through it, trembling until it passed. *I killed him. I killed my own husband.*

Forcing herself back to the present, she focused on the clock and stared at its face—so clearly defined, so precise, every Roman numeral stark, black on white. Her lawyer's muted words rolled past her like tumbleweeds as she watched the second hand mindlessly circle around and around the captive numerals.

"...Dr. Gabriel Sterling," her lawyer said, raising his voice. "From the Daedalus Institute. Are you listening, Monica? He'll be here at noon. He's eager to diagnose your condition, and with his testimony, I'd say we have a good chance of..."

Her lawyer droned on, but Monica heard only buzzing, a low hum that came from an awkward mouth in his blurred and jumbled face. She recognized her lawyer only by his voice, which was remarkable only for a sort of nasal quality, like someone with a perpetual cold.

At 9:30, a large man in a black robe ascended to the bench as the bailiff and the crowd of reporters and spectators rose to their feet. Monica followed her lawyer's lead but felt like she was the last to move and everyone was waiting for her. She kept her head down, intent on not looking up, hoping to avoid the usual trauma of seeing a room full of faceless strangers, of having her mind wrestle with the shifting, unfocused images, the features that just wouldn't stop drifting. Chimeras all, each and every face she ever saw.

It was the same every day.

Her whole life.

⧗

THE PLEA ENTERED, bail set and made, Monica was escorted out by her lawyer and a deputy. At least she didn't have to stay in prison. But the prospect of going home was intolerable; heading upstairs, walking over the spot, the bloodstains that would never come out, somehow making it past all those photos on the wall, feeling the recriminating stares from people she couldn't even recognize.

She decided she would get a hotel room. She didn't have anywhere else to go; no other relatives, no one else to help.

Monica doubled over as she left the courtroom, feeling like someone had kicked the wind out of her. Flashes went off over her head like anti-aircraft missiles. Cameras and reporters swarmed toward her, everyone jostling for a shot, a quote, or just an up-close look at what a prosopagnosiac looked like. Microphones were thrust in her face, but her lawyer pushed them aside as the deputy cleared a path.

Still, the cameras followed—news teams rushing toward her from their vans. The sun, intense for such a chilly day, bore down on her as the crisp wind bit through her sweater and sent a chill deep into her lungs. She swooned, and the world spun as people shouted and called out to her. Blurry faces bent around flashing lights and probing microphones. Somewhere above, a helicopter hovered, its blades rumbling. She smelled winter in the air—dead leaves, brittle twigs; and she thought of Paul.

Pushed into their waiting car, Monica sat while her lawyer stayed outside, giving some kind of remark to the press, something about her condition, promising to release more information after speaking to a specialist.

As Monica sat in the back seat, she risked a glance into the crowd. The reporters were still scrambling to get close. The sun dipped behind a cloud, the world flickered and turned a sepia-color, like old photographs, and she froze. She saw someone staring at her between the jumble of bodies in the way.

An old man, with thinning red hair and steel-rimmed glasses. He was wearing an ill-fitting brown suit with a midnight-black vest and a faded red bowtie; he alone remained motionless in the bustling crowd, gazing intently in her direction.

The hairs on the back of Monica's neck stiffened and her forehead started to sweat.

Oh my God.

And then he vanished—blending in with the onlookers, but not before Monica got an unobstructed look at him, *and she saw his face, his clear face.*

It wasn't the first time—she had seen it before in the only place she ever could truly see someone...in her nightmares.

She heard a mumbling sound, rhythmic like a chanting and, in a delayed reaction, she realized the man had been holding something—a gold-plated antique hourglass, another recurring image in her nightmares. For a moment, it was as if she had slipped back into one of those horrific, inescapable dreams: the world shifted, turned gray, then menacing and full of shadows. And there was the old man, leaning out of the darkness toward her, whispering something incomprehensible, something she had to hear. And there was that hourglass, glinting in the dark.

But just like in her nightmares, it was at this point she jolted out of it, shrieking awake and desperate to convince herself that it wasn't real.

Only, the vision remained, fading slowly: that hourglass, red sand inside, flowing the wrong way, sifting back up.

5

London

K aitlin Star, known to her few remaining friends as 'Kat', and until recently by her fans as 'StarKat', lead singer and songwriter for the London grunge band, PinkEye, rolled off the couch, clutching her head with both hands. She landed on a pile of stained clothing, cigarette butts, pot-pipes and beer bottles. She felt like she was lost on the moors, trekking in a fog, surrounded by a blurry landscape.

Where in the bloody hell am I? was her first thought, quickly overrun by: *What did I do last night?*

She checked her hands, relieved to find them free of blood, then looked down at her body—the lean, if too-thin figure, the ribs peeking out from her half-shirt below the still-perky breasts. She was only twenty-four, but this morning she felt more like sixty.

What had happened last night? All she could remember was getting dressed up, staining her face with the angriest crimson flames she could paint, then highlighting her hair with red and blue waves, spiking it high and fitting herself with an exotic breed of metal nose-rings and the usual silver loops through her eyebrows.

She had planned on it being a rough night for someone. Slider had finally set her off for the last time. Bad enough he had stolen the one hit song she had written in her short-lived career, bad enough that he had kicked her out of the band, broke up with her and started dating that flat-chested slut, Fennie, but then last night he had the nerve to invite her to the band's premiere at Crouch End. And once there, he and Fennie had mangled every one of Kat's songs before an increasingly drunk and hostile crowd.

At some point, when she couldn't take it any longer, she had hurled a bottle at Slider and then stormed downstairs, where she found a couple couches full of stoned-out teenagers; she accepted a joint and a glass of something foul from some boy, probably still in high school, and then...

Her flashback sputtered. She heard a sound she finally recognized as snoring. There on the couch—a young man, shirtless, with a black sheet over his waist, tangled around his bare legs. She crawled closer to him and looked at his face.

Of course, she couldn't make out anything there. Just a blur of unrecognizable sludge. *What'd I expect?* His hair—buzz cut, of course—like ninety percent of the blokes she met lately. Useless. She could tell none of these losers apart. At least he seemed close to her age.

After a moment's thought, she carefully took hold of the sheet and slowly pulled it down. *Just taking a peek.*

No help there. Nothing memorable.

She then fumbled through a pile of clothing—his pants and shirt—and there, in his back pocket, a beat-up brown leather wallet.

She opened the flap, dug around inside the jumble of cards— mostly VIP passes to various seedy clubs—and finally found his ID, just as his snoring stopped.

"Lookin' for something, sweetie?"

"Shit." She turned.

The guy was sitting up. He let the sheet fall away. "I'd gladly pay you tomorrow for another tussle today."

Kat groaned. "Don't flatter yourself..." She glanced at the name on his ID, but no longer needed to confirm it. She had recognized his voice. "Roger. Jesus, I'm sorry, I didn't recognize you..."

Roger was PinkEye's drummer, and a good friend of Slider's; he was also Fennie's ex-boyfriend. So, he and Kat had something in common—Slider had screwed them both over. Dimly, she remembered Roger coming down the stairs last night, seeing her amid all those punk kids, stoned out of her mind, immune to their pawing and groping; she remembered him pulling her free, bringing her back to his flat. A six-pack and several hits later...

"Sorry," she whispered again, holding her head. "That was some night. I—we shouldn't have..."

"Yeah, I know, doll. I know, I'm just your old bloke, Roger, but still—we have something, you and me, don't you think?"

"Not while you're still with the band. Not while I'm still..."

"Shunned?"

"Whatever. Slider's a sodding prick, and one of these days.... I—I'm going to kill him."

"Harsh, babe. Can you at least wait until we can find a new lead guitar?"

Kat laughed. "Think Fennie will ever come back to you?"

"Don't want her. No offense, but after Slider had his paws on her..."

"That didn't seem to bother you last night, if I recall."

Roger smiled. "Long-time fantasy, doll. Couldn't pass up a chance to shag with StarKat."

"Whatever." She grabbed her pants, slid into them, suddenly realizing she wasn't even wearing panties. *Screw it. Got to get out of here.*

"You really have to go?" Roger asked. "I was thinking, maybe we could—"

"I'm leaving. Thanks for looking out for me, Roger, but I'm... I'm just going."

"Kat—"

Her cell phone rang as soon as she buttoned her jeans. She pulled it free from her back pocket, grateful for the interruption and the excuse to check out, and glanced at the caller ID.

"Trish," she said, as she waved to Roger and opened his door. Tricia McKinley was her flat-mate of three years. A decent friend, if a little stuffy. Not quite as trashy as Kat, or as pierced, or tattooed, or rebellious or anything else. But she never preached, never got in Kat's way.

"Hey Kat, you okay?"

"Bloody awful, thanks for asking."

"Sorry, love. Anyway, I was expecting you'd come home last night, but I'm just glad you're okay. If you ask me, you need a break from the band and all those assholes."

"No one asked you." The door closed, and she stood in the graffiti-scrawled stairwell, alone with the smell of urine and cigarette smoke. "Sorry, didn't mean that. Listen, I'm on my way home. Save me one of those scones if you haven't eaten them all."

"You got it. But there's another reason I was calling. You know that one night we were stoned?"

"Jesus. Which one?"

"The time you told me about your problem—about recognizing people, how difficult it is for you to see—"

"Yeah, yeah." *Shit, I don't need this now.* "What about it?"

"Well, I think you're not as unique as you think."

"What the hell are you talking about?" She had lived with this condition all her life, learned to cope early on, practicing on her father—on the rare events when he came home from wherever, seeing how quickly she could point him out as different from the other men Mom had over when he was away. Hair color, the way he dressed, the way he smelled—musky with a hint of menthol from his cigarettes. How he walked, slightly hunched over as if the weight of life had finally grown just too much.

"I found an article online last night while I was waiting for you to come back. It was a news story from the States. A woman there—Monica something—killed her husband by accident. Couldn't recognize him one night when he came home early from a trip; thought he was an intruder. Shot him four times."

"Jesus, that's messed up."

"Yeah, but she got off. Get this—a doctor, from some special clinic, spoke to the jury and told them she's got this condition, right? Sounds just like what you've got. So, she's been acquitted, and she's going to this place up in the mountains, and–

Kat swooned and had to grip the handrail to stop herself from falling down the stairs. For a second, she saw, clear as the sun—the burning image of a castle in the snow-capped hills.

"Save the link," she whispered, as a thousand faceless figures circled carousel-like in her thoughts, a thousand strangers coalescing into one constant adversary: an old man with thinning red hair, holding a gleaming hourglass up to her face and whispering something unintelligible.

"I've done better than that," Trish said, and Kat imagined a touch of pride in her voice. "I made a call to this clinic—it's called the Daedalus Institute."

"No, you didn't. Trish!"

"I did, and you'll thank me for it. I told them I was you, and I answered some basic questions—just about your age, if you had any distinguishing birthmarks."

"Why would that matter?"

"I don't know, but hey—I told them about that cute triangular mark on your inner thigh that I thought was a tattoo."

A moment of strained silence when neither one spoke, then: "They said someone's coming out to interview you, to show you some pictures and stuff, and, if you're a fit, they'd like to take you back—all expenses paid. Plus provide a sweet stipend to be part of an experiment with others like you."

Kat groaned. "No thanks. I don't want to go, I'm not ready to..."

"You don't have to go alone. I'll come too. I've got nothing going on, and it'll be a great little trip. Never been to the States."

"Trish..."

"I looked up the place on the Web—it's unbelievable, nothing but snowy mountains and trees. No one around for miles, and the clinic's like this spooky gothic mansion. We'll have a blast!"

"Bloody hell." Kat held her head. "When are they coming?"

"Soon. The woman said she had someone already here in England who could stop by, which I thought was odd, but whatever. So get your ass back here soon and get cleaned up. Try to look at least a little presentable. Maybe take out your rings, wash your hair and go back to being a brunette?"

Kat flipped her phone shut and slipped it back into her pocket. She leaned against the stairwell. And she thought about Slider and Fennie, Roger, and a blur of faces and nights just as unmemorable. Her life, for more years than she could count, had been just as indistinct and forgettable as every face she'd ever met. What could be the harm in a little change of scenery? A chance to get away from this hellhole, from her old 'friends'— losers and pricks, the whole lot.

A chance to clear her head. And they'd pay her for it?

She stood on the top stair, fidgeting, trembling. Her flesh broke out, her heart raced. Then her paralysis broke. She ran down the stairs, urgency finally overcoming fear.

6

Cape Canaveral

After forty-eight hours, Jake Griffith finally emerged from the 'Pit'—what the guards and inmates of the Cocoa Correctional Facility called the four-by-six steel room with one vent, a disgusting toilet, and a dirty sink. As soon as the door opened, he got off the floor where he had been doing sit-ups in the dark. He smiled to the two faceless guards and to the massive, unmistakable shape of Officer Fenrik waiting in the hall.

"Top of the morning to you all."

"It's 6:30 at night, you dumb-shit." Fenrik glowered at him and clenched his fists. "Have a nice time in there?"

"You bet, and you know what—I thought about your wife the whole time. Figured in the dark is probably the way she likes it, anyway, right? Doesn't have to look at your ugly..."

Jake quickly retreated behind the guards who sprang into action, restraining Fenrik. He was sure he'd catch shit later, but right now it was worth it—and essential that he didn't give this weasel a chance to gloat.

"Welcome back, Griffith," said the shorter guard. "Hurry up. Your damned dinner's getting cold."

IN THE MESS HALL, the second shift of inmates was just finishing up their meals and heading out to the yard for evening exercise; a few hours later and they would be herded back for the night like sheep into their pens. Jake got his tray and trudged down the buffet line, looking over the cardboard-thin turkey slices, the dry mashed potatoes. Starving, he took a heap of everything, trying not to look up at the balcony where Fenrik was strolling, watching his every move, hoping for another slip up.

Don't mind me. Just the model prisoner down here.

He sat by himself after nodding to two inmates from D-Block who were just cleaning up. He did a quick scan of the ID numbers on their shirts, although he could tell who they were by other methods. Charlie Benson—two counts of armed robbery, a tattooed pair of dolphins under his rolled-up sleeve; and Nickie Simmons—assault with a deadly weapon and drug possession, bald with a raggedy gray goatee; each doing five to ten. Jake started eating and looked up to the small color TV hanging from the ceiling.

Jake spooned the dust-flavored potatoes into his mouth as he watched the news. On the screen, a faceless reporter stood in front of a courthouse in what looked like a bitter wind and a light snowfall. *Suckers. Should move down here with the gators and bugs.*

The reporter was talking about a murder case and a defendant who had just been acquitted, and now her doctor was addressing the media, explaining that whatever malady the woman had was the cause of her temporary insanity and had resulted in this horrible tragedy.

Jake was barely listening, glancing up only occasionally. The doctor—a distinguished gray-haired man who could have been Richard Gere for all Jake knew—stood there looking comfortable in his suit like he was used to the cold. He backed up and pointed to his patient, motioning for her to come forward.

Jake looked down at his food. All that time in solitary—it had affected him far more than he let on to Fenrik and his goons. It was like a sensory deprivation tank in there, and he had seen too many visions in the dark, in the long waking hours when he couldn't tell if it was day or night.

Of course, he had seen the hourglass: that antique-looking golden-rimmed object with gargoyles on the sides and filled with red sand. It had haunted his dreams all his life. He remembered when he first saw *The Wizard of Oz*. The evil monkeys and the Wicked Witch he could handle; but it was that hourglass, the one the Wicked Witch used on Dorothy, giving her until the ruby sands ran out, that set him off. Six years old, he went screeching from the room and his parents never let him watch it again.

He figured it was just something about that movie, the reason he kept seeing the hourglass in his nightmares.

Those dreams, he was used to. Those he could handle.

But while in the darkness in solitary, he had also seen something he had spent years trying to repress, something that made him cringe every time he saw it, even on a TV commercial: the familiar castle at the entrance to Disney World. That awful skyline, the menacing cartoon characters strolling around, Mickey, Minnie. Not to mention the ridiculous Goofy.

Helpless to avert the images swirling in the dark theater of his mind, he watched as the memories flooded back. Six-year-old Jake Griffith ran with his older brother to the front of the *Pirates of the Caribbean* ride, only to be split up at the last moment. Jake rode with an overweight, sweaty couple while Mikey went with two cute teenage girls. At the end of the ride, wet, thrilled and exhausted, the tide of people swept past Jake, swallowing up his brother and spitting everyone out on the other side.

And Jake stood there outside the ride, waiting. His brother was nowhere to found. Jake waited. Waited and waited, searching the faces of everyone in the crowd, seeing the same cloudy, unresolved features, the same unfamiliar looks.

Mom and Dad had ordered Jake and Mikey to stay together. But Mikey was gone and Jake was alone, terrified. He had to stay put, didn't he? Or should he go and find someone in charge, someone who could put out a call for help, alert his parents to come and get him?

He decided to stay and hope they'd come back for him. He sat on a bench near the front of the ride, and he waited. And waited, until a man came up to him and stood there looking down. Jake stared at him, and the sun was behind the man's head, obscuring his face—not that it mattered. He was about the right height, he had the same slouching shoulders, full of heaviness and exhaustion, the same stoop to his stance, as if he'd been running all over this park, looking for him.

"Dad?"

The man seemed to tremble, the aura of blazing sunlight shuddering around his outline, and when he moved, quick and catlike, he seemed like an angel. A rescuing angel. He didn't speak, just took Jake's hand in a familiar, fatherly grip, a tender but firm grasp.

Jake knew he was in trouble, knew Dad was angry that he got lost, that he didn't stay with his brother. He knew Mom was probably at her wits' end. That was why Dad was quiet, why he just led him away in silence, dragging him through the crowds towards the exit. Jake had his head down, somberly watching his scuffed-up Reeboks the whole time.

He was led right out into the parking lot, to the farthest end, much farther than Jake remembered parking, but in all the excitement that morning, he couldn't be sure. He was taken straight to a lone red pickup truck with clumps of dirt lodged behind the wheels like cookie pieces stuck behind molars.

That was when Jake at last realized something was wrong.

That was when he looked up and saw the bushy blond hair under this man's hat, so much lighter than his father's.

And that was when Jake screamed.

But it was too late, and no one could hear. Suddenly, there was tape over his mouth, his hands were bound with some kind of twine, his feet secured with a chain, and he lay on a mattress of potato sacks in the flatbed, covered with a heavy tarp.

He lay there, sweating, crying, trying to scream, until they got to a houseboat, until the motor started, and they sailed off into the tributaries and the dank reeds and the festering swamps.

Bad luck, he'd think later on. Just bad luck—not just his problem with faces, but the whole series of events at Disney World.

Now, Jake shook off the memories and pulled himself free just as he heard a woman's voice on the TV, the reporter again mentioning some disorder, Proso-something. And the words 'Daedalus Institute'—the second time she had said that. And then, a view of a woman being led into a waiting black Lexus by that suit-wearing doctor.

Jake frowned. A lump of thick, dry potatoes fell from his fork and landed unnoticed on his thigh. He stood up, wobbling, dizzy. Incoherent sounds came out of his open mouth.

The screen froze, capturing the woman's face—the haunted eyes full of a strange mix of fear and relief, the frazzled hair, the lines on her face from drying tears.

A face that was somehow completely familiar. Crystal clear, almost blinding in its brilliance. A beacon Jake couldn't place but couldn't deny.

He knew her!

The screen went blank, then went to a McDonald's commercial. Jake shot a glance up at Fenrik, still glaring at him from the balcony, but now leaning over, tensing.

Relax, Jake cautioned, trying to regain composure. Act natural, think clearly. Think—who is this woman? How can I recognize her?

He thought to his recent years on the beaches, in and around Melbourne, Canaveral and Cocoa Village. A steady stream of faceless women, but not one of them recognizable. He sent his memories further into the past, but as always... there was no one he could see, no one that he could see as clearly as that woman on the television.

How was it possible?

One and only one possible answer came back: one thought, one hope for salvation.

He had to find her. See her. He had to get to the Daedalus Institute.

But first, he needed to escape.

7

London

aitlin returned to her flat around ten. One of the few
Brits that never really cared for tea and made no
excuses about it, she stopped first for a double shot of
espresso at the corner before catching a bus uptown.

She had been thinking about the disorder that had, at least in
part, been the cause of so much of her self-destructive behavior
for the past decade. Since life had seen fit to give her this hard-
ship, she could hardly be judged if she paid it back in kind.
Anger and resentment had marched toward disassociation and
then open rebellion—toward her parents, her schools and, more
recently, her friends.

But her breakup with Slider and her subsequent expulsion
from the band had changed all that. Just as she was settling into
a place that had felt like home, everything had flown apart. Now,
the idea that there might be a lifeline out there stirred up a touch
of optimism.

Back at her flat, she had just rounded the stairs, a slight

bounce in her step, when she skidded to a halt. Her door was open just a crack, through which a man's voice seeped out.

She must have a guy over. It wasn't that far-fetched. Trish was a sexy little thing when she wanted to be. People always said she kind of looked like Kaitlin—but without the attitude or the punk accoutrements. But something about the man's voice didn't seem right. It didn't sound like pillow-talk.

They're sending someone over today...

Could that 'someone' have come already? Kaitlin paused with her hand at the doorknob, not simply afraid of intruding, but suddenly desperate to hear what was being said.

And why isn't Trish speaking? It was unlike her to let someone else go this long without butting in. Kaitlin peeked inside, tuned out the noise from the neighbor's blaring TV set, and tried to filter out the squealing brakes and the coughing engines on the street below.

"...I told you already. She said she saw the Gilman woman, and that was enough... Well, I didn't think to... Yes, I know I'm not paid to think, but..."

Who the hell is he talking to? Kaitlin gently pushed the door, knowing it would squeak if it opened all the way. She had been meaning to get on to the landlord to oil the damn thing already —and to fix the leaky sink and the weak shower—but she had never quite gotten around to it.

"...look, it wasn't her. She wasn't one of the Six. I screwed up, but by the time I figured that out, I couldn't let her go. She'd warn her roommate. Listen, it's under control, all right? I'll wait around for Kaitlin to return."

Committed this far, Kaitlin squeezed into the flat, pressed against the wall and inched forward. The air felt stale, motionless. The windows were closed, which itself wasn't odd given that it was November, but first thing in the morning Trish usually enjoyed a couple smokes, and she always cracked the windows for fresh air. They were closed now.

She peeked around the corner and saw the back of a tall man

in a black suit. *Undertaker*, she thought immediately. First impression. He just looked like one, tall and stringy, with disproportionately long arms and spindly legs, a narrow head and greased back hair. The kind of guy you might see at a wake, standing in the shadows while everyone lined up for their turn to kneel before the coffin.

A set of gold cuff links in a starched white sleeve caught her eye, and she noticed the hand holding a black cell phone to his ear, but then she saw the torn nightshirt on the floor. The familiar garment, stained with some of that Pistachio ice cream they had polished off two nights ago, but also with streaks of red, matching the splotches on the faded Berber carpet. And the bare leg on the floor, the rest of the body out of sight behind the couch.

Oh God, Trish... Move, please move.

"... sorry," the undertaker-man continued. "I didn't think to look for the birthmark first. Thought it was just a final confirmation kind of thing. Yes, of course I looked afterwards. It's not there. Don't worry, I'll get the target."

Kaitlin took a step back, hands to her mouth, a thousand frenzied thoughts scrambling in her mind, her heart seizing in her throat. The crimson stains... *Trish.*

She peeked out a little farther, just to get another angle—she had to be sure Trish wasn't just tied up.

She took a step inside—and the floor creaked.

Shit!

The man spun around immediately, snapping the cell phone shut and reaching inside his jacket for something.

Kaitlin screamed, turned, and fled back into the hall. Fueled by the shock of seeing her first dead body, *her own roommate*, she raced to the stairwell door and flung it open just as she heard thunderous footsteps following. Up or down? She bolted up the stairs. Two at a time.

Why Trish? But then, as if her pounding footsteps had jarred loose the real question, she thought: *Why me?*

The man—Trish's killer—raced after her, matching her stride for stride, but she couldn't look back. She imagined him aiming a gun, waiting for a clear shot. Expected any minute to feel the ice-cold punch of a bullet in her back.

She burst onto the fifth floor and slammed the door behind her, knowing it would only stop the man for a second. Running again, she headed toward the north end of the hall. There were four flats on each level, two on either side of the stairwell. She headed for the last one, owned by Niles and Benny, two standout blokes, punkers both, who had always showed up to cheer PinkEye back when she was still with the band.

She reached their door just as the killer rocketed out of the stairwell. His momentum carried him into the wall, then he regained his bearings and bounded toward her. She risked a glance and saw he did indeed carry a gun, a long, black-handled thing with one of those silencer-tips on the end. Fortunately, he hadn't seen fit to use it yet, perhaps confident he would catch her.

Kaitlin turned the knob—and screamed. *No...*

Locked. Kaitlin looked around helplessly. A fire extinguisher. Maybe that would work, she'd seen it in films before. About to make a move for it, the doorknob turned from the inside, and off-balance, she fell back inside the flat.

She knocked someone over behind the door. A second later, she could tell it was Benny. Shorter of the two, crew cut, a lot of flab around his middle. Then she kicked the door shut, got up and bolted the lock.

"Kat, wha—" was all Benny got out.

Benny had just come out of the shower; he still wore a towel around his waist and was chewing on the end of a toothbrush. He grunted, staggered back, and looked incredulously at the hole in the center of his hairless chest.

Kaitlin turned and saw the matching hole in the door behind her. She tried to scream but couldn't make a sound; she managed to drop and roll to her left, scrambling into the hallway. Two more shots burst through the door behind her.

"What the hell?" Niles stumbled out from the kitchen, a pitcher of grape juice in his hand. He took one look at Kaitlin, curled into a fetal position against the wall, then he saw Benny topple forward. Niles dropped the pitcher and sprang for the phone. Fumbled with it as he dialed.

At least he's thinking clearly, Kaitlin thought as she heard him yelling for the police.

Something struck the door. She jumped up to her feet and ran away from Benny's twitching body, down the hall to a window, which led out onto the fire escape. As Niles shouted into the phone, she shouted: "Run, Niles! We've got to..."

"Go!" he yelled as the front door broke free, slamming against the inside wall. Kaitlin reached the window, unlatched it and flung it up. She stuck a leg out, then looked back. The killer rounded the corner. Niles leapt at him and bowled him over. Kaitlin paused, for a moment wishing she'd stayed back to help. Maybe she could have—

A horrible, squishing sound, and then an eruption of red burst from the center of Niles's back. The killer stood up, pushing Niles's limp body off him. He dusted off his black tie and turned toward Kaitlin.

Scrambling out onto the fire escape, she slammed the window shut so hard it cracked down the middle. The frigid morning air enfolded her as she ran around and around, down the metal stairs, stumbling, banging her knees against the ice-cold metal. Above her, the window exploded, releasing a black shape. The killer clattered onto the fire escape after her.

Kaitlin screamed, as loud as she could, hoping to draw the attention of anyone on the street beyond the alley or in the other buildings. She reached the bottom level, but was still one story up, and she knew there was no time to lower the ladder. She got up on the railing, then leapt off just as the killer spun around the last corner, his gun raised.

She dropped, landed hard on her feet and felt the shock all the way up to her hips, but she got up, stumbling, and ran for the street. Three more steps and she'd be in the middle of traffic, three more steps...

One. Would he fire?

She could sense the killer crouching. Aiming.

Two. His superior—whoever was on the other end of that call —seemed pissed at him, and he had to defend Trish's murder. So maybe Kaitlin was safe. Apparently, she was one of six—whatever that meant. Six what? Who else was there? And why were they being hunted?

Three.

She was out. Still keeping her head down, she ducked and slipped behind a parked VW beetle, expecting a bullet to rip through the window. A double-decker bus approached, and as it passed, she sprang up and leapt into the open stairwell, clinging to the arm rail and ducking down. After another block, sure she was out of range, she climbed up, gave the driver a coin then took the first open seat.

She fished out her cell phone and was about to call the police when she thought better of it. Three murders of people she knew... No other witnesses... She'd be questioned for days. And, with her in jail, whoever was after her would know just where to look. Besides, the police were probably already on their way because of Niles's call. But she couldn't go back there, couldn't remain and wait—not with the killer around.

No, she had to get out. Away from here, maybe even away from London, until she could sort everything out.

She was trembling, her breath coming out in ragged gasps.

What the hell just happened?

She closed her eyes and saw the killer again... and what had he said before he saw her? That mysterious comment about the 'Six'.

Her eyes flew open. What was she a part of?

What else had the killer said? That Trish lied about seeing 'the Gilman woman'...

Gilman—was that her name? The woman from America who killed her husband? Why was it important that Kaitlin 'see' her, and more to the point—how could she?

Kaitlin pulled out her phone and opened the Internet. Thought for a moment, then quickly Googled 'Prosopagnosia' and 'Gilman'. A couple of seconds later, a list of articles appeared. She picked the first, a link to the Philadelphia Daily News. Impatiently, she started scrolling through the story, glimpsing mention of the break-in and the subsequent court hearing. The words, 'Daedalus Institute', and then...

As luck would have it—there was a picture.

A picture of Monica Gilman.

Kaitlin swooned. The blurry-faced passengers on the bus spun with her, the walls and seats melted, and the roof dissolved, and all of Trafalgar Square swirled into a tangled tapestry of color and sound, compressing until she was sure her senses would explode with revelation.

Staring back at her from her phone, for the first time in her life, was a face Kaitlin could see.

8

The Daedalus Institute
Vermont

Alexa Pearl snapped her phone shut. The Braille keypad's tactile sensations lingered on her fingertips, giving off ghostly after-effects. Sometimes, she thought of her skin as a sponge, soaking up numbers, letters and words, storing them close, permitting her to revisit and spend time with the images they provoked in her imagination.

So unfortunate, being born with this condition. But she had made the best of it, moving onward, learning, adapting to the latest technologies, utilizing new inventions, always keeping in mind the prize at the end of the dark tunnel.

Now, however, Alexa fought back a rising buildup of rage.

Fool! How could Malcolm botch such an easy assignment? Malcolm Byers, her liaison in Britain, was a thug at his core, a throwback to the gangster era. She had recruited him because he displayed a shred of intelligence to complement his muscle. Not enough to question orders while being paid so well and promised so much, but she had hoped he had enough brains to think for himself when circumstances deviated from the plan.

But he'd let Kaitlin Abrams escape.

Because of Malcolm's impatience, Kaitlin was not only still free, but alerted to the fact that someone—possibly from this clinic—wanted her dead.

Things were now going to have to get messy. And costly. The authorities had to get involved. Malcolm was already planting evidence to pin the roommate's murder on Kaitlin. Once the girl was in custody, locked behind bars somewhere, it would be far easier to get to her.

The same way they could get to the one in Florida. Funny how synchronized it all seemed; two of those she'd been searching for—two of the Six—behind bars. And both of them younger than Monica and Franklin, younger than she had expected.

Alexa stroked her chin, thinking, lost in the past. Their age difference was interesting, but she'd dwell on those implications later.

It was nice of Jake Griffith to call the Daedalus Institute and identify himself, to alert Alexa to his startling recognition of Mrs. Gilman. Maybe he was hoping for some of the leniency that Monica received, praying the State would allow him to come up to Vermont and receive treatment.

Jake had made the call, and others would soon be doing the same. Alexa smiled. Jake Griffith, Kaitlin Abrams, Monica Gilman, Franklin Baynes. Four of the Six.

Two more to go.

⧗

ALEXA WAS in the basement's vault room, impenetrable and unassailable, and converted to suit her purposes. The room sat back in the shadows, past the dust-heavy gloom permeating the pillared basement.

She set down the cane she had been absently twirling, passing from hand to hand. Made from smooth, polished oak, it was rounded and thick at the handle, like the hilt of a Viking's sword, and when she tapped it on the floor, the steel blade concealed inside made a subtle rattle that only her ears could hear.

She opened her laptop, feeling the immediate warmth from the screen, knowing the bright light was dispelling the vault's gloom and illuminating the treasures within. She could only imagine what the room looked like: the hieroglyphic carvings hanging on the wall; the ancient figurines, urns and statues dancing in her plasma screen's flickering light; the glass-enclosed papyrus; the stainless-steel file cabinets with all of Atticus Sterling's most treasured notes and research from a lifetime of study. In the center of the room stood computer servers and three workstations with 27-inch monitors and desks for her trusted personnel.

Her seekers, her Brotherhood. Besides the five of them here at Daedalus, she kept in close contact with sixteen others, scattered around the world, including Malcolm Byers.

The five members she had here at Daedalus had just been sent off for a few hours' rest. They had been at their stations for close to forty hours straight after the Gilman story broke, checking the news outlets, sifting through international reports, hospital records, alerting the others to be on the lookout.

Despite the London situation, Alexa still felt confident. Finally, the last chapter in the grand plan was about to begin. It was really just the tying up of loose ends now. But still, it was important, crucial in fact.

So many factors depended on each other, so many random elements needed to click together. But now at least, it felt like it was not so much a matter of If, but When.

Unfinished business.

She detested unfinished business, especially something of this magnitude; it ate away at her, as it had every day for the last eight years. But she wouldn't have to wait much longer. Soon, very soon, she would finish what had been left undone.

The Gilman woman's public exposure and Alexa's quick thinking to capitalize on the situation ensured that the others would take notice. More Prosopagnosiacs would inevitably follow, but Alexa didn't care about them—they were extraneous. Only the Six mattered. The others would make their way here, and then she could use Franklin, whose brainwaves couldn't lie, to identify those who hadn't already given themselves away by revealing their ability to see Monica. Was it a stroke of luck, Franklin being here already when she arrived? Or was it just further evidence of her destiny?

Alexa snapped open her phone again, and used the walkie-talkie feature to call Lance Critchwell who, despite her orders to rest, was no doubt parked at one of the nurse's stations. Alexa wondered if she should just have the man neutered; he might actually become reliable. The Pharaohs had the right idea with their eunuchs—for efficient service you had to rid your lackeys of distractions while simultaneously instilling them with mortal fear.

"Critchwell!" she called.

The receiver crackled. "Here, Ms. Pearl."

"Where is Dr. Sterling?"

"He's returning with the Gilman woman. He called a few minutes ago from Boston. Their flight just landed. They should be here before dark."

"Good. Prepare Franklin for a visual confirmation."

"Why? He already ID'd her picture."

She fumed, hands clenching. *Wasting time, and he's questioning me?* "Just do it! I want multiple confirmations for everyone."

"Okay, okay. What about the Griffith kid in Florida? How do we get him out?"

Alexa thought for a moment. Could she afford another mistake? Trust this most vital of missions to mercenaries? "Is our man inside yet?"

"Yes, we got him in a few hours ago as a new guard, assigned to Jake's ward."

Alexa sighed. "I want to be sure, first, before we do anything. London exposed a potential flaw in our plan. Kaitlin Abrams' roommate claimed to have the disease. She answered our set questions about recognizing Monica."

"The questions weren't specific enough to root out fakers?"

"Obviously. Interviews alone can never guarantee accuracy. Someone calling and telling us what we want to hear is insufficient. We need empirical evidence—an observable reaction."

The other end of the line was quiet for a moment, and Alexa thought he had cut out, or fallen asleep, until he coughed. "So, what do we you want done with the Griffith kid?"

Alexa smiled. It was time she tried her other talents. Other skills, long out of practice, were now demanded. Not that she doubted the loyalty of anyone in her Brotherhood; she just wanted to be doubly sure.

"I'll take care of it. Just call the prison, and when you get our man on the guard detail, put him through to my line."

9

Cape Canaveral

Jake Griffith hung up the payphone in the prison hallway. Over his shoulder, Fenrik was watching him. At his side stood the new guard, someone named Jesse Krantz, transferred in today from Alabama. Fenrik was showing him the ropes.

Fenrik, of course, was impossible to mistake: a bulky lumbering giant; and Krantz was obvious just by his contrast with Fenrik. The new guard was a desiccated scarecrow with drooping shoulders and slicked back hair; plus, he had that unmistakable circular tattoo on the side of his neck: a red-eyed snake eating its tail.

Jake had just been talking to a lawyer. The latest in a succession of court-appointed hacks, but now he was nervous. Had Fenrik been able to listen in somehow? Maybe that was it. Maybe the phones were bugged, privacy and lawyer-client privilege be damned. But what would it matter? What would the guards make of his impassioned plea for his lawyer to follow up with that place in Vermont, the place Jake had seen on the news? *Daedalus.*

The alternative was to attempt another escape but, after the last incident, they were watching him like a hawk. No privileges for at least another year, no excursions, no chance to slip away.

But he had to find out about the woman. Monica Gilman. Jake's first call, earlier this morning, had been to the Daedalus Institute, where the receptionist there put him in touch with another woman, a woman with a strange voice that almost sounded like an echo. She had asked Jake about his interest in the institute, and it was at that point he suddenly felt as if he'd made a mistake by revealing his excitement at seeing Monica Gilman on the news, his shock at finally being able to recognize someone, to retain a face. The woman on the other end of the line seemed impressed as well, promising to be in touch very soon, when they could work out a way to come visit him, or vice versa, the law permitting.

After talking to that woman, he had felt drained, completely exhausted. He'd gone back to his cell and promptly fell asleep, plunging straight into a dream, in which shifting veils of black netting obscured an occupant in a shapeless room, a room that tilted back and forth, like a boat on the waves. A shadowy form sat on a lone wooden chair in the corner. The paint was peeling from the walls, hanging in tattered spirals. Somewhere a clock ticked. And voices—that woman's voice from the phone, along with the other one, the sinister echo—were both speaking in mumbled, half-whispered phrases. The figure in the chair stirred. The shadows retreated and the light moved upwards from the floor, illuminating orange prison pants, then glinted off the item on the man's lap, the gold-rimmed hourglass with red powdery sand drifting the wrong way, into the top half, as if time was moving backwards.

The light erased the shadow as it ascended, highlighting the blond-brown hair, and a blurred-out face.

A face he somehow knew to be his own.

The mumbled words, the shifting veils, then one word pushed free, clear and precise. The dream-Jake, his eyes closed, spoke the same word, over and over:

"Daedalus."

⧖

KRANTZ AND FENRIK closed the cell block gate behind them and approached, thumbs hooked under their belts. Jake stared at their batons and the holstered pistols, then he glanced over his shoulder, hoping some of his fellow inmates were around; he had the feeling he was going to need witnesses. But the hallway was deserted. Three in the afternoon, most everyone was outside, getting exercise, smoking or just laying in the sun.

Some dudes would kill for this kind of life, Jake thought. Some of them had, he realized, but his concern now was only in saving his neck. He wasn't sure why Fenrik was after him this time, but it couldn't be good. Best to break the mood early.

"Hi guys, heard from the Governor yet? Am I being pardoned?"

Fenrik smirked as he walked past, taking up a position behind Jake while Krantz stayed in front, blocking him in. Jake looked around for the hallway's surveillance camera but saw it had been disabled, with wires hanging loose.

"Uh oh," Krantz said. "Looks like nobody's gonna see what happens next."

Jake inched sideways, flexing his fingers into fists, tensing his legs, preparing for a fight. "So, what now? Still mad about my little beach run the other day? Believe me, I've learned my lesson."

Fenrik gave him a little shove from behind. "Tell you what, Jakey-boy. You tell us why you were calling some psycho ward up in Vermont and we won't beat the living shit out of you."

Krantz shoved him back toward Fenrik. "–And blame it on a nasty spill you took down the stairs."

Jake swallowed. "So, it's going to be that kind of day? Fantastic. Okay, you got me, I'll talk."

"We're all ears."

"Listen, I need to have a doctor come down here and look at me. There's a chance..."

"That you're freakin' nuts?" Krantz giggled. "Wouldn't surprise me, given what we just learned."

"What?"

Fenrik gave him a shove, then backed out of the way as Jake threw an arm back to ward him off. "You hoping to get committed, Jakey?"

"It's not that kind of place."

Krantz faked a punch, then backed up, bouncing on his feet like a prizefighter. "Wouldn't have anything to do with a certain little boy who wandered off with a man who wasn't his daddy, now would it?"

Jake's blood went cold. He couldn't move. The guards were circling now. Fenrik moved in front of him. "Yeah, Jakey-boy. We did some digging. Turned up a file someone forgot to seal, one of your early sessions with our quack psychologist here."

"Rough life, kid," Krantz said, gloating. "Abducted from mommy and daddy when you were only a little tot." He made an exaggerated face and pretended to rub at his eyes.

Fenrik chuckled. "At Disney World, of all places. Ain't that a kick in the balls? Perverts everywhere."

Jake said nothing, warning his memories to stay back.

Krantz moved in closer. "You ever wonder if your ugly little mug showed up on the back of milk cartons?"

"Shut up."

Krantz laughed. "Wasn't so bad, though? Right? Got to live on a nice houseboat for ten years. Didn't have to go to school or do any homework."

"All you had to do," Fenrik said, in little more than a whisper, "was just lie back and let the old queer have his way."

Jake shuddered, his nails digging into his palms.

"Tell us, Jakey." Krantz moved right into his line of sight, inches from his face. Fenrik moved in close from the other side. "Do you miss his old leathery prick?"

Fenrik grabbed him by the shoulders. "Do you—"

Jake spun, his hands clasped together into one big fist that struck Fenrik square in his blurred-out face. The big man dropped to his side, choking and holding his blood-spurting nose, and then Jake was on him, pounding, punching, clawing... Choking.

Krantz leapt on his back, but Jake shook off the lighter man instantly, then went back to work, pummeling Fenrik.

Fenrik's head cracked against the ground, and his nose—now a flat pulpy ruin—took another direct hit. But that was when Krantz put all his weight into the baton swinging against the back of Jake's head.

And everything went black.

HE AWOKE in a sandy field punctuated by waist-high grass under a looming silver moon, with the sound of the surf competing with the cicadas. To the east stood the back-lit silhouette of Cocoa's correctional facility, surrounded by a glinting metal fence with a silver crown of barbed wire. Searchlights stabbed along the ground in the yard, roving, moving from the higher watchtowers.

He was a good half-mile at least from the fence.

Uh oh. How did I get out here?

Before he could even try to reason it out, two dark figures strode into his vision, one huge, the other built like a toothpick. *Oh shit*, Jake thought. *This is it*. Both men had guns, and they were just standing there, looking down at him like dispassionate mobsters, simply carrying out an assignment.

"Awake, Jakey?" Fenrik's voice sounded horrible, as if he

were still choking on blood. His nose had to be a mess, and Jake was surprised he was even walking and not in a hospital.

"We've got about ten minutes," said Krantz, waving a gun in Jake's direction. "Before someone notices you're gone."

"A lot can happen," Fenrik said, now holding a towel to his face, "in ten minutes."

"Then kill me already," Jake whispered. He stumbled to his feet, fought a rush of nausea, raised his hands and turned around. "This is probably the way you want me, right—a clean shot at my back?"

"We'll get to that," Fenrik said in a drool-laden garble. "You shouldn't have tried to escape."

Jake took a long breath, held and savored it as his last. He had to laugh in spite of it all. He turned his face to the cowering stars, to the near-blinding face of the moon, and then he closed his eyes.

Would he even hear the gunshots? The bastards were toying with him, but he wasn't going to give them the satisfaction of pleading, begging or whimpering. In fact, he was hoping they'd shoot soon. He'd suffered enough.

As he held his breath, questions struggled, vying to be answered before the end: Why had he been born this way? Were there really others like him? And most importantly—why could he see that woman on the news?

Silencing his questions, a single deafening gunshot, echoing off the distant prison walls.

A choked cry of surprise. A gurgling sound, then a collapse of something heavy.

Jake exhaled. He counted to five, waiting for the laughter, a final joke before the real shot. When he couldn't wait any longer, he turned. Slowly.

Only one guard remained on his feet, shining in the moon-light. Big Fenrik lay on the ground. His feet twitched, then were still.

"Listen to me, Jake." Krantz lowered his head, and the hand that held the .45 began to tremble. "Listen good."

His voice had shifted, turned hard, mirthless and almost unrecognizable. "In a minute, you're going to take my uniform. Then, you'll take my gun and go to the jeep—it's behind the trees right over there. The keys are in the ignition. There's five hundred dollars in the glove compartment. Get to the I-5 and drive until you hit the next exit, where you'll get out at the closest parking lot and switch cars. I assume you can hotwire a car?"

"Yes, but..."

"After that, you know where to go, right?"

Jake was still looking at Fenrik's body. "I think...I think so."

"Say it," Krantz whispered. And his hand rose, the gun coming with it.

Jake's tongue dried up as if he had just chewed a mouthful of salt. "Daedalus."

Krantz smiled. He reverently placed the gun's barrel to his own temple and, in the silvery-blue moonlight, his tears sparkled as they rolled down his face. His eyes pleaded with a vehemence that his body ignored.

Jake screamed and lunged.

And Krantz squeezed the trigger.

⧖

JAKE LOOKED BACK toward the prison, to the searchlights that were already lengthening, seeking the source of the gunshots. Dogs started barking.

Take my uniform, my gun, my jeep...

What if I refuse? Jake thought. *Sit here and surrender when they come?* Tell them the truth, as crazy as it sounded: that Krantz went psycho and shot his buddy, then himself. No, Jake doubted he'd even be given the chance to talk. Some trigger-happy guard would see the condition of his colleagues, and just start shooting.

More bad luck. Or was it something else? Whatever the case, there was only one path left now. All the other doors had been closed.

He had no other choice. He bent over Krantz and started to take off the guard's shirt. After changing and tossing his orange suit over Krantz's unseeing eyes. Jake picked up the gun and headed for the jeep.

10

Nevada

The knock at the front door came at the worst possible time, but Nestor Simms had never once believed his mission would be easy.

The Scourge would not go quietly; it might look weak and fragile, like the young woman strapped with leather belts to his bedposts, pretending to moan, bleeding those fake tears, trying to plead for her life through the duct-tape, but Nestor knew better. The demonic Scourge, living inside this girl, was far from defenseless. It had allies.

And now its minions had tracked him here, way out in the Nevada desert, thirty miles from Reno to his trailer home parked beside a wall of cactus trees shaped like infirm gargoyles.

The knocking again, insistent, demanding. And a voice, shouting through the window, "Nestor Simms?"

Nestor grimaced, pulled his two-hundred-and-forty-pound frame off the bed and gave the woman a quick glance-over before averting his eyes, ashamed suddenly, to be aroused by the demon's costume, its fleshly robes. The way her legs slid against each other as her body twisted, her neck straining... her face...

Ah, the face. At once Nestor's resolve returned. The Scourge was powerful, and other men might be ensnared by its guises, but not Nestor. He had the gift. The gift of True Sight. There it was...faces didn't lie.

That's what his father had said, right before Nestor killed him. Look at their faces, boy, and see the Devil, the Scourge. Faces don't lie.

Faces, like his own father's. Maybe no one else could truly see, but he could. He saw through the masks. Faces couldn't lie —not like mirrors. Despite what mirrors reflected, Nestor knew he had a face. He could feel it, touch the solidity of his own face. Constant, perfect, his features unchanging, not like the face he saw in the mirrors—before he broke them all.

The insistent knocking pulled him back into the present.

He'd been found.

AFTER ADJUSTING THE GAG, making sure the woman couldn't make a sound and that she was secured tight against her bonds, Nestor changed his t-shirt. He walked over crumpled Coke cans and empty Tequila bottles—the only thing able to keep the horror of his mission at bay. He walked past the frame that once held a mirror, now only fragments, shards hanging from the top frame like loose teeth in diseased gums.

When he opened the door and looked down upon the Scourge's minion—a blond-haired, blue-suited police officer with a blurred-out face and those horrid reflective sunglasses, he nearly lost his composure. But he found his inner strength and remained calm. "Can I help you, officer?"

The cop nodded, inclined his head slightly, trying to look around Nestor's considerable frame. Nestor saw the dusty police car ten yards away, noted the footprints in the dirt where the officer had obviously taken a little walk around, looking for anything suspicious.

The officer handed Nestor a newspaper. "Your Sunday paper, it was on the step."

"Thanks." Nestor took it and set it on the table beside him without looking at it, or away from the officer. "You moon-lighting as a paperboy?"

The cop shook his head without breaking a smile. "Nope, I'm here to ask about this." He held up a 6x9 photograph. "Seen this woman?"

Nestor squinted, leaned forward, suppressing a smile as he looked at the head of hair surrounding a jumbled-up mess where the face should have been.

"Nope," he said honestly. "Can't say as I have. What happened, another lost hiker?"

"Another one?" The mirrored sunglasses reflected Nestor's image suddenly, showing only the blur of his own undecipher-able features. "You hear of others?"

"Ah, always someone gettin' lost up here. Desert's a tough place for a hike."

The cop shoulders relaxed, just a little. "All the same, can you tell me if you've seen anyone recently?"

"Nope, been awhile since I seen anyone, 'cept maybe at the county store."

"How often you get into town, Mr. Simms?"

Nestor smiled, his tongue licking over yellow front teeth. "Twice a week's enough for me, officer. I have all I need out here, what with my DirecTV to keep track of the world, my water pump out back, and a couple chickens for some eggs."

The officer nodded absently, not even listening. His head was cocked and for a moment Nestor worried that his prisoner had somehow gotten free and had crawled into the path of the offi-cer's vision.

"Well then, Mr. Simms, be sure to keep an eye out for our lost hiker, and call anything in."

"Sure thing," Nestor said.

The officer turned, then paused just as Nestor was about to close the door. "Hey, I wonder if you wouldn't mind—it's been a long trip out here and I drank two cups of black coffee and I really got to go like a sonofabitch..."

"You can piss out back," Nestor said. "Against the cactus if you like."

The officer smiled. "Really, I'm sorry, but I'm thinkin' it might be more like a shit, but I didn't want to offend..."

Nestor lip quivered. "Oh. Well..."

"Really won't be no trouble," the officer said. "In and out, I promise."

Nestor glanced back at the mess in his kitchen and, before he could think of a response, the cop was stepping on in, holding his stomach. "Thanks, buddy. Really appreciate it."

As the metal door slammed shut, Nestor maneuvered to get in front of the officer to lead the way—and to make sure he reached and managed to shut the bedroom door before his guest passed on his way to the lone bathroom.

"Thanks again," the officer said, removing his sunglasses and grinning at Nestor as he stepped over bottles, empty potato chip bags and broken eggshells. "Nice place you got here."

Nestor said nothing, as he kept his hand on the bedroom's doorknob.

"Be right out," the officer said, shutting the bathroom door.

Nestor whispered a curse and finally, grudgingly, when it seemed the officer might be a few minutes, returned to the kitchen and began to clean up, picking up cans and putting them in the sink. Later in the week, he would have go into town and deposit the two-hundred and seventy-five dollars the girl had in her purse; it would join the small savings he had accumulated—spoils of war after defeating the others the Scourge had sent to test him.

It would be enough. Enough for what was to come. He had been dreaming lately, dreaming of a voyage he was meant to take. It would soon be time for him to leave the desert, his trials over, his preparation complete.

He had seen the castle in the snow. And the hourglass.

He turned on the sink to wash out the sticky cans, and a trio of big black flies buzzed out of the drain and flew up at his face. He shooed them away and turned his head slightly—where he noticed the newspaper lying on the table.

Nestor blinked. Once, twice. The flies returned and buzzed around his head. The water rose in the clogged sink and the empty tipped over. Somewhere, what seemed far away, a muffled moan sounded through the walls and a toilet flushed.

But all those sounds were like distant rumbles of thunder, beyond concern, beyond awareness. Nestor's world melted away as he lurched forward, caught the paper in his shaking hands, and brought it close to his face. His eyes darted back and forth, up and down over the headlines, the blazing block-letters spelling out a name that reverberated in his skull like the feathery wings of a thousand angels.

Monica Gilman.

It seemed this angel's eyes sought out his, and her clear, focused features were like a lost memory, a comfort he had never known, but still understood as the deepest source of his strength. His heart. His soul, there before him—the connection, the first and only face untouched by the Scourge.

Tears streamed down his eyes, his lips quivered and before he realized it, he was laughing... crying and laughing at the same time... holding that paper aloft, restraining himself from the urge to just kiss the woman's face, kiss Monica Gilman's perfectly visible lips, her eyes, her cheeks.

Monica...

Still laughing like a little boy in front of his favorite cartoon, dancing from foot to foot, Nestor didn't hear the choking gasp or the creaking of the bedroom door until it was almost too late.

"What the shit..."

The words barely resonated in Nestor's thoughts, and it

wasn't until the officer had finished fumbling with his gun, unhooking it from its holster, bending his knees, working at the safety, his eyes whipping back and forth from the horror on the bed and back to Nestor, that he moved.

Nestor turned, after first setting down the paper like it was a sacred relic. The officer tried to keep his weapon steady as he turned his head to the radio on his shoulder, attempting to call in for help.

Nestor saw the fear in the Scourge's jerking motions. It knew what it faced, and it was scared. Scared of the light and the purity in Nestor's heart. He took a step forward, calm. Certain of his fate, more certain now than ever.

It was time. The signal had come with a trumpet-blast, heralding the advent of his true mission.

The officer shouted, "Don't move! Not one more step, you piece of shit!" He glanced back to the bedroom and grimaced. "Son of a bitch, you're going to burn for this, you..."

Nestor took another step.

"I said stop!" the officer roared—and pulled the trigger.

Nestor blinked with the gun's deafening report, then he smiled. Something over his shoulder exploded and a piece of the ceiling fell behind him, clattering against the bottles and boxes.

"Stop, motherfu—" The officer fired again.

But Nestor had shifted, faster than even thought he could have. The cabinet door burst apart in a shower of splinters as he continued laughing, louder now, overwhelmed with a feeling of such utter joy and wonderment.

This is what it's like to dance with Angels, he thought, spreading his arms wide and rushing forward.

The officer shook the gun, aimed point-blank –

But Nestor slammed his hands around the man's throat and, in one quick motion, he twisted the officer's head around just as he'd wrung the neck of one of his chickens last night. He heard the satisfying snap, and then, with the faceless head gazing up at him through formless eyes, the officer's body slumped out of Nestor's grasp.

In the bedroom, the woman whimpered.

Nestor plucked the gun from the dead man's fingers, and then walked solemnly to the bed and pulled the trigger.

Her cries silenced for good, he tossed the gun aside, and began to pack.

11

Vermont

Monica and Gabriel rode the last half hour in silence. Gradually, her numbness had worn off on the long drive from Boston. Interstate 89 was far behind them and, for the past sixty minutes, Monica watched the hills and valleys give way to lush forests of swaying pines and sycamores, dizzying emerald mountains and sun-flooded branches. Route 100 had taken them north to Warren, skirting the edge of the Green Mountain National Forest. Something about all that natural land, so wild and untamed, had broken through Monica's shell; it called to her, whispering the virtues of loneliness and freedom.

She blinked away sudden tears and embraced the rising guilt —guilt that she dared to feel liberated; free of Paul, free of anyone, really, that cared about her. Free to disappoint no one but herself.

"We're close," Gabriel said, as if sensing her growing distraction and trying to bring her back. "Only twenty minutes."

Monica nodded, staring ahead at a log truck wobbling toward them. As it rumbled by, she glanced at Dr. Sterling. Keeping her gaze away from his blurred face, she focused on his hair: a lustrous silver, almost blue-gray in places; thick waves of it covering his head and smoothed back with hardened gel that seemed more suited to a hot-shot lawyer than a psychologist.

He was preoccupied too, she guessed, by his silence, by the way he had been avoiding even small talk the whole ride. He had his own problems and, whatever they were, he was heading back to face them with more than a little trepidation.

Heading back to Daedalus.

She didn't have any hopes, any feelings at all about her future. Maybe Gabriel could help get her to a better place, but she wasn't counting on it. Whatever awaited her, she didn't care anymore. She would just go along for the ride, a bitter and reluctant passenger.

She had been silent up until now, but felt it was time to say something. "Thank you."

His eyes darted sideways, met hers in a lost, yearning reach, then pulled back to the winding road. "For what?"

"Helping me. Saving me from jail."

"You weren't going to jail. No jury would have convicted you."

Monica shook her head. "I killed my husband. I belong there."

"You don't. Trust me, nothing would be served by locking you up. You're not a criminal, just a victim of genetics."

"Is that what this is? This 'Prosopagnosia'? Just genetics?"

"In your case, yes. Other patients have developed the condition after trauma—blows to the head, car accidents."

"The lucky ones, I suppose. At least they had time to be normal."

Gabriel took a slow breath. "Yes, but they have more to miss, while you, depending how you look at it, are fortunate that you never had full sight to begin with. You learned to cope from the beginning."

"Yeah, but didn't Shakespeare say it's better to have loved and lost, than... you know?"

Gabriel smiled. "But there's a big difference. Being born with it makes you stronger, gives you an edge."

"I don't know."

He gave a little shrug. "I promise you; we can teach you to think of this as a very manageable condition. You're different, but it doesn't have to limit you, prevent you from anything you want to do. In fact, it can open up new doors, new trails. In time, you might even see Prosopagnosia as something that makes you special."

"Special." The trees hurled by, each so different from the next, every trunk a different shape, with thick bark or gnarled stumps, the branches varied and definable. "Are these the kind of pep talks I can look forward to from now on?"

"Only if you'll agree to listen."

She forced her first true smile in a week. "Maybe."

"'Maybe' is a good start." He slowed and took a sharp turn as the car started climbing a steep hill while dark clouds gathered ahead, edging toward the sun.

Miles away in the dazzling acreage, where the lush evergreens gave way to a watercolor of snow-tipped pines, a dim outline drew her attention: a somber collection of red-brown walls and towers, of ivy-covered arches and glinting windows. It was set back in the woods as if retreating into a cave, avoiding the sun and the elements, withdrawing into the darkness where it could breathe.

For some reason, Monica felt it tugging at her insides, filling her lungs, quickening her pulse, sending shivers across her skin. Those towers, that outline—familiar somehow, like a childhood dollhouse rediscovered in the attic after so many years. It just crouched there, with snow suddenly falling around it as if the rumbling of Gabriel's SUV had sent tremors on ahead, shaking up the atmosphere like a snow globe.

Shivering, Monica tried to reach for the heater controls, but her hands were too heavy to lift.

"What's wrong?" Gabriel asked, slowing.

She could only shake her head.

"I've been here before."

12

Daedalus

The intrusion alarm—a shrill series of pulses—was like a shotgun blasting in Alexa's sensitive ears.

Sensing that Maria Eduardo was at her station, she shouted, "Shut that off! And then tell me what's happened?"

"We've been hacked!" Maria scampered to another terminal, scanning the screen. "Firewall breach."

Alexa was prepared for this, set to defend her secrecy from outside authorities, journalists or disturbed relatives, but for some reason, the timing of this attack, coming as it did, spoke of a different culprit. "Trace it."

"Already on it," Maria said, even as she turned off the alarm. She was a twenty-seven-year-old tech whiz who lived for computers, code and online games. An easy hire, a perfect fit—especially after Alexa had given her the first round of treatment, probing her past and finding her susceptible, eager even, to Alexa's compensation plan.

"What did they get?" Alexa asked, afraid of the answer.

"Shit. They found the encrypted folder."

Alexa lowered her head, and when she spoke, it was barely over a whisper. "You told me that file was undetectable."

"I'm sorry. It was—it should have been."

"You were supposed to be the best, Maria."

"They got lucky, found it by accident..."

"Or else," Alexa countered. "Someone was better." She shook her head. She'd deal with Maria soon enough. "Find this hacker. Can you at least do that?"

Keys tapped, followed by short heavy breaths. "Yes. There—got him. He might be good at breaking into places, but not so hot at getting out."

"Where is he?"

"India," Maria said. "Northern India..."

Alexa sucked in a breath. Despite this intrusion into her sanctuary, she was excited. This breach, coming so soon after Monica Gilman's publicity—and the mention of the Daedalus Institute—indicated someone was interested. *We may have just found one of the last two.*

Now... to reel him in. "Get Malcolm Byers on the phone. Maybe he can redeem himself."

Alexa allowed herself to smile. She was one step nearer to victory, to the end of the Grand Experiment. If this lead panned out, she would have identified five of the Six.

One more to go.

13

Jaipur, India

Pursued by the brazen intruder, Indra Velanati steered himself through the narrow doorway, stopped his wheelchair, and punched the door's close button just in time. A shining metal wall roared across the threshold, slamming shut just as the man lunged for him.

In the reverberating echoes, Indra looked up at the indicator lights.

The Panic Room was secure. He was safe.

⧖

SAFE FOR NOW.

Leaning back, he spun halfway around and drove to the main space, beside shelves full of canned goods, bags of rice, a water tank, an airplane-style latrine, and a gas-powered generator. Four small TV screens sparked to life over the counter. On the second one, Indra could see the man pounding his gloved fists against the door. A tall man, lanky with long arms and legs; dressed in a black suit.

Who was he? Indra didn't know, and right now it didn't matter. He knew why the intruder was here—because of what Indra had done earlier today. That much was certain—and confirmed again as he watched the man turn and head to Indra's desk, where he began rummaging through the mess of printouts, papers and folders, treading around the tall stacks of periodicals from around the world that teetered near collapse.

Indra was a collector of sorts; he spent every day, sometimes twenty hours without sleep at a time, poring through the world's news outlets. He was fluent in eight languages and could speed-read them all. He had an iron-clad mind with mental and intellectual skills that more than compensated for his physical disability.

He was barefoot as usual, and dressed in a relaxed white *kurta*, made of Khadi silk, and fastened along the side with gem-studded buttons. His hair was thick and unkempt, his beard ragged but not too long for a thirty-one-year-old man. When did he last eat? He couldn't remember. Not today, and most likely not since before the Philadelphia incident—before the sensational murder that made all the headlines. Before Mrs. Gilman.

Indra returned his attention to the room outside—his seven-hundred square foot apartment on the top floor of the Siddhartha Tower. His windows were painted black on the inside, so the only light came from a desk lamp and some track lighting along the far wall, above his mattress and a lone feather pillow. A golden statue of Nataraj, three-feet tall, stood beside the bed; she stood on a tortoise shell, her four arms extended in a spiritual pose—a transcendent dance willing the observer to part with the illusion of reality.

Of all the religious beliefs and icons from his strict upbringing, this one symbol was all Indra retained. All he believed in.

But since the train accident, he had spent his days learning, practicing to truly see. To peer beyond the veil of illusion. Maybe it was the blow to his head on the railroad tracks, maybe it was his shattered lower vertebrae and the severing of his potential for sexual pleasure, paralyzed as he was from the waist down. Or maybe it was the way his co-passengers that day—swarming like insects on a carcass—had ignored him completely and just moved to fill his place on the roof as others leapt onto the sides and hung onto the windows, all while he just lay there on the tracks, gasping, sure he was dead, watching the train ride off into the haze.

Indra shook his head, clearing the stubborn memories. He flicked a switch, then held down a red button and spoke into a microphone. "Hello there."

The intruder froze. Looked up, scanning the ceiling, looking for the camera. Indra pressed another button, and the lights went out. The screens all went black, then surged again, this time in an infrared view. The intruder was the lone subject on each screen, caught from four different angles, a mass of red and yellow, outlined in blue. Colors swirling.

Indra saw him turning, stumbling back to the wall, then feeling along for the front door.

"No help there, I'm afraid. The front door is bolted shut. Everything locked up tight and controlled from in here."

The figure slumped. Turned and walked in an erratic line back to the panic room door.

Indra cleared his throat. "I am speaking in English, assuming that is a safe bet. My guess is you were ordered here from, let me think… Vermont?"

The intruder's colors sparked, pulsed a brighter red.

"Oh good. I see I'm not far off. Listen, from in here I could wipe my computer's memory and incinerate the hard drive. I have all my information backed up in here anyway. I could call the police…"

"You won't," said a voice picked up by the outside speakers. The intruder stood up straight, arms at his side like a statue.

"No," Indra said. "You are correct, I won't. I do not wish to involve them. Instead, why don't you tell me why you are here?"

"You tell me. If you think you know so much."

Indra smiled, stroking his chin. "Fine. You are here because I was sloppy."

The intruder said nothing.

"I did not cover my tracks well enough when I went snooping in your servers."

Still silent.

"You traced me back here and, for that, I am impressed. It could not have been easy hacking backward through my aliases and firewalls."

"I don't know about that."

"Of course not. You're just the muscle. Not paid to think. Still, you came faster than I expected." Indra leaned back, pressing his fingers together, deep in thought. "So, will you talk?"

"About what? I only know so much."

Indra sighed. He was afraid of that. Just a lackey sent on a blind errand. "Okay, start with what you know."

"Why don't you come out of there?"

"Because you will kill me."

"Maybe not."

"I am in a wheelchair and no match for you. You will kill me like you killed that girl in London."

The red image flared again. *Two for two*, Indra thought. "Got the wrong one there?"

"How do you know all this?"

Indra leaned in, adjusting the microphone. "How did you know about the girl? Are there others? How many are you looking for?"

"Can't tell you that."

"Can't or won't?" Indra pressed another button. "The door is locked. The windows unbreakable. In a few minutes, you will hear a hissing sound, but you will not smell anything, since carbon monoxide is odorless. As you are learning, to your misfortune, I am a rather paranoid individual, prepared for the worst. I assure you: I will flood the room with gas. The vents have been calibrated quite specifically. At full strength—sixty-four hundred parts per million—you will feel light-headed and dizzy in two minutes. In ten, you will pass out. In twenty, you will be dead."

The man outside fumbled around in the dark, found a chair and sat down.

Indra grinned to himself. "Then, I will flush the vents, open this door and come out and dispose of your body down the trash chute." He waited, watching the red-hued silhouette carefully, imagining what the intruder was thinking. "You have ten minutes to talk. Tell me what I want to know and maybe I will stop the gas after you pass out. I will tie you up, and then leave you in here. After, of course, deactivating all the controls inside. Not to worry though, a man can survive in this room for two months if he is not wasteful."

"There are six," came the dull voice.

"Six?"

"That's how many we're looking for. That's all I know."

"Really? I doubt that."

"Believe what you want."

"Why are we special?"

"I don't know."

"WHY?" Indra pounded the table. "Why can I see Monica Gilman?"

"I don't know!"

He took a breath, trying to calm down. "Okay, let's start with easier questions. Do all of the Six have Prosopagnosia?"

"Do you?"

"You know the answer to that."

"Then yes."

"Who else have you identified?"

"I can't say."

"Are you trying to kill them all?"

"No. Not yet. Not until they come to Daedalus, and we can confirm their identities."

"What identities?"

"You don't know anything."

"I know enough," Indra snapped. "But I need to know more. What are their names?"

Silence.

"Who are they?"

"No. I can't... She would... She'd..."

"I understand your fear. So, why don't we play a game? I will run some names by you, and you can say Yes or No."

"What names?"

"Just a few I came across in your encrypted file on the Daedalus mainframe."

"If you already know, then why ask?"

"Maybe, like you, I need verification." He took a deep breath and read aloud from the list in his mind. "Jake Griffith?"

"Yes."

"Franklin Baynes?"

"Yes."

"Kaitlin Abrams?"

"Yes."

"Plus, Monica Gilman. Plus, me makes five. Who is the sixth?"

"We don't know."

"Why are there six?"

"I don't know. She never told us."

"How does she know there are six?"

"She just does."

Indra tapped his fingers on the console. Thinking, thinking. As soon as he'd come across the Gilman story and recognized her face, his life had been galvanized. For years before, he had been searching newspapers, surfing websites, reading magazines. Obsessed with faces, scanning everything and everybody, looking for just one thing—one person he could recognize.

After the accident, Indra turned... paranoid to say the least. He began to see threats everywhere, coming from everyone. He became a recluse, locking himself in his apartment, building the panic room. His family, once close, started to keep their distance. Oh, his father still maintained Indra's bank account, indulging his son's expensive hobbies, but there was little else in the way of family bonding. His four brothers rarely spoke to him, but his sister, Virisha, continued to look in on him from time to time. He continued to help the family indirectly with various consulting jobs for their business—a firm that Indra, as the oldest son, would have inherited had he not had Prosopagnosia, or at least had he been able to hide it better. Face-blind cripples were not well-suited to run multinational corporations.

So, he became a recluse. And his obsessions—dubbed "paranoid fantasies" by his family—became his life. He was convinced, after the train accident, that someone wanted him dead. Before the accident, he was only vaguely afraid. All the time. A disquieting suspicion surrounding everyday objects, people, unfamiliar places. Every day, he was faced with thousands of faceless strangers jammed into trains and cars, jostling, fighting, almost trampling each other for space just to walk on the street. He began to think of them as sinuous entities bent on driving him mad and killing him slowly.

Even after he learned of his condition, discovered it had a name, he knew he was different. Outwardly, he was a crazed loner, living behind black windows, installing a Panic Room in his apartment, having his food and necessities delivered anonymously to his door. Never socializing. But inside he knew. Knew he had a higher purpose. He was sure of it.

Returning his focus to the intruder, he turned up the volume. Heard raspy breathing. Gasping.

"You do not have long left, sir." Indra turned the dial on the gas, reducing the flow to half-level. "A few more minutes before you are unconscious. Anything you would like to add?"

"I'm not afraid to die."

"Why not?"

"What?"

"There are many reasons not to be afraid. Which one do you subscribe to? Loyalty, honor? Duty to your blind master? Or maybe it is something else?"

"Maybe."

Indra let the silence drag, punctuated by the desperate sounds of gasping breaths. Then he had a sudden rush of inspiration. "Do you think you'll live again?"

The red blur of a head spun around. He tried to stand. "What do you—?"

"Sit down. Conserve your energy. Is that your belief?"

The man said nothing.

"Or is it Alexa's?"

Silence. Again, Indra knew he was on the right path. Just throwing out the name of Daedalus's chief had the desired effect.

The intruder's color was bleeding out, violet turning to blue as he slumped in the chair. "It's her belief, but she has made it ours."

"Thank you," Indra said, turning up the gas. "After you're out, I will switch control to my computer out there, and I will lock down everything in this room. When you wake in here, help yourself to the food and water, but try to conserve. And do not bother screaming. No one will hear you."

The intruder, a mass of turquoise and swirling greens, slumped forward. "You won't… come back."

"You are probably correct, in which case I am truly sorry for the manner of your eventual death, but still—this way, at least I leave you with hope." He turned off the speakers and shut off the monitors.

He had much to consider, much to plan.

He was going to America. To Vermont.

To Daedalus.

BOOK TWO

THE DAEDALUS INSTITUTE

14

Nestor Simms kept the gun trained on the Kwik Fill clerk while he dialed 411 for an operator. The clerk lay sprawled on a pile of Frito-Lay snack bags, scattered when Nestor had thrown the kid into the shelves, before smashing in his face and then duct-taping his mouth and wrists. After incapacitating the clerk—the store's only occupant–Nestor had turned off the pumps and shut off the exterior lights.

The darkness was now pressing tightly against the windows. It was five-thirty in the morning, the sun still a good hour from making an appearance. Nestor had been driving all night, his third car since ditching the officer's stolen cruiser back in Nevada. Over a thousand miles lay behind him. A thousand miles from home.

A home he would never see again. He would never look back, only forward. Nothing mattered but his mission. He was getting closer. And like the man in his dreams—the one holding that beautiful hourglass—the sands were running low.

He put the phone to his ear. "Information," Nestor heard the operator say. "Directory assistance, what city and state please?"

"Bakersfield, Vermont."

"What listing, please?"

"The Daedalus Institute."

After a pause, the operator responded. "Hold for the number and you'll be automatically connected."

The clerk struggled. Nestor couldn't see anything in his face —except shades of black and blue. Whimpering sounds came from behind the tape. Nestor turned to the window, looking at his reflection in the dark pane. A blurry face swirled over his broad, sweaty shoulders, the ripped t-shirt, the Rangers baseball hat on backwards. He peered closer, trying to resolve the space under the hat, but couldn't place it, couldn't sense anything familiar.

The Scourge, still trying to break his will.

The phone answered on the third ring. A woman's voice. Professional, young. "Daedalus Institute. How may I direct your call?"

"I'd like to admit myself," Nestor said.

"Very good, sir. What is your condition?"

"I have that thing I heard about on the news. Proso-something."

"Prosopagnosia."

"Yes."

"Your name?"

"Nestor."

"Nestor what?"

He paused for a moment. "I can't say."

"I see. Where are you calling from?"

"I think I'm in Indianapolis. I'm driving to Vermont."

"Good. Tell me, Nestor, why are you calling?"

"I saw the newspaper story. The one with the woman who offed her husband."

"Yes. Ms. Gilman. And you called because of this story?"

"Because of her."

Something on the other end clicked. "Hold please. I'm going to transfer you to someone who can better assist you."

"Wait..."

A moment, and then: "Hello, Nestor?" An older voice. Feminine, but raspy, dark. And strange.

"Yes."

"My name is Alexa Pearl. I'm the head of the Daedalus Institute. I need to ask you a few questions before you get here."

"Why?"

"So we can help you better. You said you called because of Monica Gilman. Can you elaborate?"

"I *saw* her. I..." He stopped, not sure about the voice on the other end. Could be one of the demon's spies. *Must not reveal myself too early.*

"It's okay, Nestor. Keep going."

"Can you help me?"

"I can, Nestor. Yes. In fact, I can cure you."

Liar. Demon.

"Now, Nestor. I want you to listen to my voice. Listen carefully."

He frowned. All of a sudden, he felt dizzy. The room was swaying, the counter and the racks moving up and down like he was on a boat in a storm.

"We're tracing this call. I can have someone there in a few hours to pick you up. We'll get you here safely."

"No... No, I can come on my own."

"But I think you need help. You're desperate."

"Yes." The walls were tilting in the dark, shadows leeching the meager light.

"You're on the run, but you can't stop."

"No, I can't."

"Let us help."

"I can't stay here."

"Why not?"

"I just... can't."

"I see. Nestor. Do me a favor. Find a hotel, the nearest one, then call back at the number I'm going to leave for you."

Nestor shook his head. It seemed something had clawed its way inside his skull, burrowing into his brain. His palms were sweating, the phone felt wet, slippery. In his vision, that hourglass was spinning, taking shape. Red sands flying up and down uncontrollably.

"No," he whispered, fighting against a nearly overpowering weight. "I'll... I'll make it there myself. I don't trust anyone else."

"You can trust me, Nestor."

He shook his head again, violently, whipping it around and watching the faceless man in the window mimicking his actions. The image freed his mind, cleared away the entanglements.

The other end was silent for too long.

"Lady? You still there?" he asked.

"Yes, Nestor. I hear you. I wish you'd reconsider." Her voice had shifted. Lower, more soothing. The spider webs were reforming in Nestor's mind. She was powerful, *her voice...* something about it. He wanted to lay down, sit back and wait for her to send for him. Wanted to make her happy, whatever it took.

"No, I have to make it there myself. I must... see the woman."

"Monica."

"Yes. And I promise you, if I don't see her as soon as I get there, I *will* be upset..."

"You'll see her, Nestor. And others like her. Others you can see."

"Others?"

"Oh yes. Trust me, Nestor. Your curse will end. Come to Daedalus on your own, then. Hurry. Come, and I promise, you will be cured."

Nestor hung up, blinking away the decomposing webs. When his head cleared, he was smiling again. He turned and walked to the clerk who was still sobbing in a heap of potato chips. Nestor sighed. He pointed his gun at the clerk's head, at the shifting features, the demonic, sliding expressions.

The clerk grunted, shook his head.

As the echoing blast rang in his ears, Nestor proceeded to fill a large shopping bag full of high-carb foods, snacks and water. A couple of boxes of NoDoz and Tylenol. A six pack of Red Bull.

He would need his energy. He had a long way to go.

15

Daedalus

Her fingers sped over the Braille keypad, calling up information, sending orders to her people stationed around the globe, orders to prepare for the end. For their rewards.

It was almost over. The Six would soon be home, and her unfinished business at last concluded.

She shivered momentarily and pushed herself back in the chair. Atmospheric controls were kept tightly regulated down here, the temperature an even sixty-eight degrees, humidity at zero, soft lighting—only when necessary, when one of her brotherhood needed access. Like a cave down here, the vault perfectly preserved its contents, many of them already badly damaged before their rediscovery.

Wall-length bookshelves, crammed full of books, esoteric and incomprehensible to all but the sharpest and most open minds. A pity she couldn't read them directly, but she had scanned their contents and converted them through Braille translations and read them that way. Numerous times.

She took a sip of herbal tea—a special Egyptian blend of lapis-infused Chai, still hot—and then she got back to work. Her eyes, impenetrable and relentless as a grinding glacier, stared up at the darkness that teased with hints of revelation.

To Alexa, darkness and light were imaginary figments, wispy unrealities. Visionary senses, lights, darks, grays—they were all meaningless. Touch, taste, smell and sound—these alone were the conduits of reality, and blindness was not the deterrent it was made out to be. In fact, she felt she was at an advantage. Eyes could fool you; shadows and light played games with normal people, creating blind spots, causing complacency, false trust. Reliance on vision fostered a foolhardy belief in what you could see.

Alexa knew better. Reality could only be confirmed by what you *couldn't see.*

She tapped again on her keypad with one hand while the other rested on the spinning Braille wheel, its dots and raised bumps adjusting and changing instantly to the output.

When the latest transmission stopped, she swore and lifted her fingers into the air, silencing the flow of information. Her eyes shifted their attention, unerringly seeking out the panel on the eastern wall, the passage from the *Book of the Dead.*

Alexa flipped open her cell phone. The direct line was immediately picked up by Ursula, who was on the lookout in the lobby for any of their returning sheep. "Route me to Malcolm Byers, immediately."

"I've been trying," Ursula said. "No response."

"Try again."

"But..."

"Try again!" This was infuriating. Alexa was unused to her staff's hesitation and incompetence of late. She would have to use other means to deal with this inefficiency. Time was running out, and she didn't have the luxury of coddling her help.

"Okay, it's ringing," Ursula said, "but he's not going to answer. Something's wrong."

"Just put the call through to my phone." If something had gone wrong in India, she would have to act fast. The next nearest operative was in Germany. He'd have to be rerouted quickly, but he could be spared now since the Six had all been accounted for.

On the eighth ring, the call picked up.

She waited, hearing only faint breathing, then said: "Malcolm?"

"Sorry." The voice had a thick Indian accent. "Mr. Byers is... indisposed."

Alexa stopped herself from spinning. Leaned forward as if she could focus and send her essence through the phone. "Ah. Apparently, you are not as helpless as we assumed."

"You will find I am full of surprises."

Alexa nodded. "Mr. Indra Velanati. A pleasure to speak to you."

"Alexa Pearl, I presume?"

She bridled. This was unexpected. She had to play this game close to the vest. India. This outcome was unfortunate perhaps. Perhaps his country of origin gave him an edge the others didn't have.

Nothing's ever easy.

"I apologize for my associate's errant introduction, but I assure you I merely wanted to confirm your identity."

The other end was curiously silent. With her acute hearing, Alexa listened intently for any telltale noises, but it was as if he was in a soundproof box. Nothing else, no cars, no background noise, nothing.

What did he know about her? Too much, she guessed. Indra had Malcolm's phone but hadn't answered the calls before; most likely he was waiting to get somewhere safe, somewhere she couldn't easily track him. She wondered if, with his technical savvy, he had managed to block the GPS signal on Malcolm's phone.

She hoped not but didn't put the odds too high. While she listened, she typed on her laptop and sent Ursula a command to access the satellite system and begin a GPS search.

On the other end of the line, Alexa didn't like the deep and confident breaths she heard. It spoke of control and power, a power she didn't like her enemies to wield.

"So, Indra. I commend you on hacking into my system. I suppose I should thank you for pointing out security loopholes, which I've since corrected."

"Glad to be of assistance. Now why don't you tell me something?"

"Haven't you learned enough?" And just how much did you find out?

"There is always more to learn," Indra said. "Such is the nature of life. We only stop at death." He breathed out calmly, then added: "And sometimes, not even then."

Alexa's free hand clenched into a fist. *Damn.* Time to try another tack. She concentrated, drew up her strength, focused her energies. "Indra, I want you to listen to my *voice*. Listen closely…"

"No." Suddenly, on the other end, music sprang into life. Flutes and drums, Indian melodies. Hammering, discordant, jarring.

He had a stereo ready for distraction? *How much does he know?*

"Ms. Pearl, you listen to me." She could barely make him out over the pounding notes, the thumping drums. "I am giving you what you want. I am coming to you."

She dared to smile. "Good."

"You will not see me coming."

Alexa chuckled. "That should be obvious."

"You know what I mean. Goodbye for now. Preparations to make, plans to finalize. Until then, for your own sake, I would not harm the other five."

He's grasping at straws. He knows nothing.

"I don't know what you're talking about. But by all means, my door is always open. Come, we'll chat."

"Oh, we will."

Click.

Alexa pressed a button. "Ursula? Do you have his signal?"

"No, Ms. Pearl. It's been deactivated. No trace."

Of course.

She snapped her phone shut and pressed it tight between her hands and against her lips. Then she stood and bowed her head.

Now wasn't the time for anger. She was still in control, still had cards to play. Indra was paranoid, and that was her bad luck. He did his homework, trusting nothing. But still, he could only learn so much, only see so much.

It was what he couldn't see that mattered.

Alexa smiled in the dark, surrounded by the Egyptian gods and all their ancient words etched into stone. She walked four paces to her left, to the onyx table she knew was there, and reached unerringly for the sole item resting on the center of the table. Her hands touched the cold metal, the sculpted golden gargoyles, the smooth, familiar glass.

She pictured it in her mind, imagined the contents shifting, sliding. She turned it over, listening to the gently shifting sands, then set it back down on the table, heavy side up, and listened to every grain that shifted and fell within the hourglass.

When Indra came, she would be ready.

In the meantime, five others demanded her attention.

16

Outside of Bakersfield
Vermont

abriel pulled over at the last stop before Daedalus, a scenic viewing area, with four snow-draped picnic tables near a quaint, icicle-crowned restroom. A row of spruces, heavy with old snow, guarded an edge where the land gave way to a deep, narrow valley. Ahead, at the valley's narrowest point, a suspension bridge crossed over and connected with a freshly-shoveled road leading to the institute. Already the snow was building up across the ravine, coming down in thicker squalls, a blizzard in the making, further obscuring their destination.

"Why are we stopping?" Monica asked. Gabriel saw that her attention was still caught by the distant turrets peeking from the snow-shrouded façade of Daedalus. Her hands shook, and her face paled.

Gabriel peeled his fingers off the steering wheel. How to explain his gnawing fear? How to rationalize yesterday's events?

Franklin's recognition of Monica, his indisputable reaction on a neurobiological level?

"Bear with me, Monica. Please, I need to test something out first." Reaching into the back seat, he took his briefcase and brought it up front. He kept his eyes on hers as he snapped open the lid. *What does she see,* he wondered, *when she sees my face?* He had heard the descriptions from countless patients on how they visualized faces; each one was unique, but he really wanted to understand Monica's condition, partly to better protect her from Alexa, but also because, unlike any other patient, he felt compelled with the need to connect with her—in order perhaps to do the impossible and cure her. Again, he was struck by the emotion he saw in her face, the haunting, lonely eyes bearing so much pain.

"Test what?" she asked, turning her attention again to the snow-crested peaks, the swaying pines and the patient fortress looming across the ravine, retreating within the blizzard's shroud. "How crazy I am?"

"You're not crazy. But I might be, for what I'm about to do."

Gabriel found the file he had brought along to study on the plane down to Philadelphia. A thick file, everything he had on Franklin Baynes. After Alexa's last experiment, Gabriel was determined to find out what made Franklin so deserving of Alexa's focus. She had found something in Franklin, something she had been searching for. If she had a theory on Prosopagnosia, on its cure or cause, it was something she wouldn't share with Gabriel, and that infuriated him. She could have done those visual experiments with any of the patients, but she favored Franklin. Chose him for a reason that, Gabriel believed, was unrelated to the state of his disease.

Gabriel thumbed through the file until he found what he wanted, a glossy color photo of Franklin Baynes and two other men, wine connoisseurs delivering a presentation. He took the photo and pressed it to his chest. "Monica, indulge me please. I need you to take a look at something."

"Something?"

"Okay, someone."

The wind whistled around the car, icy flakes tapped the windshield, and the roiling clouds approached.

"Why?" she asked, still lost in the scenery, as if caught in the swirling blizzard, her blindness complete, the wind whipping around her. "What's the point?"

Gabriel turned the picture around. "Just look at this. One of the men here is a patient of mine, and that patient..."

Monica grudgingly turned her head to meet the photo. She blinked several times, then leaned in, peering closely, her eyes widening as Gabriel finished his sentence.

"...that patient, he somehow recognizes you."

Monica made a sound like a grunt; she snatched up the photo, ripped it from his hands, tearing it along the edge. She brought it to her face and stared. Lips quivering, hands shaking. "How is this possible? These other two, no, but him," she pointed at Franklin, jabbing the photo with her finger, "I know him!"

Gabriel's heart was thundering, and, despite the cold, his skin wet with sweat. In fact, he was burning up. "What do you see?"

Monica kept shaking her head, blinking rapidly. "His face, his eyes, everything, crystal clear. And...I don't know, I'm sure that I know him, know him so well. Jesus. Take me to him now!"

"Hold on." The fierceness of her reaction should not have surprised him, but still, he needed to proceed with caution. "Tell me, have you ever been to wineries in Napa Valley, to—"

"California? No, never."

"Any occasion to visit wine shows, or do you read those kinds of magazines, trade journals?"

"No."

He had to rule out other possibilities. Maybe she had associated some trauma with meeting Franklin and, despite her Prosopagnosia, his face had stuck somehow. This was an idea he had been toying with years ago, a cognitive-associative mechanism: tie the viewing of someone's face with a strong trigger, and maybe that could be enough to force a bond. It was a variation on the concept of how people force their minds to remember people's names at a party. Association.

Otherwise, what was happening was impossible. Gabriel felt as if he'd been hit by the same hammer that had just whacked Monica. He'd read her doctor's report, and he'd analyzed her himself. She had the most severe type of Prosopagnosia, just like Franklin—a total inability to resolve facial features, to recognize anyone by sight. She should not be seeing anything comprehensible, nothing that registered. Nothing. It was just...impossible.

Suddenly, she opened her door and a blast of icy wind rushed in, along with a barrage of snowflakes. Monica staggered out, falling to her knees and stumbling back up, still holding that picture. Gabriel went after her, nearly slipping on the ice on his first step, but he caught up by the time she had reached the chained edge at the lookout point. The wind bit hard, stinging and chilling him right through his clothes. He caught her by the shoulders and tried to steady her.

She spun and sank into his arms, sobbing against him. Her fingers clenched his shirt, her nails nearly tearing through it. A gust suddenly snatched Franklin's picture and whipped it high in the air and over the ravine.

She turned her face to the sky and whimpered: "Who is he?"

Gabriel held her back, awkwardly at first, then a little tighter.

"Franklin Baynes. Prosopagnosiac. One of the most desperate cases I've ever seen. He's completely withdrawn into himself, in a state of shock. We showed him your picture two days ago... and it was the first reaction he's given in over six years. He *saw* you, saw your face just like you recognized his."

Monica pulled away, suddenly looking ashamed of her weakness. "I swear I don't know where I would have seen him before..."

"I know." As she backed away, Gabriel stuck his hands in his pockets. He blinked against the furious snow as it started hammering down in thick chunks like exploding plaster. Already Monica's hair had turned white, and the car's windshield was covered with a heavy blanket of fluffy snow.

"Let's get back in the car," he said.

"And then what? Will you take me to him?"

"Not yet."

"Why not?" Her eyes brimmed with a sudden fury.

He took a deep, icy breath, and the stinging cold jarred his mind into gear. *Alexa.*

He could picture his blind boss, flanked by her thugs, waiting in the lobby, all of them hungry for her arrival. He thought of the tests done to Franklin. The drugs... The way Alexa had been operating all these years under a shroud of secrecy. *What does she do in that vault? What's so special about Franklin? And now Monica?*

"Dr. Sterling?"

He held up his hand. It was too dangerous. Franklin's condition had worsened only after Alexa came on board, after she had taken an interest in him. And now she was switching her attention to Monica Gilman. Gabriel couldn't let anything like what had happened to Franklin happen to Monica. She was his patient, damn it, and he wasn't going to lose control this time.

But he could only do so much, only protect her for so long. He would have to move fast when he got back. Put everything on the line and find out exactly what Alexa was doing, what danger Monica was in.

He was tempted to put her in the car and just turn around, run to another city and start over—or hide out—but the police would be on them in days if he didn't check in tomorrow. And he couldn't run from his responsibility. From his legacy.

No, there was only one way to go.

The snow swirled in miniature cyclones around their car, spinning around Monica and Gabriel. She huddled near the car, shivering, waiting for him to speak. *She trusts me,* Gabriel thought. *Trusts me to keep her safe. There's only one way.*

Back in the car, the heater competing with the cold, Gabriel told her a lie. The first and only lie he hoped he'd ever have to tell her.

"Take these pills now," he instructed, after opening his medical bag. "They'll help you sleep. We'll see Franklin in the morning, but now you need to rest."

She looked at him strangely and, Gabriel believed, for just a moment, she could actually peer through his blurry exterior and see the truth: that he wanted only to help her. Her intensity softened, melting like the flakes in her hair. She drank the pills down, finishing her water bottle, then gave him a look like she knew he wasn't being honest, but trusted him, nonetheless.

Fifteen minutes later, Monica was out. Fast asleep. Twenty milligrams of diazepam could be very effective, Gabriel thought as he drove slowly back onto the access road and across the slippery bridge. The SUV had to work hard but, in twenty minutes, the lights of Daedalus burned through the swirling flurries. A row of floodlights shone from the main façade, making it glow with a ghostly aura.

He parked outside the main entrance, where Ursula Markoff and another of Alexa's brotherhood, Gregory Stoltz, waited, bundled in scarves and long coats and trying to get in a quick smoke. Gabriel called for a wheelchair. He ignored their frowning looks as he pushed Monica into the garage and up the access ramp into the lobby. Far above, five flights up, the domed stained-glass ceiling loomed in mockery of a painted blue sky. The iron door slammed shut behind him.

Alexa glided out from the shadows.

Has she been waiting here for us all this time?

Alexa cocked her head, listening to the wheelchair's squeaking movements. "What did you give her?"

Gabriel shook himself free of snow. "Nice to see you too."

"What did you give her?!"

"Just a sedative. She was hysterical. I thought you'd want her relaxed and rested."

Alexa slammed her cane against the floor. "I want her awake and alert."

Gabriel shrugged. "You'll have to wait until tomorrow for that. I'm taking her to her room."

Alexa made a face, a wolfish snarl, then withdrew into the shadowy corridor, just as three nurses took her place.

Gabriel spoke in a low voice to the head nurse. "I want her under observation all night. No one is to disturb her."

"But, Dr. Sterling…"

"No one."

17

Heathrow Airport
London

K aitlin handed the cashier her roommate's credit card and passport. People were always saying how alike the two of them looked, once you got past the hair and the spikes and the rings. Now was the time to test it. She had gone back and taken Trish's car from the parking garage that was two blocks from their flat. Originally planning to try to sneak back into the flat for her identification, she had been relieved to find that Trish, a frequent traveler, had left her passport in the glove compartment.

She knew how it would look—her running—but she had no choice. She'd heard the murderer. They were going to pin this on her. If she stayed, she was either going to get killed, or go to prison. Neither outcome seemed particularly enticing.

The airline attendant studied the picture on Trish's passport and compared it to her driver's license. She frowned, then looked up at Kaitlin. "You really did a job on your hair."

Kaitlin shrugged. Being a punker had its advantages. "Sue my hairdresser. I did."

That got a hint of a smile. "Okay, you're all set. Gate twelve. You'll be in seat 15A. Enjoy your flight to Boston."

Kaitlin popped her bubble gum and snatched the ticket. She went on her way toward the inevitably long security line, and groaned when she saw how long it snaked back and forth, with people jostling each other and shuffling ahead inches at a time.

Stupid terrorists. Make it so hard for the rest of us to sneak out of the country when we really need to. She set her bag down, a silver backpack stuffed with only a few gift shop items: t-shirt, sweater, and a mindless romance novel to help pass the time, to get her mind off what just happened. She was trying not to think about it, keeping at arm's length the horrific and circling guilt that her roommate had just been murdered because of her.

She kicked her bag forward, put on her headphones and cranked up her iPod, then suddenly became aware of a disturbance behind her. People started making way for someone. The police—two men in blue escorting someone she couldn't quite see, cutting in front of people, moving and replacing the dividers as they brought the other guy up to the front of the line.

Special treatment? Kaitlin stood on her toes and tried to see. The cops held papers in their hands, papers they passed to the checkpoint officers.

Oh shit.

The credit card. She'd used it at the store, as well as the airline counter. By now, they had to know Trish was dead, and the killer would be the only one using her card.

Shit.

And that man they're bringing up there, in the acid-washed jeans, the Mohawk and the earrings, and...those tattoos.

Shit again. I'm screwed. They know I'm here.

They had brought Slider to identify her.

She thought about getting out of line. Turning back. But four policemen stood at the end of the line, holding those same papers. *My face on each one*, she presumed.

Better odds that way, though, rather than run the gauntlet and try to get past Slider. Bastard. He probably volunteered. Gladly doing his part to screw her over once more, without bothering to hear her side, without caring.

The line pushed ahead again. *Turn back*, she thought. *Slip out of line, head for the restrooms, and hope you don't draw attention.* Yeah, like a girl with spiked blue hair skipping out of line, avoiding the police, and trying to sneak into the restroom wouldn't attract attention.

The music blared, a cacophony of scathing drums, heart-drumming bass and screeching vocals. *I used to sound like that*, she thought. *Now I can't stand it.* It wasn't just the betrayal by Slider and her former band members. She had changed in the past few months, and now, with the brutality of death staring her in the face, her previous interests seemed so trivial.

Inching forward with the others, she wished she'd brought a hat. But really, when she got up there, what would it matter? Her earrings were out, true; she'd been concerned about the metal detectors exploding, but Slider had seen her up close without her adornments more than any other guy. He'd seen her bare face even though she had never seen his.

The boy and girl behind her started pushing each other, and the boy stepped on Kaitlin's foot. She bit her lip to hold back firing an F-bomb at him in front of his comatose parents. Instead, she glared at the boy's mom, and then dared look ahead.

Slider was no longer there.

He was walking through the line, weaving past the travelers, escorted by the detective. Taking the aggressive approach, searching the line before it got to the checkpoint.

He was only two bends in the line ahead, closing in.

Stay or run. Damned either way.

Heart thundering, biting her lip, she decided.

"Sorry." She pushed through the family behind her, then as

nondescriptly as possible, ducked under the rope and started to head for the restrooms. If she could make it that far, she'd try another change—cut her hair, bleach it maybe, put on glasses, a hat, something. There was no way she was making that flight.

Walking briskly, head down, pretending to be lost in her music, she got halfway to the restroom, across a crowded floor, before she felt strong hands on her shoulders. Two men in blue. She was turned around, the earphones removed.

"Sorry, miss, we need to ask you some questions."

"What?" *Try to appear shocked, outraged.* She pulled herself free. "Don't touch me!"

"Stay right here, ma'am." The taller one pointed somewhere behind him and motioned with his hand.

And here comes Slider. Her shoulders slumped. She took a deep breath and looked down at her pink shoes, and she tried not to give in to the rising dread, the tide of lost opportunities and wasted chances. She had been careless, too impatient.

Now, it was over. She had to assume the frame job was too clever. She didn't have an alibi, people must've seen her go into her flat around the time of the murder, and she had tried to leave the country. No one would believe her tale of assassins and mistaken identities.

She continued staring at her feet, even as Slider's signature boots stepped into view. The same polished steel-tips, black and imposing—they always made her think of the monoliths in *2001: A Space Odyssey*. Slider loved those boots.

Should she just give up? Lift her head, and just smile and hold out her wrists for the cuffs?

She looked up. Met his eyes, eyes that she couldn't recognize but knew didn't belong to anyone else, not with that signature rooster-like Mohawk, those flaming red eyebrows and the black ring through the right ear. She opened her mouth, then waited, frozen as he stared at her. As he scrutinized her.

"Well?" asked one of the security team, the bald one again.

"Umm..." Slider leaned in and, for a heart-thudding

moment, Kaitlin was sure he was about to sniff her, as if her fear or lingering sweat would give her away. *What's he doing? How can he not recognize me?*

"I don't know," he whispered. "I..." His eyes softened, his lips quivered, and his voice, when it came again, had dropped a notch to that familiar tone of Slider's, the one he used after sex, in those rare moments of contentment when he actually felt everything was right with the world. "No, it's not her. Sorry."

"You sure? She might have changed her appearance."

"Listen, jackoff." Slider turned to the cop. "I fucked the girl for two years, face to face—among other positions. I know what she looks like, and this isn't her." He turned back and gave a smile to Kaitlin. "Sorry, love, you're cute and all, but you're just not my type."

Kaitlin stared at his shifting, faceless expression, and gave a small nod. She mumbled something, turned, and slipped her earphones back on.

Heart thundering, nearly drowning out the music, she kept walking, finally making it to the restroom where she ducked into the first stall, gasping for air, and fighting to hold back the rush of nausea.

She was free, she was going to make it.

Move, she yelled to herself. *Get to the ATM, take out some cash...* But then what? She'd still need to use Trish's passport—or her own. The police would be looking for either one. She could try switching seats with someone or stealing another ticket if she got past security, but that was a big If.

Five minutes later, back in the main terminal, wandering with the tide of rushed travelers toward the food court, she was still running through the alternatives, and finding none. *This isn't going to work.* She wished she had some friends connected to the black market—someone to get her a fake passport. Didn't Interpol admit there were something like seven million passports reported missing? Surely one of those could be a passable match for her, if she could only find one, or have someone doctor up a new one.

But it would all take time. Time, for some reason, she didn't believe she had. *Red sand running out in an hourglass.* She trembled. Why did that image bother her?

Chin resting on her hands, she continued thinking, dreaming, trying to come up with something, and was so lost in thought that she didn't notice the man in the wheelchair pulling up in front of her until his raspy, breathless voice shattered her concentration.

"Sorry, miss. I saw you while those men were interrogating you."

Kat shrugged, still not looking up. "Yeah? So what?"

"You don't understand." A hand reached over and touched her arm—a soft, tender grasp that nonetheless jolted her. She backed away, staring into the face of the crippled man, expecting to see the usual unfamiliar blur.

"You do not understand," the man repeated. "I said I *saw* you."

Kaitlin's mouth hung open as she stared at a face she somehow knew.

"My name is Indra Velanati and, by that look in your eyes, Kaitlin, I am guessing you can see me as well."

She grabbed onto his arms for support, analyzing every feature, every familiar mark on his face, desperately trying to retrieve her memories, to remember why, how…

Indra smiled. " Fortune smiles upon us. I know where you are headed—the same place I am going."

"They're looking for me," Kat whispered, still not blinking, afraid to lose this image even for a second—the first tangible, visible face she had ever seen.

"I know," Indra said, taking her hands and giving them a light squeeze. "But do not worry. I have access to a private plane. Come, we are going to Vermont."

18

Outside of Springfield, MA

en miles before the last stop, Jake Griffith prepared to leap out of the train car where he'd spent the past eight hours, fitfully bumping against the wall, trying to sleep. He had shared the car with three cows and another fellow traveler, a homeless man.

Now, Jake bid his traveling companions goodbye, slung his backpack over his shoulder and jumped into a snowbank, rolling halfway down before gaining his feet.

When the last car had rumbled past, he stepped on the tracks, the steel planks twinkling in the silver-blue moonlight. He gazed over the crystalline landscape, where several inches of frosty snow blanketed the farmlands for miles, soaking up the luminescent starlight.

Jake started walking. *Keep heading north. That's all.*

In the morning, only a few hours away by the look of the spreading glow in the east, he'd find a gas station or a diner, get some breakfast, find a map, then steal a car.

Piece of cake.

He'd made it this far without a hitch.

Maybe his luck was changing.

⧗

FIFTEEN MILES OUTSIDE OF MONTPELIER, VT, driving a hot-wired Chevy Impala from a Marriott hotel parking lot, he saw the sirens in his rearview mirror.

What was I just thinking? Shaking his head, struggling not to laugh, he started slowing. *Bad luck, my old friend, where have you been?*

Pulled over by a state trooper for speeding—100 in a 55 zone.

No license. No registration. The only saving grace was that maybe the car hadn't been reported missing yet. The way Jake saw it, he had only one chance. If he was taken to the station, sooner or later, unless everyone in the local police department had Prosopagnosia, they'd spot Jake's resemblance to the escaped convict from Florida, and he'd be done. Caught and sent back down there for good. And didn't they have the death penalty? Two dead guards...

So, with the policeman shivering, holding a wavering flashlight, the flakes swirling around in the beam like hungry moths, Jake tried to give his best sob story.

"Sick mother up in Vermont. Going to visit her. She doesn't have long left."

The cop coughed, narrowing his eyes. "Aren't you the good son, eh? So, you just dropped everything, rushed to your car, and forgot to bring your wallet?"

"That's right," Jake said, looking up into the flashlight that had been roaming around his car, seeking anything suspicious in plain view. He shrugged. "I'm an idiot. I don't know how I'm even going to pay for dinner."

"I'm sure dear old Mom'll cover it. Probably got a home-cooked meal all ready for you. A little steak, potatoes and gravy?

What's her number, son?" He handed Jake a cell phone. "Give her a call and tell her you'll be a little late."

More bad luck. Jesus. Keep improvising. "I'll call her, but she may not answer. And she won't be making any hot meals. She's... in an institution."

The cop kept smiling. "I assume you know the number."

"I do." Jake dialed, thankful for his memory, honed by years of practice with details.

When someone picked up, he cleared his throat. "This is Jake," he said. "Um, from Florida? Alexa Pearl knows me; we talked the other day. Oh, good, she's there? Yes, put her on. Thanks."

The policeman ducked his head in and pushed the speakerphone button. "Let's all hear this."

"Jake? Where are you calling from?" Alexa's voice. He recognized it at once, chilling, numbing him to the bone.

"Hi, Ms. Pearl, I'm calling about my mother. I'm coming to visit her, you know, like we talked about earlier. But... I've been stopped by a friendly state trooper, and I fear I won't get to see Mom before she passes. Can you..."

"I'm sorry," the cop said, snatching up the phone. He turned off the speakerphone and placed it to his ear. "Who am I talking to?"

He frowned, silent for almost a full minute, wobbling in the wind. Finally, he nodded, glanced at Jake, then cocked his head. "I... see. Yes, but... Okay. Yeah, he's fine. A good son, like I thought." His eyes had glazed over, like someone had brushed a thin film of wax over them. "Definitely, Ms. Pearl. Give him an escort the rest of the way? I could do that, yes. Take him in my car? That's a better solution. Yes. Thank you, I'll make sure he gets there before the snowstorm gets any worse."

The cop hung up the phone, still smiling like he had just talked to an old, dear friend.

"Come with me, son. Wouldn't want to keep Mom waiting."

19

Daedalus

Monica woke to something less than full consciousness, not quite dreaming, not nearly awake. A strange room, dark, narrow. A hint of light issued from a window above the outline of a shadow-heavy door.

And a silhouette of someone, man or woman she couldn't tell, sitting in an ornate chair beside the bed. A low mumbling came from the figure, inaudible words spoken just for her, spoken to her deepest self, lifted out of her dreams.

This is real, real, real...

She listened but couldn't make sense of anything. The words failed to fit into patterns that made any kind of sense. It was like trying to identify faces.

But still, she knew, deep down, that if she did hear those words, if she gave in to their implications, followed their orders, her life would be over.

So, she willed herself to drift back into the world of dreams, yielding to the tugging pull of the dark. The figure shifted—was it a lady? One moment it looked like a thin, skeletal woman. The next, a gnarled old man.

Something glinted in the faint light, a gold-rimmed object held in the figure's hands.

And the unmistakable sound of sand whispering through an hourglass.

20

I n the corner office on the eastern wing on the top floor, a single, green-shaded banker's lamp bathed Gabriel's desk in a bubble of soft, trembling light. He sat, rubbing his neck as he studied the files, clippings, articles, and notes strewn in front of him.

It was 3:00 a.m. and he had made no progress. The answer had to be here, in his father's notes. Atticus Sterling had kept meticulous records. Everything he did, each observation of every patient. All his articles. His receipts, his journals.

But there were gaps.

Missing dates.

Whole periods of time. In 1968, Atticus had taken a sabbatical from his position as head of psychiatry at Green Mountain College and gone to Egypt. What he did there, what he found, where he visited, stayed, and studied—whatever he did, it was never spoken of, never recorded.

Or at least, not in his records up here. Maybe... the vault?

Upon his return, Atticus had promptly retired from the College and devoted his full attention to the institute he had founded five years earlier, dedicating himself to the study of genetic psychiatric disabilities, especially Prosopagnosia.

But then, things had gone south.

Gabriel scanned the headings of clippings from the local newspaper and science journals.

Renowned Psychologist Censured. Board Votes to Oust Sterling... On and on.

Atticus had begun delving into questionable practices, testing radical theories, using something he termed 'Deep Hypnosis.'

He was compared to Rasputin. Religious groups called him a warlock. Public institutions shunned his name, his papers were ridiculed. Patients checked out of Daedalus. His staff left in droves.

But the money never dried up. Instead, he always seemed to find new funding. Rich benefactors came to visit him, spending weeks at a time. There was something about the rich and powerful; they needed to believe they had been destined for their current greatness, and that their past lives were just as special.

Atticus filled a niche, like some traveling snake charmer of old.

When Gabriel began to pursue his own career, he suffered ridicule and discrimination, based solely on his association with his father. Through sheer determination, Gabriel had overcome the land mines Atticus had dropped in his path and made his own name for himself. However, there was one dream he shared with his father: He was still determined to treat this disease.

Atticus had dismissed his own son's ambitions. Gabriel was, in Atticus's words, a "waste". and his father made it clear he had no plans to leave him any part of his legacy. Gabriel began to wonder if his father regretted having a son in the first place. Before his father's trip to Egypt, Gabriel had some fond memories of a decent family life with a father who was a good man, if a little too busy. He was stern, distant, and unemotional, but never cruel.

All that changed after Egypt. Right up until he took his own life almost ten years later, Atticus never attempted to reconcile, never spared a single kind word or any notion of pride in his son's accomplishments.

Gabriel pushed the stacks away. Rubbed his eyes. This was getting him nowhere. He had gone over and over the same material. The same articles and journal entries. He had studied the patients' cases repeatedly, astonished that they actually believed what they had 'discovered' under his father's unique brand of hypnosis.

Past Life Regression.

There was the Senator who had been told he used to be a Druid around the time of Stonehenge's construction. An actress who was a Major in the Revolutionary War. A CEO that had been a 6th Century Persian Prince.

On and on. Every entry sickened Gabriel. He imagined his father, getting older and older, still managing to keep his intellect, his creativity strong. Giving his rich clients an even richer story, leading their subconscious minds, and filling them with such rubbish.

Gabriel stood up. He needed air. He needed answers. Outside his iron-rimmed windows, the snow beat steadily, into its sixth hour without pause. He peered outside, where the floodlights were obscured by blowing waves of white and shifting, rising drifts.

With the weight of all that snow pressing down on his thoughts, he realized where he had to go.

There was only one way to figure out what was happening, what Alexa was doing here. Obviously, she had some connection to Atticus. Maybe she was a daughter of one of his clients. Maybe his own daughter, one he conceived and never got the chance to see.

Gabriel could have walked away. Left Daedalus in Alexa's hands. But he wanted to reverse the stigma that Daedalus had suffered; he wanted to restore the facility and help these people his way. It wasn't enough that Alexa emulated his father's theories and methods; that she was a rabid follower of the same bizarre notions. No, she had *the key*. She had his legacy.

Whatever happened in Egypt, whatever his father discovered there, she had inherited it. And whatever it was, it had to be in that basement vault.

But now the stakes had changed. This wasn't just about his feelings of being cast aside or about his need to understand what happened to his father. Now, patients' lives were in danger.

There wasn't much time. Monica would be waking up soon. The others were coming, some of them already here. He had to learn what she planned for them. What she believed.

He had to get into that vault.

He strode out into the hall, listening to the door creak, breaking the silence of the darkened corridor, the shifting shadows punctuated by dimmed overhead lamps. He turned to the elevator doors, reached for them just as they opened, admitting Nurse Stamers.

"Oh, excuse me, Dr. Sterling." Her eyes were glazed, like she had just woken up. And she moved around him, strolling as if on her usual rounds.

"Nurse Stamers? Naomi?"

"Yes?" She paused, right foot in mid air.

Gabriel shook off a feeling of intense disassociation, like he had just stumbled into someone else's dream. "Why are you here? I left strict instructions for you to spend the night shift watching over Monica Gilman."

She turned, wobbling. Smiled, reached into her left jacket pocket, and removed a syringe. Pulled back the stopper. Still smiling.

Gabriel had the sudden impression of a marionette, its arms jerking listlessly with the motions of its handler.

"What are you--?"

She jabbed the needle into her wrist, deep into a vein.

"No!"

She pushed the stopper down, and then her eyes went white, and her head lolled to the side.

Gabriel caught her, ripped out the needle, setting her down as gently as he could. Her hands clenched, scratching at him, and then her arms dropped, and she lay still. *What was in that syringe?*

For a few scary moments she didn't take a breath, and then Gabriel found a pulse, extremely weak, and heard her take a small gasp.

He immediately ran for the phone in his office and called down to the infirmary. Then he went back and held the pale, cold nurse, rocking her slowly, waiting for the elevator doors to open, for the nurses to come, while only one thought raced through his mind.

Monica.

21

Alexa navigated the empty hallways, listening to the wind and the sound of her footsteps. She reached the doors for the stairwell and climbed up the eastern turret to the third floor, where she quickly caught up with the aides taking Franklin Baynes back to his room.

Frustrated that she couldn't wake Monica, couldn't have her conscious enough even to glance at Franklin, she ordered him taken away. She'd try again later.

Inside, after they had Franklin situated back in his bed, lightly sedated, she sent them away. She took a chair and pulled it up beside his bed. She slid her big leather purse off her shoulder, unzipped the bag and dug inside.

She pulled out the object and set it on the bed. On Franklin's chest.

She heard him gasp.

"That's right, Franklin. You remember this."

She heard him wheeze, felt the mattress tremble, and smelled urine as his bladder let go.

"Don't take your eyes off the hourglass, Franklin. Watch the sands."

It was time. Time to tie up loose ends. Unfinished business.

With Monica here, soon to be under her control, she didn't need Franklin. He was too much trouble. High maintenance. She knew the identities of the Six, and so he was no longer necessary.

"Franklin." She smiled, reached down, and touched his hand. "Our sessions were very informative, and you proved to be everything I had hoped for. For that, I thank you. And for that, I'll make this short and sweet. But don't worry, I'm sure the next life will turn out better for you."

She leaned in, her hair tickling his sweating face. "Picture your vineyards, Franklin. You're strolling through them, touring your Napa Valley estate, touching the grapes, tasting them, inhaling their wonderful scents. Are you there?"

"Yes." He always spoke so smoothly under hypnosis.

"Good, Franklin. Enjoy your walk. But keep your eye on these sands. When the top glass is empty, you're going to do exactly as I tell you."

22

Interstate 89
Vermont

Shortly after passing a slow-moving snowplow and veering back into the right lane, the police cruiser hit a thick drift, spun in a wide circle, and slammed into five feet of snow on the west side of the interstate.

Pure stupidity! Jake thought. *Not bad luck, not this time.* He wrestled with his seat belt, freed himself and turned to help the state trooper when Jake saw the blood fountaining down his face from the deep gash on the trooper's scalp and shattered nose. Still, his eyes rolled around in a sea of crimson and locked on Jake… just as the car's interior lit up like a solar flare.

The snowplow!

Without thinking, implicitly understanding that the cop was a goner, Jake lunged. Got the passenger door open and burst out, slipping and sliding across the street, praying the snowplow didn't veer left out of reflex.

Jake looked back, squinting through the onslaught of snow

and wind. Saw the police car crumple like a balsa wood model, then flatten into the snowbank as the plow drove it off the road.

Oh shit.

The plow skidded a little further, then ground to a halt.

Jake stumbled back onto the street, desperately looking back down the road, hoping to see another pair of headlights through the driving snow and the swirling darkness. But he remembered hearing on the police scanner that Vermont had issued a state-wide No Travel Advisory until the morning. No one was going to be out here except other snowplows. Or cops.

He dug his hands into his windbreaker's pockets after zipping up its meager collar. Teeth chattering, legs weak, ears already numb and tingling, he approached the plow. Smoke coughed out from the mashed cruiser, snatched immediately by the wind. *Maybe the snowplow driver's dead, too, or unconscious.* Jake had the wild hope that he could just take the plow and cruise the rest of the way.

The plow's door opened.

No such luck.

Jake stood still—just as the driver saw him and froze, too. Jake had an instant of doubt. What to do? He couldn't run. He'd be dead in a half hour, lost in the dark, unable to distinguish road from field. Frostbitten in no time, and then... he didn't want to think about it.

The snowplow was his only chance. Heat was his only chance. Now Jake wished he had thought ahead and grabbed the trooper's gun before bolting from the car.

The driver was huge and waving him forward. Jake stumbled ahead, still thinking about a way to overpower the driver. But then he saw the other man, another passenger. Just as big.

Damn it. Give me a break.

The driver was shouting back to his friend, and over the howling winds Jake made out the words, "Police" and "accident" and "hurry".

So, here it ends.

So close.

If not for the damn weather. If not for bad luck.

What were the odds that when the police got here, they wouldn't recognize him, they wouldn't ask what he was doing in the police car? Bad enough he would be blamed for the murders of Fenrik and Krantz, now they'd tack on 'cop-killer.'

Imagining he could already hear sirens, Jake slowly made his way to the snowplow's cab.

Right now, shivering so hard his bones were chattering with his teeth, he actually looked forward to being recaptured. He missed the humidity, the heat, and the bugs. Missed the palm trees and the scent of the salty ocean.

Just before climbing in, he gazed longingly ahead, to where the storm collided with the darkness. Goodbye Monica, and goodbye Daedalus.

Goodbye answers.

As he was about to confront the men inside the cab, head-lights appeared. Intensely bright, up high like a truck, or an equipped four-by-four. Coming fast.

Jake started to laugh. *Here come the cops. Or the National Guard.* Either way, he was screwed. Shaking his head, he raised his numb hands to ward off the lights. The other men were out of the cab now, one of them lighting a flare and signaling the approaching vehicle.

"It's not the police," one of them shouted, with surprise in his voice.

23

Nestor Simms found the snowplow shortly after 4:00 am. He had been driving a Ford F-50 with chained 22-inch mag wheels and a front plow, going dreadfully slow for the past twenty miles since the roadblock.

He had used the stolen vehicle's On-Star Navigation system to track a side route and bypass the National Guard's checkpoints, driving through the swirling blizzard and navigating the deserted roads with his fog lights.

Nestor looked ahead, to the outline of a mountain, and something on the way up: dim, flickering lights. Beacons, pointing the way. He was almost there, but now, this setback. Was it another test, or was it the Scourge making a last-ditch effort to throw him off its trail?

His headlights speared into the angrily whipping blizzard, and he could make out a massive vehicle set up high on thick tires. A plow truck sat on the side of the road, lit by a couple of meager flares, and three men waving their arms.

Then he saw the destroyed police car, and a mangled arm hanging out the window.

He slowed, meaning to pass around the men and just keep on his way; he couldn't afford any distractions. But one of the men, the smaller of the three, huddled with a blanket around his shoulders, turned his face to Nestor's car.

"Holy shit!" Nestor slammed on the brakes, skidded sideways and slid back to center. He threw the truck into park and leapt out before the truck had even stopped skidding. He raced around to the man whose face had appeared in the storm like a perfect beacon of clarity; he grabbed him by the shoulders and stared into his eyes. "Holy..."

"—shit!" the young man said, gaping back at Nestor. The winds tore at their voices, but circled around the two of them, almost protectively. "You can see me?"

Nestor nodded vigorously, snowflakes dancing across his vision. This was it—one of the signs! Miraculous things were happening. He shifted into action. "Get in my truck quick!"

"Hey!" One of the snowplow guys came closer. "We've got a dead cop back here, and that guy there... we don't know..."

Nestor pushed his new ally behind him, sent him skidding and tripping toward the truck. "Go," he shouted, and when the man had reached the door, Nestor turned around, facing the two demons.

⌛

JAKE GOT INSIDE, immediately enveloped in a soothing, warm cocoon. He closed the door against the harsh wind, and continued shivering as he looked out the windshield at his unlikely rescuer. *First the woman on TV and now this man.* His whole life, Jake hadn't been able to see anyone clearly, couldn't form the most basic of connections, but now...what the hell was happening?

Ahead, the snow swallowed up the big man and the two retreating snowplow guys, but not before Jake thought he saw his rescuer reach into his coat for something. Jake leaned forward, straining to see.

There were two bright flashes amidst the storm, followed by

muffled pops. Jake swallowed, still trying to make out anything but the angrily swirling flakes. A silhouette emerged, arms at his side, head down like a warrior-monk in prayer. Jake sat motionless as the big man rounded the truck's edge, paused in the headlights, grinning inside to Jake with that incredibly detailed and memorable face. Then the man was inside, sliding next to him behind the wheel, shaking off the snow.

"Name's Nestor," he said, extending a cold hand and shaking Jake's in a bear-grip. He slammed the door and put the Ford in gear. Jake pulled his hand away quickly, mumbling his own name as they skidded away from the crash scene.

"What did you...?"

The Ford's headlights angled away, down the drift-covered highway, and Nestor smiled at his passenger. "Nothing to be concerned about, my friend. Next stop, Daedalus!"

24

Boston, MA

The Lear Jet-60 belonged to Indra Velanati's father. One of three company planes, it seated seven comfortably in leather couch-like seats. A 27-inch plasma screen with DirecTV was mounted on the left wall, currently running CNN.

They would have landed in Boston eight and a half hours after departing London on any other day, but today they had been circling Logan International Airport for the better part of an hour, and their fuel was running out. They would have to land soon, snowstorm or not. The airport had been closed for three hours, with plows and deicers fighting a losing battle against the storm. One runway had been cleared for emergencies, and Indra's plane was fifth in line.

Kaitlin had slept for the last four hours, after washing her hair and cleaning up in the Lear's lavish bathroom. When she finally awoke, she saw Indra, his bony feet outstretched, a tabletop over his knees, piled high with folders, stacks of papers and glossy photographs. An Indian woman with long straight black hair, dressed in a blue-striped suit, stood beside him, sorting through the files.

Kaitlin stretched and blinked away an odd assortment of dreams and memories. Trish was dead. Her past life was over. All of England thought she was a murderer.

And she was on the run with this man, a stranger by all accounts but, somehow, she recognized him, knew him. Indra's face was warm, clear, and responsive, and she still couldn't believe that she could see him, that his features stayed locked in place.

"I thought it was a dream," she said.

Indra shook his head. "Welcome back. This is my sister, Virisha. You didn't get a chance to meet while we were taking off."

Kaitlin nodded. The woman's face was a blur surrounding a single dot on her forehead.

Virisha's voice was silky. "So, you're like him? You can't see faces?"

"Except for his," Kaitlin said, still staring at his eyes, his lips, his nose, every feature triggering some primal sense of understanding, a burning desire to know more, to grasp and hold on to an elusive lost treasure before it could be snatched away again. "And that woman in America. The one on the news."

"Monica Gilman," Virisha said, holding up an enlarged color photograph, a printout from the Web. Kaitlin trembled, staring at Monica's face, seeing the clear, recognizable features. She knew she shared something with Monica, with Indra, something profound. But whatever it was, it was elusive, slipping from her grasp after every attempt to understand it.

"Tell me," Indra said, looking up. "Do you know where you have seen her before?"

"No," Kaitlin whispered. "But... I feel like I've known her a long time. Like... she's important." She continued staring right into Indra's eyes, only barely aware of his sister's presence.

"Same with you. I haven't been able to 'see' anyone my whole fu... sorry, *freakin'* life. How's this possible?"

"That is what I am trying to determine," Indra whispered.

Virisha took a seat beside her brother. "What do you two have in common, then, besides this disease? Besides Prosopagnosia?"

Kaitlin shrugged and raised her eyebrows at him. "I'm guessing you don't like gothic punk music? Ever heard of *PinkEye*?"

"I had it as a kid, I think."

"We're not long-lost twins or something?" Kaitlin asked, attempting a grin. "No offense."

"None taken." Indra sighed. "But we are also not related to the other four."

Kaitlin gave Indra a puzzled look. "Other four?"

Virisha groaned. "Here we go. You must understand what a conspiracy nut my brother is. The whole world's out to get him. Hence, the panic room in his apartment."

"It saved my life."

Virisha nodded. "Even I have to admit there's something incredible going on here. Something that you two are a part of."

"Something," Indra added, "that is bringing the six of us together."

Kaitlin frowned. "Bringing us where?"

"To the Daedalus Institute."

"But why us, and who are the others?"

Indra rattled off the names from memory. He told her about the incident in his apartment, about the files he retrieved from Daedalus's server, about the call he intercepted. "Including the two of us, that's five; five of the people Daedalus had in their secret file. They are still waiting for one more, apparently. Or at least they were, as of yesterday."

Kaitlin shook her head. "I'm sorry. None of this makes any bloody sense. Why did they send someone to kill me? To kill you? Why do they want us dead?"

"I do not believe they intended to kill us. Not yet…"

Kaitlin thought about that for a moment but wasn't convinced.

"Why can I see you and Monica? Will I recognize the others too?"

"Probably," Indra said. "We share something. What it is—that is what we must find out."

Kaitlin crossed her arms and sat back, sighing. "Do you have any ideas?"

He regarded her for a moment. "A few. But first, we should eliminate obvious solutions."

"Okay. Go."

"Have we met before?"

Kaitlin tried to tune out the TV, a commercial between news segments. "No."

"Ever have any missing time?"

"What?"

"Any blackouts, any surgeries that left you unconscious for a long time, or in a coma, or…"

"No."

Virisha got up. "I'm going to check on the pilot, see how we're faring with the landing clearance."

Indra paid his sister no attention. He tapped his fingers together. "How about psychotherapy?"

"What?"

"Ever been treated by a specialist? Ever been hypnotized?"

Kaitlin kept shaking her head. "No therapy, but I probably should've been committed years ago." She leaned in, tugging at her left ear absently, feeling the holes the earrings used to fill and finding herself longing for their comforting presence. "What about you? You have any of those things? Have you been to Vermont?"

"Never. But I have been hospitalized, obviously." He tapped his withered legs. "Drugs, long periods of unconsciousness. I often wonder what might have been done to me during that time. Perhaps my brain was altered, memories implanted. Something..."

"But I don't remember anything like that. I've never had surgery. When would someone...?"

"It's just a possibility," Indra said. "There are other scenarios."

"Such as?"

He held up a steady hand. "Not yet. I need to know more. More about the Daedalus Institute and Alexa Pearl."

"Alexa who?" Kaitlin glanced at the TV, with its scenes of the snowstorm, of the thousands stranded at JFK and Logan International, of the state of emergency in Massachusetts and Vermont, the closed expressways, the power outages.

The plane lurched, dropped, and swerved to the side. Kaitlin gripped the arms of her chair. Indra picked up a file, opened it and showed Kaitlin a photo. "This picture is one of only a few she's ever allowed to be taken. This was from eight years ago. During her first week at the Institute, addressing the staff."

"I can't see her face," Kaitlin said.

"Nor can I." Next, Indra held up a printout from a local Chicago paper from 1994. "And this one was from when she was only fifteen years old."

"She's blind?" Kaitlin looked closely, saw the thin girl with the dark glasses and the cane, the headlines about her winning a scholarship despite her disability.

"Since birth," Indra said.

"Yale at sixteen," Kaitlin murmured, reading the text. "Must be academic hot-shit. What'd she go for, medicine?"

Indra shook his head. "You would think so, but no. Law. And also, surprisingly, she never graduated. As you can see by the size of this file, I've been busy digging into her background."

"Why'd you do that?"

"I like to be prepared."

"You saw Monica Gilman on the news, I take it. And then you checked out the institute?"

Indra nodded. "My gift, my curse. Suspicious of everyone. I felt an almost incomprehensible longing to seek her out."

"Jesus," Kaitlin said. "Me too."

"It was so intense, so extraordinary, I knew it could not be anything natural. And since I had no conscious memory of this woman..." He shrugged. "Sorry, my cynical nature made me seek out a potential villain in this scheme, and who else but the one who has promptly sought out and brought Mrs. Gilman to her?"

"What could she possibly have to do with all this?"

"Appearances are nothing," Indra said dismissively, patting his legs. "In any case, I made some calls to Yale's admissions, and I learned that Alexa Pearl dropped out unexpectedly, right in the middle of her senior year, another straight-A semester. Disappeared, in fact."

Kaitlin scratched her head. "Family problems?"

"I thought the same. Looked up her family. Called her father, who is living in the same home she was born in, down in Austin, Texas. Mother died when Alexa was a child, and they only had the one child. Dad loved her dearly despite her handicap, you could tell, but..."

"But?"

"But he claims she just... became someone else right after she dropped out of school. He didn't want to talk at first, but because of my promise I made to share anything I found with him, he relented. He told me that, for a while, he thought she might have been brainwashed by some cult. All of a sudden, she started acting as if she had just found out she was adopted and wanted nothing to do with her father anymore."

"Was she?" Kaitlin asked. "Adopted?"

"She was not. But her father felt disowned all the same and has been an emotional wreck ever since. He lost touch with her for years, until finally he brought in a private detective to track her down, which is how he found her at the Daedalus Institute."

"How'd she get that gig, anyway?"

Indra smiled. "That, as they say, is the million-dollar question. Why does a blind twenty-one-year-old young lady with no degree, no prior experience in psychology or medicine, just waltz into a private research facility and become its manager overnight, displacing, as I've found out, the reasonable alternative—one Gabriel Sterling, son of the original Daedalus founder?"

Kaitlin stared at Indra again. "But still, I'm dying to get there, to meet Monica. The others. You don't understand. It's like suddenly I know I have family, and..."

"Believe me, I do understand. The attraction is devastatingly powerful. Which is why I am being cautious." He studied the picture of Alexa Pearl again, the one of her poised like a high priestess on the grand stairway inside the Daedalus Institute, with a flock of attendants below her.

"Thank you," Kaitlin said, as tears welled in her eyes, emotions threatening to crumble her from the inside out. Finally, she wasn't in this alone anymore. Finally, her life had a direction. She was headed somewhere. Somewhere dangerous, for sure, but that didn't bother her as much as the curse of stagnation, the lack of a future.

She was about to ask Indra what else he knew, or what she could do to help with his research, when she heard him gasp, drop the folder and stare over her shoulder. She turned and felt as if the air had just been knocked out of her lungs. On the TV— another face she recognized without knowing how or why. But this one... it was even more powerful, and she reacted as if thousands of volts were ripping through her bones.

She stared at the man in a red jumpsuit, his hair long and wild, eyes hardened yet touched with an unfathomable sadness —the hint of a young boy who had never had the chance to grow up.

"Turn it up," Kaitlin whispered, but Indra was already reaching for the remote control.

"Meet Jake Griffith," he whispered, and for the next minute

they listened to the report about a manhunt up the east coast for an escaped convict who had murdered two guards. He was believed to be heading north, past Philadelphia and could be trying to reach Canada.

"Not Canada," Indra whispered. "Daedalus. He's headed there too."

25

Daedalus

Gabriel burst into Monica's room. In the darkness, for just a moment, he was sure he saw the outline of a spectral shape bending menacingly over Monica's sleeping figure.

He flicked the lights and the shape vanished. Monica slept on her side, eyelids trembling, her breathing deep and relaxed. Gabriel scanned the room, looked inside the closets, behind the door, then back to Monica. *On edge. Seeing things.*

He gently pulled up her covers and nudged the hair back from her face. He stopped. What was he doing? *Don't get emotionally involved. Not with patients.* Wasn't that his rule?

But where did that leave him? Forty-eight years old already, a family life passed over in pursuit of finding a cure for Prosopagnosia, an obsession that had consumed his youth, his relationships, and his future.

All for what?

He stood staring at Monica, at his trembling fingers inches from her face, thinking about the lost past. He lowered his hand slowly back to his side.

Turning off the light, he edged out of the room and eased the door shut. He took a deep breath, steeling his thoughts, and headed for the staircase. The lights flickered and the hallway seemed to glow in a blue haze, as if a phosphorescent fungus had overrun the walls. Three flights up, past his office on the top floor, past the records room and the conference room. He strode past the library, past more patient rooms, to the last door on the eastern wall. Again, the lights flickered, and he suddenly worried the power would fail tonight, the heat would die, and the lights would vanish. They had an auxiliary generator, like most care facilities, but with everything going on tonight, with everything seemingly going Alexa's way, it would only be fitting that the lights went off so she would have an even greater advantage.

Alexa. Just her name got his blood boiling. He had to confront her. No more waiting, no more digging through records, no more speculations, rumors, and gossip. This had gone too far. A nurse had almost died, and one of his patients had needlessly been placed in danger. There would be an inquiry, and he would make sure Alexa burned for this.

He stormed toward her office as the lights dimmed again and the windows on the east side trembled and rattled, and spearlength icicles swayed from the roof. Reaching her door, he turned the brass knob and stepped in. Two large flat screen monitors sat on her enormous oak desk, and Alexa sat between them, arms spread, hands working both keyboards simultaneously while she stared straight ahead as if expecting him.

One of her aides—Critchwell, the bald man in a black turtleneck—stood on the right side of the large office, the office that used to be Gabriel's and, before that, his father's. Behind Alexa's chair, on the wall above a glass-enclosed bookshelf, hung a six-foot tall, framed portrait of Atticus Sterling. His father's visage looked down on Gabriel with an expression that seemed to be an eerily similar match to Alexa's own glowering look.

"Dr. Sterling." As if reading his mind, she said, "Who else would be so inconsiderate to barge into my office unannounced? And at such a late hour? Don't you have a bed somewhere?"

Gabriel fumed, took two more steps to the desk, but then felt his legs withering under his father's scowling face. That portrait —he had stored it in the basement, in the back of the archive rooms, but Alexa had found it, brought it up and hung it back in its old place where Atticus used to stare at it every morning, as if in awe of himself. That same damn suit in the portrait that he always wore—the brown striped jacket with a black vest, and the red bowtie clumsily secured around his neck.

Making two fists, aware of Critchwell's tense stance, Gabriel said, "Why did you send Monica's nurse away?"

"Why did you drug Mrs. Gilman?" Alexa snapped back.

"Because she was hysterical."

Alexa cocked her head. She reluctantly took her hands away from the keyboards and folded her arms over her chest. "Did she have this reaction when she saw the Institute?"

"Yes, she did and..." Gabriel frowned. "What are you saying? Has she been here before?"

Alexa sat motionless, not responding.

"What have you done to her? Why did Nurse Stamers just try to kill herself?"

Alexa opened her mouth. "Ah, Nurse Stamers. How is she?"

"Resting in the infirmary. Sedated. We'll get her to the hospital tomorrow."

"If the roads permit."

Gabriel narrowed his eyes. "You didn't answer my question. What did you do? I demand..."

Alexa cut him off. "You're in no position to demand anything. As I said, you're only here for appearances sake."

"Screw you."

Alexa stood up, placed her palms down on the desk. "This is my institute. You... you're nothing but a waste."

Gabriel paled, took a step back. Looked up at his father's painted eyes, burning at him. *A waste. That's what he used to call me.* He could never please his father, never. No matter what he did, how well he excelled in his studies, none of it made an impact. And after his father's death, nothing changed. What had Gabriel really accomplished? No cures, no progress, nothing. He *was* a waste. His efforts were never good enough: not then, not now.

"Something to say, Dr. Sterling?"

His voice cracked: "I want to know."

She shook her head, the twinge of a smile on her lips.

"These are my patients," he said. "I will protect them."

Alexa shrugged. "You have your treatment methods. I have mine."

"We'll see which of ours the Board of Ethics approves. I'm calling them, having my staff document each and every violation. They'll be here at the first chance."

Alexa held up her hands. "I have nothing to hide. Now, if you don't mind, I'm very busy." She leaned over the desk and began scanning again with her fingers.

"Doing what?" Gabriel asked.

But the man with the snake tattoo was moving forward, coming to usher him out.

"Get some rest, Dr. Sterling," Alexa called without looking up.

Gabriel made a decision. He would not cave in to her again, and he wouldn't wait for the Board and their long process of investigation. Monica needed help now. He was sure that any further delays could be fatal. He had to act.

But before he could move—attempt to get around Alexa's associate and rush the desk...turn the monitors...see what she was doing—the door at his back flew open and slammed against the wall.

A nurse barged in. Celia Woods, from reception. Her face was red, and snowflakes were still melting on her hair.

"Ms. Pearl… Dr. Sterling—there's been an accident. Franklin Baynes…"

"Yes?" Alexa said, without a note of concern.

Gabriel couldn't move. He was rooted to the spot, staring at Alexa, at the unmistakable smile on her face.

Nurse Woods continued, "He jumped. Found an unlocked window on the fifth floor in an unoccupied room. We heard the sound from the lobby. He landed in a snowdrift, and it took time to find out what the noise was—I'm sorry, we thought it might have been a clump of snow falling from the roof, but we went out and finally found him."

"How is he?" Gabriel asked, not taking his eyes off Alexa.

"We took him to the infirmary. Severe hypothermia. Broken collarbone and some ribs. Internal bleeding, it looks like. He needs to be in a hospital."

"We can care for him," Alexa said, and Gabriel noticed that her smile had faded, replaced by a darker expression he couldn't quite place.

"No, we can't," Gabriel said. "We're nurses and psychologists, researchers. Not surgeons."

"We have a well-stocked infirmary," Alexa countered. "And no one's getting out in this storm. He can wait."

"It's not your decision," Gabriel said, reaching for his cell phone. "I'm calling 911. Both he and Nurse Stamers need hospitalization. Now."

He looked down at his cell phone, where the words 'No Service' blinked back at him.

"Shit." He looked up to Nurse Woods. "Are the phones–?"

"Out," she said. "A few minutes ago. Wires are down everywhere. Cell phones are having trouble finding service, more so than usual out here."

He stomped out into the hall, pulling Nurse Woods out with

him. The door eased shut, and the last image he saw was his father looming over Alexa, both of them wearing matching smirking faces.

26

They were almost there. And, as Nestor ground up the last mile and toiled up the last hill, his passenger slunk in the seat, huddled and looking shell-shocked.

Nestor couldn't worry about him now. Maybe Jake would rise to the challenge and become a valuable ally, but Nestor wasn't counting on help from anyone. Nothing else mattered but his mission. Finding and defeating the Scourge.

And finally, he was there, sliding to a stop as the snows parted to reveal the gothic spires, the crimson-eyed windows, the icicle-draped rooftops, and the great iron door opening before his headlights.

Welcoming him to Daedalus.

⧗

"Come this way, I'll show you to your rooms."

Jake stepped onto the marble staircase first, holding onto the polished brass rail, while Nestor followed him. He was in awe of the view up from the lobby: the impossibly high, tower-like stained-glass ceiling overhead, the outer railings of the five levels overlooking the marble floor below. Dizzy, he lurched after the woman in the tight black v-neck sweater and black pants.

"I'm sorry," he said, "Nurse–?"

"Markoff. Ursula Markoff." The lights dimmed and flickered suddenly. The nurse's face, the usual mass of blending features, seemed even more blurred somehow, as if that quarter-sized tattoo of a snake eating its tail on her neck was shedding its skin, further obscuring the nurse's face.

"Can't we take the elevator?"

"No, not during a storm. Can't risk a power outage. Don't want to get trapped in there all night, do we?"

Jake was about to say something clever about not minding being stuck in a small room with a hot nurse, but decided it wasn't appropriate. And besides, Ursula creeped him out, and Nestor... It was unnerving to be in the presence of someone he could actually *see*.

He followed close behind Ursula, watching her hips, the nonchalant movements of her arms that didn't quite mask the fact that she was tense.

A few steps behind him, Nestor quickly caught up and moved ahead of Jake. "Where's Monica?" he demanded, as they rounded the second level. "We came here to find her."

"You'll all meet in the morning," Ursula said without turning.

"All of us?" Jake asked, stopping, out of breath. "Who else is here?"

Ursula turned up to the next flight of stairs. The third level was dark, doors in each direction shadowed and murky. "There are others. As I said, you'll all meet tomorrow."

Flashing Nestor a look, Jake shrugged. "Don't you just love meeting new people?"

NESTOR'S ROOM was down the hall, the last one before the stairs, next to a small sitting room. Jake's was in the opposite wing.

Nurse Markoff lingered in the doorway for an uncomfortable moment, as if expecting a tip, before she bade him good night.

"Get some rest, and we'll see you in the morning."

Jake peeked at the digital clock by his bed. "So, in a few hours." He glanced around the room, tiny by most standards, but still like a hotel suite compared to his jail cell. "Is room service still open?"

"Breakfast is served between 7 and 10 in the morning. I advise getting there promptly at 7. We will be coming for you at 8."

Coming for me? The door closed and he held his breath, expecting to hear the sliding of a deadbolt, locking him in, or maybe some creepy organ music coming from some other floor?

Best not to waste time even trying to sleep. He waited a few minutes, then opened the door. Out in the hall, he stood, wavering. Should he go to Nestor's? See if he was up for talking, try to figure this out together?

No, there was something about the big man that made Jake uncomfortable. Better to stay on his own right now. Without another thought, he headed for the stairs.

A FEW MOMENTS later he saw the cameras. Blinking red lights on each floor, in the back corners of every hallway. *Tight security,* he thought. *Am I back in prison?* He supposed the patients needed to be monitored so they didn't hurt themselves or anything. Insurance.

But it raised a red flag, and suddenly he felt vulnerable, in danger. He moved quickly, silently on the soles of his bare feet; his sneakers were back in his room, drying on the radiator. The floor was cold, but served to sharpen his senses, kept him alert and awake. He stuck to the shadows, hoping that whoever was watching the monitors was either asleep or otherwise too busy to look carefully.

He scouted out the next two floors down, finding only more of the same—twenty or so patients' rooms, several sitting rooms and conference areas, snack machines, linen closets and shared rest rooms and showers. Then he crept down to the lobby level and paused, still out of sight of the main desk. It was too quiet down there; he couldn't go exploring the lobby, not yet.

Jake followed the stairwell down to the lower level. One flight up, the nurse Ursula was talking excitedly with someone, and Jake thought he heard the names, 'Nestor' and 'Ms. Pearl', and something about arranging a meeting. Then he was out of earshot, rounding the bend and descending into the darkness.

Might as well explore down here, he thought. He turned, rounded the corner, and then suddenly felt as if he were stepping into a marsh, dragging his legs through thick, swampy water. His chest seized up, and his throat tightened. All at once, he started to sweat.

The feeling crept over him, nearly as intense as the sensation in the pit of his stomach when he first looked up from the lobby at all those winding stairs. Or when he first saw Nestor, and Monica.

He'd been here before.

Shaking, grabbing the rail for support, he went down slowly, needing to regain his will before proceeding. Then the stairs ended, and he was at the entrance to a large area, lit sparsely by a few domed lights on a low-hanging ceiling crawling with pipes, air ducts, wires, and cobwebs. Deep shadows lurked in every corner and congregated around concrete pillars spread out like a maze around the floor.

From somewhere, he heard the echoes of a slow, steady drip, drip, drip. Jake moved carefully, imagining black-clad guardians poised behind the pillars or masked in the shadows, ready to pounce and silently slice his throat.

Steel doors glimmered, almost glowed, every so often on the walls, with small plaques on them. He got close enough to read the series of dates, 1950-1960 and 1960-1965. Archives. Jake tried the first door but found it locked. He kept walking, heading deeper into the room, where the lights were sparser and the shadows the thickest. He couldn't tell if the basement ended there or continued, but he knew... He just knew that there was a door up ahead.

A silver door. A thick door, like a bank vault.

How did I know that?

A door with something on it... a carving.

An hourglass.

He froze at edge of the light's meager reach. Ahead lay only thick and soupy blackness. He reached out a hand, waved it around in the inky gloom to make sure there wasn't a wall or some other immediate obstacle, and then resumed walking.

Five steps. Ten. He was in complete darkness now.

Still that dripping sound, getting closer.

Fifteen.

He glanced back. The light seemed an impossible distance away, a dying star in the black void.

But he knew where he was headed.

He'd been here before; he was sure of it.

How? When?

His whole life had been spent in Florida, most of it in seclusion aboard the houseboat. Every year since his escape was either spent on the beach or in jail. He had never been here.

And yet...

Five more steps and he came to the wall. His hands sought it out, felt the cold concrete, then moved to the right and felt the outline of a metal door, cold to the touch. And there in the center, a raised imprint. Jake's hands backed away. He had no desire to trace out what he knew was there, the hourglass. Instead, he reached for the door.

Just as it opened on its own.

A stabbing light, a narrow crack at first, then an immense rectangular slab. And a large hand caught his shirt and a man's voice boomed out, "Mr. Griffith. You're not allowed down here."

Jake backed up, blinking, his eyes screaming, unable to focus. He could make out just the blurry shape grabbing him, outlined against the light.

"Sleepwalking," he muttered, thinking fast. "Got lost, sorry." *Does everyone know me here?*

"Get back to your room." The grip loosened.

"Yes, sir." Jake took a step back, allowing his eyes to adjust a little more. He peeked over the bald man's shoulder to see a room with red walls, all sorts of things hanging on them like museum pieces and, in the center of the room, a mass of electronic equipment, computer screens, servers and wires.

And then the door slammed shut behind the man who stood there in the resurging darkness like a nightclub bouncer.

"Go," he said.

Jake turned and headed for the distant pinprick of a light, following it like a lifeline.

What seemed like hours later, after an uneventful climb back to the third floor where he saw and heard no one, he eased into bed.

Eventually he drifted off, fighting the certainty that his dreams, if they came at all, would be anything but pleasant.

27

Franklin Baynes woke just once, shortly after 5:00 a.m. It was his first moment of lucidity in nearly four years. The sedatives had worn off, and now he only felt a comfortable numbness, a little like sitting too close to a raging fire. He couldn't move, that much he determined at once. *Straps holding him in place?* He was lying on a bed with an IV hooked up to his left arm, and a tube up his nose. His ribs felt like he had been run over. Something was beeping.

The room was dark, but he could see a wall of windows ahead, exposed to a gloomy hallway.

And outside: a figure pressed up against the glass, looking in.

Franklin felt all the heat in the room leave at once. Shivering, he tried to raise his head, but couldn't move a muscle. Something was wrapped tight across his forehead, holding him fast. His wrists were bound. His legs too.

And with a rush, his memories returned. Memories of sitting propped in a wheelchair, a blur of changing faces on a screen or a white wall. One after another. Hundreds, thousands. Every day. Forced to stare at them as drugs numbed his body and clouded his mind. Unable to think, to dream, to remember.

Remember...

He could remember now, little things at first, tumbling into his thoughts and gaining clarity along with momentum.

A rolling series of smooth hills baking in the sun under a cloudless azure sky. The smell of grapes, the sound of bumblebees. Oh, sweet grapes. Each taste, a magnificent explosion of sweet and sour, blends of flavors so palpable, so potent. Bottles and vats, cases and more cases. He remembered it all. The meltdown at the awards ceremony. Checking into Daedalus. Meeting the woman.

He shuddered again.

The woman with the dark glasses. The woman with the voice that chilled his soul, flayed his thoughts and subdued his brain. She didn't need the drugs to keep him susceptible, they only augmented her already-indomitable control over his mind. He would do anything for her, at the slightest suggestion.

Even jump out a window. It was easy. It was what she wanted, and so it was what *he* wanted. He remembered the plunge and the impact: a wave of white, and a feeling as if he had been knocked out of his own body.

He had thought it was over, but now he was back. Needles and heating blankets, IV drips and bandages.

He was back.

But he couldn't move.

And someone was coming in, the same someone who had been silently watching him from the window.

At first, he thought he recognized her, the woman with the dark glasses, the woman from his memories, the years of experiments, the years of drooling, the years of staring at faces. So many faceless faces.

He thought it was her, but now he realized he was wrong.

So wrong.

It wasn't a woman,2 at all.

An old man hobbled towards him, cloaked in darkness and

haloed in a crimson radiance—a man with receding red hair and searing eyes.

A grinning man clutching an hourglass.

28

28

onica woke before dawn to the sound of someone prowling around her room. She sat up straight and reached to the side of the bed, expecting to find the nightstand, and the 9mm. But then she blinked in the light filtering through the iced windows. Floodlights from outside... she remembered seeing them once in the night, when she awoke and saw that strange woman studying her hungrily.

This wasn't her room. She was somewhere else, somewhere unrecognizable, yet still familiar.

She remembered now. There was no gun here. They had taken it away before the trial. After... Paul. She felt suddenly weighed down with a crushing despair. One mistake, brought on by a lifetime of fear, a setback from a disease she never asked for. Was this it, all there was to life? One chance, one roll of the dice, and then live with the consequences? No opportunity for a re-roll? It was too unfair—the universe couldn't be that cruel, could it? But there was hope, perhaps a light at the end of this dark tunnel. A photograph, someone she recognized...

Again, something moved in the room.

She blinked, shook her head, tried to get the shadows to

cooperate and stop moving. Then she finally caught a glimpse of gray hair, someone coming out of the darkness.

Gabriel. Dr. Sterling. Relief surged and memories fluttered back to her, as if returning after a long winter. The snowstorm, the long drive. He had brought her here, to the Daedalus Institute, had given her sedatives that put her out. He had been worried. Terrified.

And, by the look in his eyes, nothing had changed.

"Put this on," he whispered, holding out a white nurse's outfit. "I'm moving you, and you can't attract attention."

Monica frowned and pulled the sheets up, realizing her nightshirt had come undone. "Where? What time is it? What..."

"No time for questions. I'm moving you to a safe place." He helped fit the shirt over her head. "At least, I hope it's safe. Next to my office is a supply room and, in the back, there's a utility closet."

"You're putting me in a closet?"

"No one will think to search there for you. And it's big enough."

She tried to squeeze some humor out of it. "Color TV? Private shower?"

"Sorry, strictly fourth-class this time around. But let's get through this and I promise I'll put you up in the Ritz."

"Do I have to? I'm..."

"Scared, yes I know. But there's no alternative. Trust me."

Monica tried to smile as she swung her legs out over the bed and then she remembered something. The picture he had showed her before she took the pills. "Can I see that man first— the one I recognized? Franklin Baynes?"

Gabriel looked away. "Sorry... I just learned...it's why I'm moving you. He's dead."

"What?"

"It might have been accidental. They're saying it was an overdose of his pain medication, but I can't take that chance with you."

She backed away. "What's going on here?"

"I don't know, not for sure."

"Isn't this your place? Your clinic? You're the head..."

"Not really." Gabriel's voice was pained. It seemed like he wanted to say more but failed to find any words. He turned around and looked down as she changed, and then he led her to her a pair of comfortable slip-on shoes, warm and spongy just like the pair Paul had bought her for her birthday last year.

"Are there others?" she asked as he reached the door. "Others like me? Like Franklin?"

"Yes. Two others just arrived. They came looking for you."

"Oh my God." She felt dizzy again, the room spinning. The winds battered the windows and the hardening ice creaked along the panes like nails on a blackboard. "I've brought them here to die."

"No. If there's any blame, I should shoulder it. I've let this go on, failed to protect my patients. I won't let it happen again. And I've got to..." His voice hitched. "...make this right."

She gripped his wrist as he opened the door with his other hand. *I don't want to go out there. Out with them... with the faceless ones, the strangers. Nurses, other patients.* She wanted to stay in her room, hide in the closet or under the bed, and continue to believe in the darkness where nothing was necessarily *real*.

"Come on," Gabriel whispered. "Let's get moving." The door opened and a heavy-set black woman in a white uniform stood there. "This is Nurse Elsa," Gabriel said. "She'll take you to your hideout. Stay there until I return."

Monica backed away. "You're not coming too?"

"Too dangerous if anyone sees us together. She'll be looking for me. There are cameras, and..."

"She?" Monica staggered forward and had to lean on him. "I saw a woman in the night—thin like a ghost, wearing sunglasses in the dark."

Gabriel shot a glance at Elsa, then gripped Monica's shoulders. "Alexa Pearl—she was here? Did you talk to her, did she wake you?"

"No," Monica replied. "She tried to wake me up, but I couldn't rouse myself. I sensed she was really angry—pissed off that my drowsiness—I don't know, it upset her somehow."

"Good, you should be okay then." He released his grip. "Keep your head down and move quickly. Any other orderlies that approach you, beware of them—look for a mark, a tattoo." He touched the side of his neck. "A snake, eating its tail, right here. Anyone with that tattoo is part of Alexa's personal guard. They don't work for me, so don't trust them."

"What will you do?"

Gabriel tried to smile. "I do have other patients, you know."

"The other two?"

He nodded. "I've got to make sure they're safe as well. And see if there are any others coming, anyone else Alexa is expecting."

"How can she be expecting others? Have you figured out why I could see Franklin?"

"No, I haven't. Not yet. Listen, I need to check on the roads. If the storm lets up, maybe we can all get out of here in the morning."

Monica felt a nervous pit in her stomach. "Why do I have the bad feeling that tomorrow's too late? What about trying to leave right now? Got one of those snow-treaded all-terrain vehicles?"

"A Sno-Cat? No, sorry."

"Snowmobile? Skis? Snowshoes?"

"Sorry. We're a little remiss in our winter survival gear," Grabriel said. "A fact I'll remedy for next year."

"Assuming I have another year left."

"You will," Gabriel said after a moment's pause, speaking with such an abrupt shifting of conviction that Monica couldn't object. "And I promise we'll leave at the first chance. I'll get you all somewhere safe while I return with the authorities."

As he eased her out the door, Monica dared to hope. But as

soon as she let go of his arm and followed the nurse into the shadowy hallway, she had the sudden, sinking feeling that there were no second chances, no re-rolls. No fresh starts.

The blizzard had her sealed inside Daedalus, heaping snow over her like dirt over her casket.

29

Logan International Airport
Boston, MA

Kaitlin helped Virisha put their bags in the back of the Hummer, which had pulled up to the curb around the line of buried cabs, police cars and maintenance vehicles. The storm hadn't abated, only taken a small respite, but in the window of opportunity, flights were landing, and ten plows were busy on the exit ramps and in the parking area, industriously moving aside the heaps of crystalline ice and snow.

Her hands were numb within seconds, her nostrils frozen and her lungs burning, but she did her best to assist Indra out of his wheelchair and into the backseat while his sister folded up the chair and set it in the back.

"All set?" asked the driver, a Mr. Hank Bristle, an associate of Virisha's. As soon as Kaitlin slid into the backseat on the other side of Indra, and Virisha took the passenger seat beside Hank, the Hummer lurched forward, and a blast of warm air blew across her face.

The snow began to fall again. The flakes trickled from the purple-black haze of the sky, glimmering and sparkling in the predawn gloom. An army of snowplows and salters preceded them on the roads.

"Highway's opened just now," Bristle said. "But the state is still under a 'no unnecessary travel' order."

Indra grinned at Kaitlin. "Doesn't apply to us. Special privilege."

"How?" Kaitlin asked, again wondering at his resources. "What exactly does your family do?"

"A little of everything," Indra said. "Contract work for various governments."

"Jobs others don't like to do," Virisha added.

Indra continued rubbing his hands together for warmth, and Kaitlin wondered if his legs felt cold, or if they were completely immune to sensation. "My father's company specializes in obtaining knowledge of systems, security and defenses—and especially people. Lucrative. But not always ethical."

"For someone of my brother's high standards," Virisha amended. "Believes himself a little farther advanced than the rest of us. Isn't that right, brother?"

He shrugged. "Believe what you will. Progression is not a matter of heredity."

Kaitlin blinked.

"What he's saying," Virisha told her, "is that the family bond isn't really that meaningful once you get right down to it. It's more about who you are at a spiritual level."

Kaitlin shrugged. "What does it matter? Someone's trying to kill us."

"It matters," Indra said, "and someday you will learn why. But you are, of course, correct. For our current situation, we need only simple practicality and, for that, my family's resources are going to prove useful."

"So we've got permission to travel. What else? What do we do when we get there?" Kaitlin tugged at her ears, still thinking about London, about her dead friend, about the hunt that must be raging across England for her.

"Actually," said Indra. "*We* are not going. Just you."

"What?"

"Too dangerous for me, just yet. They will be on the lookout for me and, despite my family's resources, nothing can be done to get me out of this wheelchair." He patted his legs. "No, I would only be an impediment. And besides, there is something I must do first."

"So, what about me, then? I'm just going to march in there? They're looking for me too, or did you forget they want me dead?"

"I remember." He reached into the front and took a black briefcase from his sister. Tapping open the locks, he studied Kaitlin. "As I said, my father's company is good at information. Not only obtaining it, but... modifying it where necessary. In here, lies your new identity. You've already disguised your appearance enough, I believe, to get past their initial scrutiny."

"Lucky for us," Virisha said, "your appearance was quite... eccentric before. No one will recognize the real you."

"Great," Kaitlin said. "All those years of trying not to look normal, and now I've got to embrace it."

"You'll go in," Indra said, holding up a folder, "as Abigail Freise from Marlboro, Massachusetts. You've got Prosopagnosia, and you saw the news program and heard about Daedalus. Get yourself admitted, but don't answer questions about Monica in any way to tip your hand. And try to lose the British accent."

Kaitlin grinned. "What, you mean no 'gits' or 'buggers'? Or 'bloody hell'?"

"Exactly. Guard your expressions," Virisha added, "in case they show you her picture. Or Franklin's."

"Or Jake Griffith's," Indra said.

"Or the other one?" Kaitlin put her hands to her forehead. "There's one more, too that I might be able to see. You know what it's like. I don't think I can control my reactions around them."

"I know," Indra agreed. "But you will have to try. Avoid doctors at all costs. And do not trust anyone. Appear as normal as you can, just another Prosopagnosia-sufferer seeking relief. Get settled in and learn what you can."

"Snoop around, you mean?"

"Exactly."

Kaitlin tried to smile. "Snooping, I'm good at. Singing, not so sure. Running, escaping, not at all."

"Oh, I don't know," Virisha said. "I think you've done a pretty good job so far."

"And," Indra said, "I bet *PinkEye* is a complete loss without you."

"Maybe. But I feel I'm only free, and alive, thanks to you," Kaitlin pointed out. "I'm lucky you saw me."

"There is no luck," Indra said. "Good or bad. There is fate, and there are spiritual connections, but no luck."

"Okay, Mr. Fortune Cookie. What else should I do?"

"We'll give you a satellite phone. Security-issue. Boosted. Untraceable and scrambled. You can call me at any time, and I'll need to contact you when I'm ready. Find the lay of the land, and determine a way I can get in, wheelchair and all, if I have to. Myself—and possibly a guest."

Kaitlin glanced at his sister.

"No," Virisha said. "No cloak and dagger for me. I'm the geek in the server room, doctoring up passports and playing video games. I've got to keep up appearances at the state offices."

"Who, then? Police?"

Indra shook his head. "Too early to involve them. Someone else. Someone I need to see, someone who may hold the key to all of this."

"Where?" Kaitlin asked, feeling the vehicle slide slightly, then correct, as they took a turn onto the Interstate.

"In St. Claire, not far from Daedalus. A nursing home." Indra closed his eyes and leaned his head back. "She's eighty years old and, I only hope, still lucid enough to talk. That her memories are intact—or at least still reachable."

Reachable? Kaitlin shuddered, and again she had the image of a man holding out an hourglass, whispering to her, reaching into her soul, into her memories.

"Now," said Indra. "I suggest you get some rest during the ride. We are all going to need it."

30

Daedalus

Nestor paced, counting off steps in the small room, wringing his hands like an expectant father. A single mission-style lamp highlighted the room in a soft amber glow. He eyed the paintings on the walls, the quaint landscape scenes, the snow-capped peaks, and cabins in the woods.

He'd had enough of the snow and the cold. Enough of this frozen misery. Enough waiting. He still wore the same wet, chilled clothes, the socks, pants and sweatshirt he had been wearing for two days.

This was intolerable. He stopped and glared at the door. Why weren't they coming? He was here, at the end of his quest. He had to see the woman, Monica; had to pry the secrets from her, one way or another. Or he would have to try with Jake. He...

The doorknob turned and the door creaked. It opened slowly inward, agonizingly slow, as the shadows beyond stretched out to him.

Nestor froze, turning toward the hazy figure outlined in the dark beyond the lamp's feeble reach. Someone, alone. Thin, so thin he almost wasn't sure anyone was there.

"Nestor," came a whisper.

His lips cracked; his mouth dried up. A bone-white hand emerged into the light, and without thinking, his own stretched out meet it. Fingers touched, grasped, and then he was gently, slowly, pulling her forward.

A faceless woman, so thin and frail, yet composed and powerful. Ash-gold hair spilling down her face. He felt as if she held back her strength and, if she wanted to, she could tighten her grasp and shatter every bone in his hand. Her eyes—what he could make of them, were glossy-white and *wrong* somehow.

"Nestor," she whispered again as the door eased shut. "Thank you for waiting." In a blink, she was pressed close to him. He gasped and his lungs cleared, and he breathed in a cool, fresh scent like the freedom of death.

"I—I have come to destroy the Scourge..." He tried to form the last word, but she placed a finger on his lips and his lips felt like they had turned to brittle parchment.

"Ah yes, the Scourge."

"Where... is it?"

"I'll show you just how close it is."

He choked, desert air whispering through his bone-dry teeth.

"Just listen to my voice, Nestor."

He nodded, eyes swimming in and out of focus.

"Think of an hourglass."

Nestor's breath lodged in his throat.

"It's in a room, a vault—deep, deep in your soul. You are in the dark, heading there right now."

"Is the Scourge down there?"

"Yes, Nestor. Be patient, you're almost there."

He shuddered as the blackness descended across his vision, everything else dimming—but not before he noticed that the paintings on the walls had changed, their colors more vibrant—and now they were populated. People standing outside the cabin, toiling up the mountain. People that seemed familiar. Some wore hiking gear that he remembered; others he recognized only by the pattern of blood splatters down their shirts. Dozens of them, standing in the wilderness, heads down. Throats slashed, eyes gouged out, punctures, slashes through their flesh.

He had a moment to wonder how he could be seeing all this, when he felt someone's lips brushing against his neck, a breath in his ear, and then the room disappeared, replaced by near-darkness.

"Are you seeing it?"

"Yes, but I'm lost. I can't... So dark..."

"Just wait... now, you should see a dim light ahead."

"Yes, I see it."

A hot breath across his cheek, and an echoing whisper: "Follow it."

"I'm there," he said, after gathering his courage and striding forward into that nether-realm, the world he knew had to be the entrance to Hell. Quick, confident steps ahead. *This is it...*

"Are you there?"

"Yes."

Another tingling brush of her lips, followed by words—soothing, long-awaited words. Powerful words, syllables, phrases, echoing so deep, past his muscles, boring into his bones and drilling like a sonic charge through the wall of his spirit.

He had backed up—or he had been pushed—then lowered onto the bed. Still the whispers came, seeking, probing around in his soul until isolating one dark, occluded place, a lonely, secret place he never knew existed, a place as ancient as memory, existing long before Nestor Simms ever did.

More words—strange sounds full of consonants. Resonating in power and fury.

Then, something at last he could understand: "Open the door..."

"Yes..."

"Step inside…"

"I'm in…" Nestor gasped, and his rolled-back eyes were opposing mirrors of Alexa's as his inner vision beheld the source of all his pain. "An hourglass…" He almost choked on the words, his chest heaving as he saw the lone object hanging suspended in the dark, glimmering with a crimson radiance.

"Break it, Nestor! Do it now…"

In his mind, he watched himself move with purpose, with power. Here it was, right here, diabolically lodged in the very core of his soul. And now he understood at last…

This woman, his savior, had led him to it, made him face the nearly unbearable truth: that he himself carried the Scourge. A blur of motion, and he swept the hourglass up in his huge hands, then hurled it against the far wall.

It shattered into a hundred shards that hung poised with the sand crystals for several seconds—and then everything scattered as if blown by the wind into the resurging darkness.

He shuddered, trembled, and relaxed.

"You're free, Nestor. Open your eyes."

He did, and then he took a breath—a clear, open breath. And he saw—*saw* the face above his. The sharp, witch-like hair falling over her eyes, slicing, tickling his skin. The slim lips, the high elfish cheekbones and the blazing opaque eyes—turned away from his own, as if refusing even this minor aspect of intimacy.

Suddenly, he became aware of himself, rock-hard beneath her, and her hands moving, adjusting, freeing, and then he was inside her, and she was smiling, her tongue darting snakelike into his suddenly wet mouth.

"Free," she whispered, slamming her hips down upon him. "Free… You can see again."

"The Scourge…" he stammered, getting the words in between her fierce kisses, the biting, almost tearing snaps at his neck. "It was in me all along, but you've taken it away."

"Oh yes."

"All those people I killed…"

"It wasn't you. And now you're free. Free of the past, free of demons and ghosts alike."

"Who are you? An angel?"

She smiled. "An angel... I like that."

He grunted and the room continued to spin, faster this time as he felt her nails digging into the flesh of his back, scraping his spine, and he had the abrupt, certain fear that she would sink her teeth into his neck and rip out his jugular in the height of her passion.

He exploded within her, a blinding crescendo of pain and pleasure. And just as quick, as if disgusted with herself, she was off him, backing away, into the shadows.

Nestor's pulse subsided; his breathing relaxed. And then he heard her silky voice. "You're special, Nestor. Different from the others. And because of your... talents, I would ask of you a favor."

"But those things I did..." He held his head, and a crimson montage of faceless, writhing victims flashed in his mind.

"Yes, I know you feel the need to atone. Trust in me, and I will give you the opportunity for redemption."

Nestor swallowed, tasting a gritty residue. He looked down and saw himself, vulnerable, exposed, yet paralyzed still in the aftermath of an experience too exquisite to believe. One he might just have to reconcile as a dream.

"I am yours," Nestor whispered. "What can I do?"

"There are others," she said, gliding back toward the door. "Others with the Scourge."

"Monica. Jake."

"Yes, and two others. They too, must be cured. Exorcised."

"Like... what you just did to me?"

A chuckle. "No, no. You were special. The others can be freed by my voice alone. But you... I came to you tonight because I believe you can help me. The Scourge is strong, it seeks to evade me even now, when I'm so close. There are others here who seek to defend it, hide it from me, to keep me from my sacred duty."

"No..." His heart lurched again, pounding. Anger suddenly boiled in his veins.

"Yes, Nestor. Listen carefully. I need you."

"But you have other strong men—I've seen them."

"They lack your skills, skills you have proven on your journey here. Your single-mindedness. And besides, my other assistants... will not be with me for much longer. You will now be my eyes and ears. The others—those with the Scourge—go to them, act as one of them. Get them to trust you. And come back to me when you have learned what I need to know."

Nestor sat up, suddenly finding the strength. He fumbled with his zipper, then staggered forward and dropped to his knees as she retreated completely into the shadows.

He glanced at the paintings, but saw they were once again unpopulated. Barren mountaintops, empty landscapes. His soul felt just as empty. But it was a good empty, a cleansing empty.

He was free.

He bowed his head as the door opened.

"I am yours."

31

Daedalus
7:00 A.M.

lexa convened the meeting in her office. She positioned herself with Atticus Sterling hanging on the wall at her back. She knew his painted face looked on in anticipation, although she also felt his recrimination. His disgust at what she had just done.

She felt disgusted too. Revolted the few times she'd had to do that in the past eight years, but... Wasn't it wise to use all the resources at one's disposal, all the powers in one's arsenal in the pursuit of such a goal? But she shook off the feeling. In a few more days, possibly as soon as hours, this would all be over.

Then she could start again. Fresh, clean. Virginal and pure. Everything would be different, and it was impossible—against all odds, really—that it could be any worse next time.

Three large-screen monitors were each displaying an eight-way split, with different faces appearing in each. All of the sixteen men and women were marked with similar tattoos on their necks. Inside her office, Critchwell and Stoltz stood with Ursula on one side of the desk, and Maria Eduardo and Dominic Greiner stood on the other. She could feel their presences, and, in some cases, she could smell them—their perfume, or in Critchwell's case, that repugnant Polo aftershave, lingering after two days still without a shower. She had kept them all busy. Especially in the past week, but busy enough during the past eight years.

"The wait is almost over, my friends. Our task almost complete." She spoke calmly, forcefully to the ceiling, her arms at her side. "For those of you in the field, your work is done, and you have my eternal gratitude. We have four of the Six here, and the two I had feared lost have been located." She nodded to the middle screen, where she knew Edmund Vrees was watching, accepting her acknowledgement. He'd done good work, tapping his contacts at Homeland Security, keeping a lookout for a pair of passport flags.

"Indra has been accounted for. And a woman fitting the description of Kaitlin Abrams was aboard Indra's private flight from Heathrow, which landed in Boston an hour ago. Our sources confirm they took a chartered Hummer and made it to the Interstate, heading west." She beamed at the room. "Heading here."

A rumble of satisfaction broke out in the room. "We have only to wait and greet them at the door." She turned to face the back wall, the portrait of Dr. Sterling, Sr.

"You have all done a tremendous job, and each of you will get your promised reward." She pointed to her left, along the wall, where two cardboard boxes sat. "The champagne is here for my team and, in the field, each of you have your prepared vials. Mix it with the champagne and raise your glasses. It's time. Time for those of you outside of Daedalus. Very soon, we will all be together, but for now..."

Murmurs among the others on the intercom; in the room, excited whispers.

Alexa spun around with cat-like quickness. Her hair was coming undone after a lame attempt to fix it following Nestor's... conversion. It fell over her face, her glossy eyes shining through the dark glasses. "You may raise your glasses in celebration. Drink, and fly to your predecessors in eternity. We shall reunite very soon."

The five members of her local team came forward and stood close around Alexa, hands in their pockets as they watched their brothers and sisters on the monitors. Watched them pour something into their celebratory glasses. Pour, and then raise their glasses.

Each one had a glazed look in their eyes, an afterglow of an immense passion that had left them drained, susceptible and compliant. The people on the monitors toasted each other, bowed to Alexa.

And drank.

Everyone in Alexa's office hung their heads as one by one, the faces in the monitors contorted, eyes turned white, tongues lolled and blood spilled from their noses; they dropped from view, or collapsed back in their chairs. After another minute, the screens sparked and went black.

Alexa sighed. "It is done."

Inwardly, she smiled. They were fools to believe she'd share the secret with them. Sure, she had gone tinkering in their minds, but never to the extent necessary for what they wanted. Never as deep as with the Six.

No, where she was going next, she'd go alone. Much better that way, or else such power and knowledge would need to be shared. And that was simply not acceptable.

What was the point of Godhood if it had to be shared, even a little?

"Do not fear," she said to those around her, holding the

hands of the two closest. "Your time will come. Do your jobs today. Find and subdue Indra and Kaitlin. Keep the others from leaving."

"When will you attend to Monica and Jake?" Ursula asked.

Alexa closed her eyes and took a deep breath. "Now."

32

Daedalus
7:30 A.M.

Jake awoke to an insistent knocking at his door. Groggy, he rose and met Dr. Gabriel Sterling outside.

"Where's Nestor Simms?" Gabriel asked, his eyes shifting to the hallway cameras as he spoke.

"Dunno," Jake replied, yawning. "The big guy is a little odd, and… well, despite the fact that I can actually see his face, let's just say I'm glad we didn't have to share a bunk."

"You can see him," Gabriel asked, "really see his face, visualize it, rationalize the features?"

Jake nodded. "The whole shebang. And that woman on the news, too. They're the only ones."

"Ever?"

"Ever. My whole life."

"And Nestor—he had the same reaction to you?"

"Exactly."

Gabriel nodded, as if checking off a box on a questionnaire.

"Okay, listen. We need to talk. You, Nestor, and me. He's not in his room, so let's go check the cafeteria—they opened at seven. Maybe he was hungry."

"I know I am," Jake said, and had to stop himself from making a crack about prison food. He forgot, only the woman he had spoken to—Alexa—knew about him; this doctor might just as easily recognize his name from the news and turn him in.

Jake had to hold back all his questions until they made it down the stairs, crossed the lobby and entered a large room with diners in several lines gathering around the food stations, a coffee area and a drink machine. He followed the doctor to a small table in the back where they found Nestor leaning forward, arms folded, staring down at a cup of steaming coffee. He seemed at peace, remarkably relaxed, Jake thought, compared to his agitation last night. At the table, Jake had to pause and marvel again at how Nestor's face seemed so perfectly resolved, the details fixed in acute clarity.

Gabriel cleared his throat, reached over and shook the man's reluctantly-offered hand. "Nestor Simms? Good morning. I'm Dr. Gabriel Sterling. And obviously you've met Jake Griffith..."

"Sure have," Nestor said, smiling.

"Just yesterday," said Jake. "But I'm hoping you can help us remember where we've met before that, cuz nothing makes a shit's worth of sense anymore. Not since I saw Monica Gilman's picture on the news—and then saw Nestor on the road last night."

Gabriel took a seat, and Jake did the same. "I'm sorry to say, I'm as much in the dark right now as you, but I can tell you that you're both special in some way. We need to try to determine why you all can see each other. But I'm afraid the process won't be easy, or quick. And unfortunately, we don't have much time." Gabriel glanced around nervously, and Jake noticed that his attention lingered near the entrance to the cafeteria, at the large bald man standing there as if on guard. The same one from last night—at that strange basement door.

"Unless either of you are different, you probably don't remember ever being here, or…"

"It's weirdly familiar somehow," Jake said. "That's why I took a little tour last night."

Gabriel stiffened. "You what?"

"Sorry, but this is a sinister little place you got here, doc. Especially the basement."

"You've been down there?"

"Didn't get too far," said Jake. "WWF-type guy—that's him at the door—turned me back around." He frowned, studying the doctor's reaction. "I take it you haven't spent much time down there either? They don't let you in that room in the back?"

"No." Gabriel said, and merely shook his head. "Okay, listen. Here's what I know, and feel free to stop me at any time. There are four of you so far. The two of you, plus a patient who… died a few hours ago. Monica…"

"…Gilman," Nestor said, perking up. He leaned forward on his big arms. "Where is this woman? I came looking for her, expecting her. Why isn't she here?"

Gabriel lowered his voice. "She's hidden away. For now. And that's what we need to talk about. I believe you're all in danger. The other patient I talked about? His name was Franklin Baynes."

Jake cleared his throat. "You said he died last night?"

"Yes. Look, we don't have much time. A woman named Alexa Pearl runs this facility."

"I spoke to her before… before I left Florida," Jake said. "But this morning, when you introduced yourself—I figured you were the head honcho."

"That's what I thought too, up until Alexa showed up eight years ago. So yes, she's in charge. She's blind, but before you ask any stupid questions about why we can't just sneak past her, believe me, she has better senses than the rest of us. And her goons—others like that WWF type you mentioned, Jake—they back her up. They're her eyes and her muscle."

Jake asked, "So what does she want with us? And why can I see Monica—and this big guy here?" Glancing at Nestor, Jake was surprised to see he seemed distracted, as if he had somewhere else to be, or something else to do.

Gabriel shook his head. "I thought I'd have the answers by now, but I've got nothing but more questions. I've followed this condition, Prosopagnosia, for decades, and I've never seen anything like the reaction you two have experienced. It's like you have selective sight, selective recognition. It shouldn't be possible because the sections of the brain involved with facial pattern recognition don't work that way. It would be like someone who's color-blind being able to see just that one red stop sign on Main Street, and no others. It doesn't make any sense."

"But Alexa Pearl," Nestor said, lowering his voice and speaking reverently, as if in church. "It must make sense to her."

"I'm sure it does. And I'd venture to say your arrival is exactly what she came here for, what she's been preparing for all these years."

"Well," said Jake. "That just takes the creepiness factor up a notch."

"I don't know," Nestor said. "Maybe we should keep an open mind."

Jake gave Nestor a look, but then snapped his head back to Gabriel. "Wait—I had a thought. You said it's like we're experiencing 'selective sight'?"

"Yes," Gabriel said. "It's not a technical term, mind you, just something that I think fits."

"Well, what if it's the other way around? What if it's really 'selective blindness'?"

Nestor blinked at him. "What the hell are you talking about?"

Jake's heart quickened. Here he was, in the midst of strangers, telling a professional how to do his job. "I find whenever I'm stuck with some problem, I try flipping it. Looking at something from the opposite perspective changes the whole thing and gives you new insights. It's one of the ways I coped with this face blindness thing."

"So," Gabriel said, the words coming quickly, "you're suggesting that, instead of the miracle being that you two can see each other, the real mystery is the fact that you're blind when it comes to everyone else?"

Nestor grumbled, "Isn't that the same damn thing?"

"No," said Gabriel. "I think I see where he's going with this."

Jake smiled. "Thanks, man. Just trying to help."

Gabriel rubbed his temples. "Selective face-blindness. There's actually nothing physically wrong with your ability to see others, but for some reason your brain is blocking out everyone's faces—except for a certain few." He scratched his head and, for a moment, Jake thought he might have fallen asleep or put himself in a trance, but then he perked up. "But why—and how could the brain have been reprogrammed with such specific instructions?"

Jake reached for his coffee and took a deep gulp. As the silence dragged, he finally said, "So, where does this leave us?"

"Nowhere," Nestor said. "This is stupid. Let's go get this Monica woman and see what she knows."

"Not yet," Gabriel said.

Nestor's face darkened. "Why not?

"Because," Gabriel said, "I believe she's in danger. You all are. I don't think Alexa's interest in you is professional, by any means."

Jake sighed. "If my recent bad luck is any indication, I'm betting you're right. I didn't have time to tell you this before, Nestor, but I'm scared more than a little shitless right now. Some weird crap happened to me on the way up here. Stuff that had me thinking someone really wanted me to get here. And fast."

Gabriel looked at him strangely. "What do you mean?"

"Let's just say I was running from some people, and they should've caught me, but I made it."

"I thought," Nestor said, "that you usually have bad luck?"

"Exactly. I never should have made it here. Not without help. What about you, amigo? Anything weird happen on your journey?"

Nestor stared at him coldly before shaking his head. "Other than the snowstorm, piece of cake."

"Okay, okay." Gabriel sighed. "This has only made me more suspicious, and certain that I have to get all of you to safety. And that means out of this institute."

"But the snowstorm!" Nestor protested. "We shouldn't go anywhere."

"I know, but the roads are clearing." Gabriel glanced at the ice-crusted windows and the drifts piled high. "We might have an opportunity to get out, find a safe site nearby, and then I can come back with inspectors and officials and..."

"Wait, wait!" Nestor stood up. "I'm not sure about you guys, but I came here because I thought I could be cured. I came because of that woman, Monica. And nothing else matters. I came for a cure, and I'm not leaving until I find it. Or at least, until I talk to Monica and anyone else whose face I can see."

Jake nodded. "Sorry, Doc—I kind of agree with Nestor. But I'm also sure we need to be on our guard."

"Please," Gabriel pleaded. "Think this through. Something happened to you, something... maybe in your past. Something Alexa knows about."

Jake twirled a sugar packet in his fingers. "You saying she did this to us?"

"No. But only because that's not possible. She's only twenty-nine, and you've all had this condition your entire lives, correct?"

Both nodded.

"Unless," Jake said, "maybe we do have this Prosopagnosia, but somewhere along the line someone came along and implanted a little—I don't know—recognition program, a microchip or something programmed with each others' faces, and ..."

Gabriel was shaking his head. "Can't work that way."

"Why not?" Jake asked. "Maybe Alexa's got some new technology you don't know about. Some experimental shit."

"But how did she find all of you?"

Jake tried to reason it out but came up blank.

"You didn't exactly broadcast your condition," Gabriel continued, "And if she wanted test subjects, she's had access to more than enough, right here."

Jake was silent. His eyes met Nestor's for a second, then they both looked away. "Wait a minute," Gabriel said finally, rubbing his hands through his hair. "This is absolutely crazy, but I want to test something." He took out a business card from inside his coat pocket, held it in front of his face. Then flipped it and set it down between Jake and Nestor. The reaction was like a lightning bolt. Jake backed away and nearly leapt from his chair as he stared at the Daedalus insignia: an hourglass superimposed over the castle façade.

And Gabriel whistled. "Jesus."

"That goddamned thing," Jake whispered. "All my life, as long as I can remember, just seeing one of those things freaked me out. Especially in that movie…"

"What movie?" Nestor asked.

Jake trembled and said: "It had red sand. In my nightmares, it's always red sand in an hourglass."

"You say it was red?" Gabriel rubbed his eyes like he was trying to wake up from a bad dream. "It's not possible. But…"

"What movie?" Nestor asked again.

Gabriel stared at them all for a long moment. *"The Wizard of Oz."*

Nestor blinked at him, then at Jake, who said: "I'm guessing you're not much of a movie buff?"

Gabriel stood, rubbing his chin. "My father… He made connections in the film industry and treated a lot of old-time producers. He bought the set prop."

Jake scratched his head. "He bought the hourglass? Why?"

"He was a fanatic, a collector. A colleague and friend of Frank Baum early on. They were both into the occult, members of the Theosophical Society."

"The what?"

Gabriel waved a hand. "Mystical nonsense. Secret knowledge, magical energies. Latent powers in every human being, spiritual progression—that sort of thing. Baum actually worked a lot of these beliefs into his books. Oz itself is short for the Egyptian god, Osiris. Many of the quests the characters went on were symbolic, and..."

"Get to the point," Nestor snapped.

Gabriel sat back, scratching his chin. "Maybe someone else is using the same thing, the same technique now." He glanced up. "Using it on you."

"You lost me again, Doc."

"My father used the hourglass in his sessions. Used it as other hypnotists might use a candle, or a stopwatch. He thought it held a universal attraction for some deep level of our subconscious. The whole 'sands as a measure of life and time' kind of thing." Gabriel took a breath. "By using such an aid, theoretically, he could access deeper levels of the patient's awareness and spirituality."

"How deep?" Nestor asked.

Gabriel said nothing, looking at the two of them. Finally, he lowered his head. "I need to verify something. Give me a little time to make sure you're not in danger. You've waited this long, please just lay low and don't do anything rash."

Nestor grumbled. "I'm not waiting any longer. I can take care of myself."

"No," Gabriel said quietly. "I don't think you can. Please, I think you should stay together. Resist any treatments or drugs not approved by me directly. If anyone argues, send them to me."

Nestor shrugged. "I still want to meet Monica. Where is she?"

"She's..." Gabriel glanced at each of them, then looked around and lowered his voice. "In a supply room in my office. I'll take you to her, but later. I need to talk to her first. I'm going to try something that may help reveal what the three of you share."

Jake asked, "What are you going to do, play twenty questions? Charades?"

"No. Hypnotic regression."

Nestor laughed and shook his head. "No way you're hypnotizing *me*."

"Don't worry, it's not like what you might have heard. Honestly, it's a technique I usually frown upon. My father used it improperly, but in his day it was a new and potentially groundbreaking treatment. Now we know its limitations—susceptibility, false memories, all those kinds of things."

"But it can help people?" Jake asked.

"Yes, it can. For certain ailments. Psychological conditions, addiction. A properly trained hypnotist can get a patient in a suggestive state and open up the possibility of behavioral change."

"But nothing drastic?" Jake asked. "Like making someone believe he's a spider-monkey or an opera singer?"

"As I said, depending on patient susceptibility, there are varying levels of potential."

Jake leaned back, frowning, thinking. "What about something really radical? Like can a hypnotist suggest that someone kill himself? Put a gun to his head?"

Gabriel stopped short of a laugh. "No, definitely not. Although, maybe..." His voice drifted. "...she could have the patient believing himself to be somewhere else, taking a walk when he's really out on the roof..."

Gabriel backed away in his chair, looking deathly ill. Jake stood and thought about reaching out to steady him. "You all right?"

"Yes, yes." He looked at them again. "Listen, remember what

I said. Stick together. Go and check at the front desk for the latest weather details, and tell them I sent you to see if a car can get in or out."

"You calling the cops?" Nestor asked.

Gabriel shook his head as he turned to leave. "No, not until I learn more."

"When can we see Monica?" Jake asked. "Shouldn't we all be together?"

"Soon," Gabriel fired back. "Stay in sight of each other, stay with a crowd, and I'll return as soon as I can."

When he had gone, Jake glanced at the food line. He turned to Nestor. "You hungry, dude? I'm famished, and I don't want these other nut jobs eating my share."

Without waiting for a response, he headed to the line; but when he glanced back, Nestor was still seated in the same pose, watching Gabriel leave.

33

Daedalus

Kaitlin Abrams walked in the front door at eight-thirty. Indra's driver had dropped her off after following a plow through to the end of the road, into the circle around the Daedalus Institute's main doors. Kaitlin thought it looked like a scene from a natural disaster movie. A pickup truck had been snowed in right in front of the doors, and some men were digging it out, just as others were trying to shovel out their own cars and scrape off windows. Two snow blowers were going, clearing the entrance as the winds continued to buffet them and hurl barbs of ice at anyone who dared try to leave the building.

Before entering, she gaped at the icicle-draped rooftops, the towers and frozen ramparts. It didn't look real—more like an architect's grand dream rejected out of sheer difficulty, tossed into a snowbank and left to the elements. But whatever it was, Daedalus resonated with Kaitlin. She knew it. She could picture its interior: winding staircases and ornate wood-carved banisters, a stained-glass dome above the lobby, marble floors and hooded lamps; she could feel the oak railings, smell the musty curtains. Daedalus was lodged in her spirit, a splinter burrowed deep then sealed in behind layers of flesh, muscle and skin.

"Been here before?" Indra had asked, back in the car.

"No. Yes. I don't know—I don't remember, it's not possible, but..." Kaitlin leaned forward and stared, taking everything in—the walls and edges gleaming with blue-silver ice, the blankets of snow piled high around the base, the frothy winds stirring up cyclones that roared and smashed against the walls; the windows blinking in the clouded dawn. She shivered and, when she stepped outside, she almost turned right around and got back in. She didn't want to do this, not alone.

But finally, hefting her travel bag over her shoulder, hugging her purse with her new identification, she waved goodbye and started walking, head down.

Indra's car turned slowly. Kaitlin stopped, scarf around her face, while the plow passed around the circle, and then she was left wobbling in the wind before the looming structure and its lofty, spear-tipped icicles arching precariously toward her.

⧗

INSIDE, her tension drained as she admitted herself with little excitement. It seemed that the nurses and orderlies had more urgent things to worry about; some of them had been here for two days now, unable to get home to their families. Other patients were sitting in the lounge, an attractive common room with soft lights, a plush carpet, and several cozy couches around a gas fireplace. Some were reading day-old newspapers or playing chess, others were vainly trying their cell phones.

A receptionist took Kaitlin's information perfunctorily, as if, with a rush of applicants recently, this had become second nature. She was given a number and a room and told that it was one of the last three they had available. They were being forced to turn away new callers for the moment.

Heeding Indra's warning, Kaitlin kept her wool hat on to keep up her disguise. If one of the other 'special four' happened to catch a glimpse, her cover was blown.

Before taking her up to her room, the orderly, a big bald man with an odd tattoo on his neck, showed her the cafeteria. "After you settle in, come back here and grab something to eat before they close. Lunch is at..."

But Kaitlin had tuned him out. Her legs had gone weak, she trembled and almost toppled, then started to lurch forward before pulling herself back.

No—don't give yourself away.

She gaped at the table near the right wall, where two men sat eating breakfast and having coffee. She had a clear view of them, and could see their pure, perfectly visible faces.

The bigger, older man she only glanced at, taking in his features before studying the younger one. The one with long, stringy hair; he was laughing, and when he turned suddenly, Kaitlin had a horrifying moment where she thought he sensed her and had turned to see, but he only bent down to pick up a dropped fork.

In that moment, she recognized Jake Griffith with a bolt of searing white energy that roared from her eyes straight down to her toes. It felt as if her body was paralyzed but her mind wildly alert.

First Monica, then Indra—and now these two. Four of the Six. Who were they? What the hell was happening to her? And why was her reaction so much stronger with Jake than the others? She clenched her hands into fists and dug her nails into her flesh. *Think of something else.*

She started humming her hit tune, *Baby, baby. What's the score?* Good old *PinkEye*.

"You all right, miss?" The orderly gripped her shoulders. She looked up and into the swirling ripples of his face, the unblinking eyes roaming the crowd, seeking.

Kaitlin stepped away slightly from the table she had been looking at. "I just... the smell of all this food is making me queasy. Haven't eaten in a while and..."

"Then go and eat, and then come get one of us to take you upstairs."

"That... that's okay," she said. "I'd really rather get changed first. The drive here was nerve-wracking, and I feel like I must have sweat out a couple liters."

The man stared at her, and Kaitlin felt as if his shifting features would somehow form into a devilish visage, an inquisitor's glaring, accusing eyes, and she'd wither and admit her true name and why she was here.

But she somehow formed a smile, pulled away and headed for the door. In the window, she saw his reflection, saw him still glancing around until he found the table with the two men she had recognized. His head spun back to her, his brow furrowed.

He knows, she thought. Or at least, suspects.

She pushed her way outside and started walking briskly to the stairs. He came after her. Long, determined strides.

"Critchwell!"

Kaitlin looked over her shoulder. The big man had stopped, and a young nurse ran up to him. "We're needed upstairs."

"But..."

"Get someone else to take this one to her room. Alexa's asking for us."

Critchwell's eyes darted back to Kaitlin, narrowed, then nodded. "Let's go." He waved to another orderly, a portly man with a splotchy face, and called him over. "Brian here will take you up to four-eleven."

"Thanks," Kaitlin said, bowing her head as Critchwell and the nurse ran by. For some reason, curiosity made her steal a glance at the nurse's neck. And there, just under the collar, the same tattoo as Critchwell's: a segmented snake with red eyes, eating its own tail.

SHE FOLLOWED Brian up the stairs, around and around, almost getting dizzy. Holding onto the ornate wood banister, trying not to look down, Kaitlin asked about the facilities. "How do you get supplies up here during storms like this?"

"Oh, don't worry," he said. "We've got a large garage on the west wing, with an entrance to the lobby and a loading area that backs right up to the kitchen—and the basement. Trucks can pull right in there, and we load everything up a short ramp."

"Then we won't starve."

"No, ma'am."

They rounded another flight, then headed into a corridor with paintings hanging just slightly crooked, and overhead lamps that seemed too dim for safety. A few patients were strolling around, some looking out the windows, others heading back to their rooms.

"How many doctors are there here?" she asked on the way.

"Three specialists, a couple interns and a whole lot of us orderlies and nurses." He smiled at her, his swirling face moving like a Mr. Potato Head with the features all jumbled and jammed in haphazardly. "Dr. Gabriel Sterling is the head doctor. It was his father who founded this place. Atticus Sterling. That's him right there."

He pointed to an oval picture at the end of the hall, just next to room four-eleven.

Kaitlin couldn't quite see his face either but, with a start, she recognized the hairline, the brown cross-stitched suit with the black vest and red bowtie. And something about his eyes. She never could pick anything out from a person's eyes, even Slider's. Other than color, unless it was something distinctive. But something about this man's eyes... The way they bored into her, flickering with a red glow; they seemed to follow her approach, looking at her with utter distaste, revulsion. And... was it— expectation?

Like he knew she'd be back.

Her mouth went dry.

"Ma'am? You all right? You're room's right here."

She shook her head, still locked in a stare with Atticus Sterling. She thought of a golden hourglass and had a stark vision: this man leaning over the desk, leaning towards her, telling her to watch the sands, imagine that they were moving upwards, and to watch—and listen to his voice.

"My God," she whispered. "Is he...?"

"Colorful guy," said the orderly, "from what I hear. But sorry, you can't meet him. He died, oh... thirty years ago, at least."

Thirty years... Kaitlin swooned. Impossible.

What the hell was happening to her?

She lurched into her room, mumbled her thanks, then slammed the door. Fell to her knees, and peeked back through the crack under the door, expecting to see another shadow coming towards her—maybe Atticus himself, stretching and ripping and tearing his way out of the portrait, dropping to all fours and clawing his way toward her with hungry red eyes.

34

abriel stood outside his office, pretending to fumble with the doorknob. He kept an eye on the cameras, then pushed through the door. He wanted to make sure they saw him going in; he needed them to assume, with his absence, that he would be working diligently inside. Elsa had confirmed that Monica had made it inside without notice—she and Elsa just appeared to be going in, delivering the morning reports.

He had cancelled his morning appointments, a fact he imagined wouldn't bother too many of his patients. The storm had left them all out of sorts, more concerned with watching the news in the lounges, tracking the extent of the damage, or just drinking hot chocolate and enjoying what amounted to a snow day.

Gabriel paused, thinking about the conversation down in the cafeteria. The hourglass. It was his father's signature hypnosis aid. Gabriel was only twelve but he remembered when Atticus came back from a trip to Hollywood, how proud his father was, showing off the actual prop used in *The Wizard of Oz*. Even then, Gabriel was unimpressed; the gargoyles and the red sand were nice touches, but otherwise it was nothing special. Later, Gabriel had to admit, it worked. Patients focused on the red sifting sands, and it worked to dull their mind, to correlate with a sense of time, the prospect of infinity and their own relation to it. And soon enough—they'd be under.

But how were these new arrivals involved? How could they be? Gabriel opened the door, heard it creaking slightly on its hinges, then stepped into the supply room, and across, to the other side, to the door that was already opening.

Monica stood there, a fire extinguisher in her hands.

Gabriel stopped, giving way to a smile. "Where's the fire?"

She lowered it, set it down against the wall. "Sorry, doctor. Old habits. Heard someone coming in, and I..."

"You were right. Don't take chances."

She looked down, breathing heavily. "And another thing—to help me recognize you, if you don't mind, please keep the same clothes on for a while."

"Sure, no problem—at least as far as I'm concerned. My other patients might start complaining about the smell around me, but otherwise I'd be happy to not change for you.

"At least that shirt, the white collar and blue stripes are distinctive. And your hair."

"Yeah, my gray. Happened at twenty-two. I should color it, but..."

"No. It's..." She stared for a moment, then looked down. "Perfect. For your position, that is. Lends respect."

Gabriel laughed. "Thanks, I think. Now, come on out, have a seat. There's little time, and we've got a lot to do."

Gabriel had her sit on the couch, a leather recliner with deep cushions.

Monica said, "Wait, did you meet the others?"

"Yes, just now. Two men."

"Who are they?"

Gabriel held up a hand. He had taken off his suit coat, rolled up his sleeves, and now sat in a maroon leather studded chair in front of her. "Who they are can wait. It's what they told me that matters now. It's got me baffled. Just when I think I'm under-standing, I'm thrown for a loop."

"So, what do we do?"

Gabriel leaned forward, his silver curls falling over his eyes. "With your permission, I'm going to try hypnosis. It's something I rarely use, but I don't know what else to do."

"What's it going to prove?"

"I don't know. We've got a kid from Florida who's never left the south, a guy from Nevada who lived in a motor home for half his life, a winemaker from California, and then... you. It's possible some of you came here years ago and then repressed the event, but I remember all my patients, everyone who has come through these doors. I would have known." He took a breath, then continued. "I'd like to try this. The only way we're going to find out the truth is by taking you back, freeing your mind and seeing if I can uncover what you've forgotten."

"If anything's there."

"Something's got to be there."

"And you've done this before?"

Gabriel nodded, suppressing a shiver. *And I've seen it done—enough sessions watching Dad at work.* Gabriel had tried it on some early patients when conventional procedures weren't working. He had some success, at least in overcoming patient's paranoia, allowing them to cope a little better, adjust and function in society.

Monica looked nervous. "So, what do we do? Do I follow a candle's light? A pocket watch on a chain?" Suddenly her eyes glazed over, her lips trembled, her teeth chattered. "...an hourglass?"

Gabriel leaned in. *Her, too?* "Why did you ask that?"

"I... I don't know." Her fingernails were digging into her legs, and Gabriel reached over and took her hands, steadied them, tried to soothe her.

"I know where to start, then," he said. "Now, I need you to relax. Forget about where you are, forget about everything. Just think about the snow falling outside, and the wind, and then listen to the sound of my voice."

He got up, dimmed the lights, and returned to his chair. "Comfortable?"

"Getting there," Monica said, her breaths coming out deeper, more subdued.

"Good. Here we go."

⌛

"Go BACK to the last time you were here at the Daedalus Institute."

It had taken nearly fifteen minutes to get her under completely, and she had struggled, her mind wandering, her thoughts resisting. Gabriel had to try a couple different tactics of distraction and relaxation before succeeding.

"Tell me where you are."

Monica shifted, frowned. Her eyes were closed. "In an office," she whispered. "Dark, a few candles on a desk, and one glowing on the wall."

"You're at the Daedalus Institute?"

"Yes."

Gabriel put aside his shock at the confirmation that she had indeed been here before, somehow without his knowledge. "Do you know why you are here?"

"Yes. I came. I volunteered."

"Volunteered?"

"Yes," she said, her lips curling into a smile. "I fit the profile."

Gabriel scratched his head. He had no idea where this was going, but most times it was best to follow where the patient led you. It often ended up at the source of the problem. "What was the profile?"

"I had a birthmark."

"You did? Okay, where?"

"My back, just under the right shoulder blade."

Gabriel frowned. What did having a birthmark have to do with anything the Daedalus Institute did? This wasn't helping.

"Back to the office. What else can you see?"

"There's… someone sitting there, behind a desk, someone—no, I don't want to look at him. I won't."

"Okay, relax. Tell me something else."

"I won't look at him."

"Don't. Just look away." *Who was she talking about? Just where the hell was she?* He decided to try something else.

"How old are you?"

"Thirty," she answered promptly, tension easing from her voice.

"No, not now." That was Monica's age, or at least close to it. *Was she rounding?* He dismissed the inconsistency. "I mean, how old are you back in the past, when you first came to the Daedalus Institute?"

"Thirty."

That's impossible. Could she have come here just last year? He would have known it, would have seen her, even if Alexa had some secret project on-site. Daedalus just wasn't that big a place.

"Tell me, when you were here last, did you see a woman—a blind woman?"

"No." Monica swayed slightly, like a tree in a light wind.

"Think carefully. In the room, or greeting you when you arrived. A woman with dark glasses?"

"No."

Gabriel scratched his chin. "What time of year did you arrive?"

"July. The fifteenth, I think."

Last year, in July or four months ago? Impossible.

He rubbed his hands together. *Time to work in the others.* "Are there more volunteers? Like yourself?"

Monica smiled, nodding. "Yes."

And now, Gabriel thought, the million-dollar question… "How many, including you, are in your group?"

"Six."

Gabriel blinked. *Six?* He knew of four, but also suspected Alexa was still expecting more. *Two more?*

"What do you all share in common?"

"Just birthmarks."

"The same kind, the same place?"

"No. Just a birthmark, something noticeable."

"Okay. Are these others in the room with you now?"

"No… he sees us one at a time. But afterwards, we can meet and talk and eat together. Some of us…" She smiled. "We're making friends."

"Friends?"

"Yes. We've been here awhile. I think two of them are hitting it off."

Gabriel frowned. "How long have you been here?"

"Two months."

What the hell? That was impossible—she would have missed two months of her life. A huge gap like that—and so recent? And if she were here for two months, he would surely have remembered it—there weren't many patients as striking as Monica.

Damn hypnosis. So unreliable. He sat back, shaking his head. This wasn't working… or else he was just bad at it. False memories. Had he been asking leading questions? This was why hypnotized people were so often reporting alien abductions and obscene sexual experiments or early childhood abuse.

This was all just a waste.

Like him.

Gabriel kept running his hands through his hair, tugging at it. He got up, started pacing. *What else to ask? Just take her back.* Go into her childhood, see if there was something traumatic buried there. Maybe she was juxtaposing dates, confusing the past with her present situation. That had to be it.

But why did she say July? Age thirty he could understand, but she wouldn't have misplaced the date, not when the snowstorm was so prevalent.

"Tell me, Monica, is it snowing outside?"

Monica sat there, swaying, eyelids flickering as if dreaming.

"Monica?"

Her lips were sealed tight.

"Is it snowing where you are?"

"No."

Gabriel frowned. *Why the delay in answering?* He thought back over the questions, replaying each one, and her responses, in his mind.

No, that couldn't be it.

His lips dried up, his heart started thundering in his chest. "Monica?"

She didn't answer.

"Monica, if you're hearing me, say 'yes'."

She said nothing.

Gabriel tapped his fingers together. *Time for 'Simon Says'.*

"Okay... say 'yes.'"

"Yes."

"Monica, how old are you?"

Nothing.

"How old are you?"

"Thirty."

Oh Christ. Here goes.

"What is your name?"

She smiled. "Elizabeth. I prefer Lisa, though. Lisa Ellison."

35

When Jake returned to his room to wash up before running back down to meet with Nestor, Alexa Pearl was waiting. He saw her, froze, and tried to back out, but the big bald guy was there behind the door, along with the nurse, Ursula. The man slammed the door and hauled Jake inside.

"Not too rough, Mr. Critchwell," said Alexa. She stood up, motioned to the desk chair, which had been set out in the middle of the room, and Critchwell set Jake down in it.

"Thanks for not keeping me waiting," Alexa said.

Jake struggled as Critchwell held him down and Ursula secured his arms behind the chair with duct tape. "What the hell are you people doing? Seriously, now's not the time for this kind of kinky shit. Really, I..."

"Quiet," Alexa said, gliding in and placing a finger against his lips. "Don't scream, this won't hurt."

"Wha—?" A needle slid into his arm. Ursula's tattoo seemed to revolve in his vision, spinning around and around, the snake devouring its tail over and over again. And then he realized the snake wasn't moving at all: the room was. Spinning faster and faster.

His head lolled back, and Alexa's dark glasses seemed the only constant in the whirling room. They pressed in close, and he could see beyond the lenses: twin pinpricks of white, watching with cold impatience.

🏿

"ARE YOU WITH US, Jake? All better now?"

Alexa leaned in, lightly slapping his cheek. Smoothing back his hair. She wiped the sweat from his brow with a wash towel.

"Yes," he murmured, eyes glossy, body limp, hanging forward.

She nodded to Critchwell and Ursula. "Wait outside."

When they had gone, Alexa sat on the bed, crossed her legs and leaned forward.

"Listen to my voice, Jake Griffith. Listen well. Trust me, we're going to some interesting places, you and I."

He nodded, his head lolling from side to side. "Mikey," he whispered.

Alexa flashed him a look of annoyance. "Who?"

"My brother... Mikey... I lost him. Didn't stay with him. Mom, Dad... I'm sorry."

Alexa nodded. "Oh, such a sad tragedy. So, your brother... you want to see him?"

Jake nodded.

"It's why you've come here, right? To be cured, to see again. To find your brother, maybe your parents?"

"Yes."

"Poor Jake. Poor, poor Jake." She took a deep breath. "Don't worry, you'll see him again."

He tried to lift his head to the sound of her voice. "Promise?"

"Cross my heart," Alexa whispered. *And hope to die. When I'm done here.* "Are you ready to be cured?"

🏿

TOO EASY. She brought him under without any setbacks. Between the relaxants and her skill with the Voice, it was simple. And given his willingness stemming from his guilt about losing his family... *Too easy.* More difficult was navigating the labyrinth of his mind and finding the exact route to the vault. The core of his consciousness, which had been constructed to resemble this very basement vault. The room with the symbol over it.

And inside... the root of all his problems. And the lingering obstacle to her plans.

She had already done this for Franklin Baynes and Nestor Simms—eliminated the danger there. Two down, four to go.

"Jake, are you there?"

"Yes."

"What do you see?"

"A door, with... with an hourglass on it." He shuddered. "I don't want to go in."

"I know," Alexa said, suppressing a grin. *I bet you don't.* "But trust me, we have to. So you can be cured, so you can see your brother. Do it for him. For Mikey. Open the door."

"Okay."

Almost done.

"Are you in?"

"Yes."

"What's in there, what do you see?"

"Just a table, and that hourglass. A big one, gold trim."

"The sands—which way are they going?"

"Up," he intoned. "Always up."

"That's right." She smiled, proud of that image. "Now, Jake. Listen carefully. Look down at your feet. There's a sledge-hammer there. A ten-pound sledgehammer with a long handle and a silver head. Do you see it?"

"Yes."

"Pick it up."

"Okay."

"Both hands low on the handle. Approach the table, bringing the hammer behind your back."

"Okay."

"Now… swing!"

Jake's legs tensed, his arms twitched. His head rocked from side to side. His torso swung as far as the restraints would allow.

"Is it done?" Alexa asked, leaning close. In her blindness, she imagined the scene in his mind. "Destroyed?"

"Yes," Jake whispered, his voice taking on a note of awe. "Shattered. So many pieces… the sand everywhere. Dissolving, and the pieces… they're fading."

"The room?"

"Empty now."

"Good. You've done so well, Jake. The sledgehammer's gone. You can close the door, the door that's now just a blank silver door, no symbol on it. There's nothing left in there. Your problem is gone."

And so is mine. Almost. Just a few more loose ends. Three more pieces of unfinished business.

"When you wake, you'll be able to see everyone's faces. No more blindness, no more need for your tricks, or memory games. But there's one more thing, Jake. One more piece of unfinished business, without which you'll never be cured. Do you want to be cured?"

"Yes, yes."

"Good. Here it is. You have to do something for me, after you wake, after your nap. Will you promise to do as I say?"

"Yes."

"Good. When you wake, get up, put your coat on. Go downstairs to the garage and pick the first vehicle you see. A Jeep Cherokee. The keys will be in the ignition. Do you understand?"

"Yes."

"Very good. Get in and start driving."

"Can I look for my family?"

"Sure, Jake. Go wherever you like. But here's the catch—

when you're approaching the bridge just outside of the institute, this is what I need you to do..."

Alexa lowered her voice, speaking still to that secret part of him, the niche in his *Ba*, the place she alone knew how to reach. It had all been there in the *Book of the Dead*, if you read the passages properly, if you took them beyond their words, read into the secondary meanings. The *Ba*, depicted as a human-headed bird, was the soul, the part of a person that lives on after the body dies. It was that essence that lived on and came back. The trick to doing it right was in the preparation...

Jake sat completely still as she finished her instructions.

"Do you understand, Jake?"

"Yes."

"I'm sorry, but it's the only way. Will you do as I ask?"

"I will."

"Thank you." *Piece of cake. Just one more thing...* "But before we leave, before I bring you out and before you can sleep off the medication, I want to take you back. Farther back. Deep into your past. Are you ready?"

"Yes."

"Good. I want you to peel away the years. See your life as a movie played in reverse. Go all the way back. Back... to the first time you saw the Daedalus Institute. Your arrival. The first time you came up the long winding road, the first time you saw those spires in the distance."

Jake trembled, breathing slowly.

"Are you there?"

"Yes. We're driving..."

"Who else is with you?"

"A man, another volunteer."

"His name?"

"Nick DeWolfe. We met at Boston's airport and shared a cab here."

Alexa smiled. "Ah... I know you now." She clapped her hands. "I remember you talking about destiny, how excited it all seemed that you had found each other. Let me ask, are you a man or a woman?"

"A woman, of course."

"Good. Just one more thing. Why are you coming here?"

"Saw the advertisement. Figured I can earn some money while I'm out of work."

"What a good idea."

"Yes. But I'm scared."

"Why?"

"This place. It looks... creepy."

Alexa smiled. "Yes, sometimes it does."

"Okay," Alexa said. "I think I know enough. But just to be sure..."

She leaned in close, right next to his ear, and whispered.

"What's your name?"

36

Nestor Simms slipped out of his room just moments after entering. He glanced up and down the corridor and didn't see Jake. They had agreed to just get back to their rooms, wash up and meet again together in the lobby in a few minutes. Stay together, that's what Dr. Sterling had ordered.

To hell with that.

He had more important things to do. A promise to keep. Alexa was right. The others had it—the Scourge. And it was up to Nestor now; he was the one to deliver them, to save them. Gabriel Sterling wasn't to be trusted. He was one of the Scourge's minions, that much was clear. Despite his professed ignorance, he knew.

Alexa alone had proven she could vanquish the Scourge. He owed her his life, and now he had to give back. Help those who were suffering, just as he had suffered, up until only hours ago.

He slipped into the hall, nodding to a few other patients walking about, marveling to himself that he could see them, see their humanity, their faces in all their unchanging perfection. Every one different, memorable, perfect.

He climbed.

One flight. Two. Glancing out over the side as he rose, seeing the immense domed ceiling overhead, the sparkling crystal lights drifting stardust down to the lobby floor.

On the top floor, he made a bee-line for the last door in the eastern corridor. It opened just before he reached it, and a large man, nearly bald, dressed in black, stood there as if expecting him.

"Well?"

"I need to see Alexa."

The big man shook his head, and a circular snake tattoo contracted and expanded with the motion. "She's with a patient."

"In there?" Nestor stood on his toes, trying to look over the man's shoulder.

"No."

"Can you get her? It's important."

"You can tell me."

"I only speak to her." Nestor was getting frustrated. This oaf was standing in the way of his mission.

The man sighed. He pulled out a walkie-talkie phone from his back pocket. Pressed the button down. "Can you speak to Mr. Simms?"

The speaker crackled. "Put him on."

Nestor took the phone. Pressed the button and brought it to his mouth. He turned away from the guard and lowered his voice. "You'll save the woman? Liberate her?"

"Who?" came the sinewy voice, arching through the speaker. His spine tingled, and he recalled the feeling of her breath on his skin.

"Monica. Mrs. Gilman."

"You have her location?" Alexa asked.

"You'll save her?"

Silence, and he had the sudden fear that her next words

would lash out at him in anger and impatience. "I told you I would cure her, Nestor. You know I keep my promises."

He took a deep breath, a cleansing, cool breath. His eyes darted down the hall, to the opposite end, where another door waited, the other office. Sterling's office.

"Then yes. I know where he's keeping her."

37

Gabriel went down to the lobby in search of Nestor and Jake, and he hoped they had stayed in the common room after he had gone to check on Monica. Reaching the bottom, he paused and looked out the nearest window. There was a commotion outside—one of the Institute's Jeep Cherokees, revving its engine. Its rear wheels were caught up high in a snowbank, and it looked like it had fishtailed drastically.

What the hell? He sprinted around a few nurses and patients, and ran to the door behind the lobby desk, the door leading to the garage.

"Who's in that vehicle?"

"Sorry," said the nurse standing there. Ursula. A thin smile. "One of the patients just ran out and stole it."

He nearly throttled her. "Who, damn it?"

Ursula gave him a weak smile. "A Mr. Jake Griffith."

"Shit!" Gabriel opened the door and winced with a blast of frigid wind.

"Sorry, Dr. Sterling," Ursula said. "Someone must have left the keys in one of the Jeeps. Or he hot-wired it."

Gabriel ran back around her to grab his coat. His mind raced. *What happened?* Had someone gotten to Jake? Had…

But as he ran into the lobby, he saw movement above him—two flights up. A black-clad man, Gregory Stoltz, rushing up the stairs. Moving fast, with purpose, to the top floor.

Going to Alexa's office, or mine?

He yelled back to the desk, where two of his orderlies stood at attention. "You two—go outside! Get Mr. Griffith back in here." Then he turned and bounded up the steps, three at a time.

The stairs seemed impossibly tall, each step higher than the last. He paused for a half second on the third landing, his heart pounding, then burst into action again.

Finally, at the top, he faced Alexa's door. Closed. One lamp overhead, providing dim, ghostly light. He turned, looked past four equally spaced lights, and faced his own door. *Closed, thank God.*

Please...

It opened, and Critchwell and Stoltz emerged, dragging Monica Gilman out behind them. Critchwell saw Gabriel, let go of Monica, and moved to meet him.

"Back away, Dr. Sterling."

"Leave her alone. She's in my care."

"Not anymore. We've determined that you neglected her treatment. Ms. Pearl will file a report, and your actions will be reviewed—along with the irregularities concerning Franklin Baynes's suspicious death, and Jake Griffith's escape..."

Gabriel snapped. Lunged—just as he saw, in the corner of his eye, Monica raise her head, her eyes pleading.

A huge fist came at his face.

He dodged just enough to miss the full brunt of the punch, but still suffered a glancing blow to his temple. His vision darkened for a second, but then, finally giving vent to years of frustration, he clasped his hands together and swung upwards like he gripped a baseball bat. He connected, knocking Critchwell's chin straight back. He heard a sound like a crack, and the big man went stumbling backwards.

At the same moment, emboldened maybe by Gabriel's

arrival, Monica grabbed Stoltz by the hair, twisted his head back, and then delivered a swift knee to his groin. When he backed up, doubled over, she kicked him in the face and knocked him on his side.

Critchwell looked over, in shock as he rubbed his chin, and then Gabriel was on him again, slamming him into the wall, and delivering a barrage of fists to the back of his head. One of them, finally, was enough to send Critchwell to the ground, unconscious.

"Jesus," Monica said, suddenly at Gabriel's side, helping him up. "Look at us."

"Couple of street fighters."

In the middle of the hall, the elevator doors opened. They both turned. Taking one step out, Alexa Pearl paused, head cocked.

"No chance for subtlety anymore," Gabriel whispered. "We need to run."

38

He had to listen to the voice in his head. Had to obey her wishes. Jake had come this far. Taking the Jeep from the garage, driving out into the storm. It was rough going at first, but he finally found traction and got himself on the road.

Find the bridge. And when you see it, speed up.

Yes, that's what he had to do. That's what she wanted.

Speed up, then veer to the right, and drive over the edge...

But as he neared the bridge and the ravine, he saw something out of place. Out there in the blinding storm, someone was running alongside the Jeep. A woman without a coat, her short brown hair whipping around her face. Jake leaned forward and peered through the frosted glass. His chest tightened, and then he felt like someone had reached in and grasped his heart. Seeing Monica and Nestor's faces had caused a stunning, powerful reaction, but this was something else entirely. Even from just a glimpse, seeing this woman's face sent him reeling.

He knew her, somehow, but... But there was more—they shared something deeper than mere familiarity. He started to brake, then suffered a crushing sense of dizziness.

Drive to the bridge...

Blinking, he gripped the wheel, pulled his eyes away from the woman, and found himself stepping on the gas and turning the wheel. *To the bridge,* came Alexa's voice, still echoing in his mind, but now with a hint of desperation.

Jake turned his head. This other woman was closer now, struggling to reach him.

He moved his foot to the brake.

Drive... Alexa's voice rose in his mind for one last attempt. *Drive... off... the edge...*

Jake stared at the woman, now right outside his door, desperately reaching for the handle and shouting something lost in the winds.

The bridge...

Caught in a moment of indecision, his body reacted. He stepped on the gas.

⌛

KAITLIN HAD FOLLOWED JAKE, at a distance, to his floor. Overwhelmed with her reaction, desperately needing to see him, to touch him and confirm that he was real and not just some dream, she was about to run to him when the door opened, and the big bald man and the crazy-eyed nurse appeared in the doorway. They pulled Jake inside. Before the door closed, Kaitlin saw her—Alexa Pearl—standing in the shadows within the room. She leaned on her cane, and her head moved slightly from side to side, as those black glasses seemed to survey everything in her path.

Kaitlin ducked her head back around the corner and dared not look, not yet. Not until she heard the door close.

And then she waited. Against all her impulses, she held herself back, remembering Indra's advice to not give herself away. If it was just Alexa in there with Jake, she might have risked it, but not with those other two. She'd be dead meat. So, she waited—for nearly forty-five minutes. When she had almost given up and had been about to just go in and interrupt whatever they were doing and take her chances, Jake's door opened.

Alexa left first, striding confidently away, then back up the stairs, followed by the others. Only the big bald man remained behind; he crossed his arms and waited by the door until, minutes later, Jake emerged. He looked glassy-eyed and exhausted, as if he hadn't slept in weeks. But he moved with a sleepwalker's sense of purpose, heading for the stairs.

Kaitlin left her hiding place and followed at a distance, trying to appear unobtrusive, until he went into the garage, and the big bald man went back upstairs.

Not good. Whatever they did to Jake, she had to stop it, warn him, help him somehow. Warning bells rang in her head—Indra's instructions to remain out of sight.

Sorry. She looked out one of the lobby's leaded-pane windows and saw the Jeep tear out of the garage, turn into the circle, and then fishtail immediately, slamming into the snow bank. And then she was out, running through the door, into the whipping winds...

THE JEEP FISHTAILED AGAIN, slid off the road and stuck this time, nose-first right into a deep drift.

The edge... Alexa's voice still thrummed in his head, but now Jake saw that other woman, running up to the Jeep. Her face, so clear and brilliant. *Are those tears? Is she weeping? Laughing?*

The door opened—and the wind almost slammed it closed. Jake added his strength when she pulled again, and then he was out. Standing in front of her, shivering along with her. Running toward them, out of the storm, came two orderlies in heavy coats.

But right there, right in front of him... Whoever she was, she glanced back nervously as if she didn't want the others to see her. She brushed snow off her hair.

And Jake couldn't help himself. He stepped right up to her, face to face. Their eyes searched each other's. Their hands touched.

"What were you doing?" she asked meekly.

"I... don't know. I think... I think I was trying to kill myself."

The girl's eyes flickered, and she gripped his hands tighter, almost ripping his skin with her nails. "Don't you dare."

"It's okay. You somehow broke the spell—or whatever was making me crazy." And Jake realized it was true. Alexa's voice was gone, his mind quiet and calm. "Seeing you, it just blasted through this other voice in my head."

The girl leaned in close. "What's happening to us?"

"We're freezing," he said as he suddenly hugged her close. And then he pulled his face back, studied hers, and then kissed her. Hard. She kissed him back, threw her arms around his neck, squeezing. Pressed herself to him. Kissing with surprising ferocity.

Finally, hearing footsteps crunching through the snow, they broke apart. Arm around her shivering shoulders, they stepped back as the orderlies approached.

"Who are you?" Jake whispered quickly, his eyes still locked on hers as if they were stealing his vision, welding it to her skin.

"I could tell you," she whispered, "but I don't think it means anything."

"I'm..."

"Jake Griffith, I know. I saw you on the news... briefly."

Oh shit.

"No," she said wrapping herself around him, speaking into his ear. "Don't worry. I know... you couldn't have done anything too bad."

"I didn't... at first." He swallowed hard, tried to pull away and show her his eyes, let her see he was serious. "But I had to escape."

"To come here, I know. I understand."

They ducked their heads as a snow drift fell from the roof,

caught in the wind, and slammed down onto the orderlies. Temporarily blinded, they rubbed their eyes, backing away— and Jake pulled the girl with him as he rushed back towards the main door into the lobby.

As they ran, more snow descended, another blast of the icy blizzard from the darkening morning sky.

Inside, they skidded across the floor, into a group of other patients, then ducked through them and ran toward the stairs.

"Down," the girl said, looking over her shoulder. "Maybe we can hide out."

As they descended, half-slipping down the stairs and around the first bend, Jake shook his hair, freeing the snowflakes and trying to clear away the maelstrom of emotions. "I think I knew you'd be here. Please, who are you?"

"I'm Kat. Well, Kaitlin Abrams. London punk band, Pink-Eye," she added. "Every heard of 'em? Hit song, *'Baby, Baby, What's the Score'*?"

Jake grinned, shaking his head. "I promise I'll download it once we get out of here."

"Don't bother. I don't get royalties anymore. So, now that we've found each other, what do we do?"

"There's another guy waiting upstairs, and also that woman who whacked her husband—Monica—and we've met a doctor we can trust. We're trying to bust out of here soon, before the next storm. We..."

"No," she said, backing up. "We have to wait. There's help coming. I've met someone else like us. He knows about the Six."

"Six? So, there are six of us?"

"Yes. And my friend, Indra, he knows other things too. About this place. And he has..." She half-rolled her eyes. "Resources."

Jake gripped her wrists. "What sort of resources?"

"I– I'm not sure. He told me to find somewhere he could get inside unnoticed. He's bringing help. I have a satellite phone with his number, and..."

Just then they heard someone shout upstairs. Ursula's booming voice. "Where did they go?"

"Oh shit!" Kaitlin gripped Jake's arm so hard he nearly cried out. "I don't think we can go back up."

They retreated, further into the darkness, Jake leading. "Down here, I know where we can hide."

39

abriel ran down the last few steps, with Monica's hand in his. *Getting tired of these stairs*, a silly thing to notice in spite of everything. Only 9:00 a.m. and already the windows in the lobby were darkening, the storm suddenly returning with a vengeance. It sounded like howling banshees were at the windows.

He headed for the desk and was about to ask the receptionist if she'd seen the two guys he'd been talking to during breakfast, when he saw Nestor's big outline in the lounge. Gabriel skidded to a stop, then ran into the room.

"We have to go now," he said, between ragged breaths, speaking low enough that only he could hear. "Did they find Jake?"

Nestor shrugged, staring at Monica now, his mouth open.

One of the orderlies spoke up. "Mr. Griffith came back inside, but we lost where he went—he just ran off."

Nestor blinked at Gabriel. "What happened to your face? Get in a fight?"

"Yes," Gabriel said. "Let's start moving. Nestor, take Monica to the garage now. We have to beat the storm. I'll find Jake and then we'll be right behind you."

Gabriel turned back to the lobby, keeping an eye on the nurses. *Come on Jake, where are you?*

A commotion. There, on the stairs. Critchwell and Stoltz came running down, out of breath. "Dr. Sterling! Where are you going?"

Gabriel swore. He glanced back in time to see the door to the garage closing, Nestor and Monica safe for the moment. Critchwell was striding toward him, and behind him, easing down the steps, Gregory Stoltz and Dominic Greiner, with Nurse Ursula in front of the lobby doors, her hair full of snow.

Critchwell's face turned red. "I asked you where..."

"I heard you. We're leaving."

"I don't think so, Doc."

Gabriel balled his hands into fists. He glanced around, aware of the other staff members looking on with concern. Could he count on them for help? He doubted it. He was good at his job, but never earned the kind of respect that would lead mere employees to put their lives on the line for him.

He opened his mouth and was about to try to talk his way out, when Ursula, standing on her toes, looking down the stairs, shouted something. Then she was leaning over. "The Griffith kid! And a woman—looks like she could be Kaitlin!"

Gabriel cursed and lunged forward, but Critchwell shifted, blocking his path. He shoved an arm in his chest and knocked him backward. "Stay there, Doc." Critchwell turned and raced after the others, into the stairwell, chasing their quarry into the basement.

Stoltz and Greiner advanced toward him, fists clenched.

Gabriel decided. Save Nestor and Monica. Get help, come back and—

The lights above blinked. Flickered first, then died.

A scream. A series of shouts.

Then the auxiliary power kicked in, the generator supplying the minimum power to get a few lights on, keep the refrigerators going and the heat pumping.

And the storm raged outside, shaking the walls and rattling the windows, celebrating its first breach in Daedalus's defenses.

At least it's cover. Gabriel turned and raced for the garage.

⧗

THEY STARED out into a world of swirling white. A drift a foot high covered the drive. "Get in," Gabriel shouted, pointing to the only Jeep left, the one without the plow.

Damn it, Jake! Why couldn't you have waited for us?

"I'm driving," said Nestor.

"No way," Gabriel answered.

"I've had the experience. Drove all last night in a truck. This'll be easier."

"Nestor, it's my..."

"Boys!" Monica was sliding into the backseat. "Someone please just drive. Get us the hell out of here!"

Shocked with her tone, Gabriel ran to the passenger side and got in, while Nestor jumped behind the wheel, strapping himself in. He turned the key, floored the accelerator, and they were off, barreling through the drifts, crunching across the main drive. Gabriel glanced back to see two men running into the garage, taking a few steps into the snow before the blizzard swallowed them up.

"Can't see shit," Nestor said, hunched over the wheel; he turned on the wipers.

"Trees on the right," Gabriel said. "And a steep ditch near the bridge, so stay in the center of the road, if you can tell where it is. And don't go too fast."

"Okay, okay."

Monica made a whimpering sound behind them, and Gabriel turned around. "It's going to be okay. I know a place, a farmhouse a couple miles away. We can get there and send for help, and..."

"Seatbelt," Monica said, pointing to Gabriel's unused belt.

He smiled, said, "Thanks," turned and reached for it—when he caught a glimpse of something in Nestor's expression. Something cold, colder than the winds outside. Calculating, scheming. A tight smile had formed on his face.

"Sorry, Doc."

"Slow down, Nestor," Monica said at the same time.

But then they were skidding off the asphalt, and Nestor was turning away from the skid, purposely trying to flip the already top-heavy SUV. Gabriel felt the wheels leave the ground and they tilted–

Once, twice, a violent slamming, hard on one side, then the other, crunching into the drifts, pounding and skidding finally along the roof through the snow, careening like a sled.

Gabriel had no time to think, no time to reason what had happened. He tasted blood, felt it burst from his nose, and was dimly aware of lying on the ceiling in an impossibly twisted position, when the car crunched into the tree and sent him head-first into the glass.

Just as dimly, he felt cold winds kissing his face, numbing his injuries. And he noticed that the driver's side was empty, and a big shape was crawling into the back, freeing Monica, who was just lying there limp and shell-shocked. Gabriel reached for her.

But then Monica was dragged out into the snow.

And everything went white.

40

The Hillside Nursing Home was set back in the outskirts of St. Albans, just twenty miles from Daedalus. While its setting shared some characteristics with Daedalus, Indra thought the architecture couldn't have been a better study in contradictions: stately white pillars, ornate window dormers, a grand brick facade and a colonial-style roof underneath mounds of snow and ice.

The rest of the town had just lost power, but Hillside's generators were keeping the interior warm and the elevators operable. Indra made it past the front desk. He preferred to think it was his skill at persuasion, rather than any pity for his handicap, that won out. He was admitted as a visitor, and allowed up to the third floor. After the elevator doors closed, he drove his chair toward the fifth door on the left and promptly knocked with fingers still cold and nearly senseless from just a few minutes spent outside. He could hear the TV on inside, so he knocked again, louder.

Someone promptly yelled, "What the hell do you want?"

Indra opened the door, maneuvered through it and rolled in. He smiled at the blurry-faced old woman with the snarly gray hair, the pink cotton bathrobe and mismatched blue slippers. She didn't seem too bad off—a little thin, spine hunched with age, but still mobile. He couldn't speak to her mental condition yet, but he had been told she was mostly coherent, one of the better ones.

"You're no nurse," she spat. "What the hell're you doing in here? You ain't takin' my roses away."

Indra raised his hands defensively while looking around the room. There were no flowers of any kind in sight. "I'm only here to talk, Mrs. Sterling."

"Mrs. Sterling's my mama's name. Call me Darcy or get the hell out."

Indra stifled a laugh. "Okay, Darcy."

"Who the hell are you?" she asked. "You're wheeling around like one of my old fart neighbors, but you ain't that old."

"Who I am," Indra said, "doesn't matter right now. Not as much, I believe, as who I *was*."

Darcy blinked at him. She reached for the remote, clicked off the TV.

"Shut the damned door."

☒

INDRA ROLLED to the other side of her bed while she took a seat in a reclining chair by the window and a card table littered with old magazines—*Cosmopolitan*, *TV Guide* and *Star*. She snatched a box of tissues from the window ledge. Indra expected her to offer him one because he was sniffling from the cold, but instead she dug around below the tissues and came up with a glass ashtray, a silver lighter and a pack of Camel cigarettes. She lit one, then switched on a small bedside fan to blow away the smoke.

"Okay, Mr. Gandhi, or whatever your name is, explain yourself. Why're you here? Although I can guess."

Indra leaned in closer; he studied the jumbled face before

him, trying to make sense of it. "Guess, then. It might save us both some time."

Darcy took a deep drag. "Time, I got plenty of. Do you?"

Shaking his head, Indra said, "No. And neither do five other people at the Daedalus Institute. Five others who are about to die. If you cannot help."

Darcy breathed out a long cloud of smoke and watched it scatter in the fan's breeze. "Six, including you?"

"Yes."

She took another drag, and finally stared into his eyes for several moments. After another exhale, she leaned back and gazed up at the ceiling. "Son of a bitch. That bastard actually did it."

Indra said nothing.

Darcy sighed. "Guess you know then, or think you know."

Indra nodded but thought: Not really. Just a couple of wild theories...

"Atticus, Atticus..." She flicked the tip of her cigarette into the tray. "I never thought he had any real talent, you know. Just a smooth talker. A con man. Playing for serious stakes."

"Tell me," Indra urged.

"The circles he ran in. The articles he published, the ads he put out. Lots of people came to him. Usually of a certain type."

"Wealthy?"

"Stinkin' rich, more like it. And everything that involves. Usually huge-ass egos. And my Atticus, he was like those fake séance people, he knew how to tell folks what they wanted to hear. Hell, that's how he got me to marry him, wasn't it? Naïve little tramp that I was."

"His clients... he would regress them back—"

"—to a past life. All that hypnosis shit." Darcy rolled her eyes and took another drag. "But like I said, I didn't figure he was anything but a showman at heart, despite the medical degrees and all those books. All a big game to him. He knew how to get to people, get inside their heads and stroke their egos." She laughed and then coughed out a cloud of smoke. "All those rich clients, paying ungodly sums? You can bet he told each of 'em they were something special in the past—a prince or a philosopher, or a general or some shit like that. Oh, and what little talent he had, he wasn't above snooping around in their minds for some dirt, some blackmail material to beef up his usual fees."

Indra's heart was racing. They were getting off track, and he had to steer her back without giving away his ignorance. "The Six…"

Dropping ash on the floor, she carried on as if she hadn't heard him. "Atticus had no talent. None. Leastways, until Egypt."

"Egypt?" Indra's ears perked up.

"Yeah, that six-month sabbatical he took in '68. Gave me a nice little vacation from him too, mind you. Although most times he wasn't around anyway, always holed up in that dank room in the institute's basement. Had me some affairs behind his back, and the old goat never even noticed. Ha!"

"Okay, Mrs.… Darcy. We were in Egypt?"

"He was, yeah. Went on a tour with some of his occult study buddies. Whack-jobs, all of 'em. Rich old men afraid of death, wantin' to take all their gold with 'em and leave nothin' for their families. They forgot that their lineage was supposed to be the only immortality any of us get." She frowned at the dying cigarette, put it out and reached for another.

"So, dear old Atticus had this theory. He'd been reading about the pyramids and the pharaohs for years, obsessing about it, even hiring a tutor from the University to teach him how to read hieroglyphics."

Indra swallowed. Something in his vision darkened and a gloom settled about the room, almost muffling her voice.

She went on: "So he and his batty friends took off, gone for half a year. He had me run the place in his absence, and I brought Gabe along too; thank God he didn't share his daddy's problems. Good thing too, my boy and I, we knew enough to carry on when Atticus was out of the picture."

She breathed in, coughed, and continued. "So, when he got back, I asked Atticus: why Egypt? What the hell was he doing when he had patients to help, a clinic to run, and a wife and a young son who idolized him."

"And he said?"

"Well, that's what it comes down to, don't it? He spouted out some crazy theory that I promptly filed in the same mental cabinet where I shoved all his other nutty beliefs. The ones that eventually got him censured and ridiculed." She blew out a perfect smoke ring, and then sat back, admiring it. "You know about them pharaohs, right?"

"What about them?"

"How they built those obscenely big pyramids? Built 'em as tombs, right?"

"That's what they say."

Darcy shook her head. "Ain't what Atticus said. In fact, after reading up on some ancient writings, some Book of Death or something—"

"The Books of the Dead?"

"Whatever. Atticus had himself the bright idea that the pyramids were actually supposed to be more like safe deposit boxes. Like in a bank vault. All that loot locked away behind nasty booby traps that'd kill anyone who didn't know where they were —who didn't have the key, in a sense."

"But," Indra said, "the Egyptians believed the treasure inside was for the Pharaoh, for when he came back to life. He—"

"Nah, that's bunk. Think about it. He'd be trapped in a pyramid under the sands with the skeletons of his former aids, concubines, and dead cats—and yes, a shitload of treasure—but he would have no way to escape and spend it."

"I never said it made sense," Indra responded. "It was supposed to be symbolic."

"Atticus thought the opposite. According to his theory, he thought the pharaohs did it for practical reasons."

"Tell me," Indra said. "Although I think I've guessed."

"Then save me the time," Darcy said.

"Okay." Indra let his fingers, still numb, trace the cool edges of his wheelchair's handles. "Atticus thought that the Pharaoh believed he would be coming back for that treasure." He licked his lips. "Coming back..."

Darcy smiled. "Coming back through the damned front door." She raised her cigarette in a salute. "You get it? The old rotting mummy was nothing, a red herring I guess you'd say, never meant to be any kind of resurrection vessel. All that preparation for the afterlife—all bunk. I'm guessing only a select few knew the truth, had the real answers. Only they knew what the Pharaoh did. What they all tried to do."

"Find a way to come back."

"To be immortal. Here on Earth." Darcy grinned. "Atticus even figured that some of the tomb raiders, the looters who came centuries later and seemed to know where to look, knew how to get in and rob everything? They knew because they weren't simple thieves."

"They were the pharaohs."

"Coming back to get their stuff."

"What about Tut?" Indra asked. "And the others whose tombs were never robbed?"

"Too young when they died? Or they didn't learn how to trans-whatever their souls, how to preserve their inner selves, reawaken their memories or whatever, in the next life. I always wondered about reincarnation. What if they came back as a stinkbug or something, and had to work their way back up to a human, what then?"

"It does not work that way," Indra said. "I believe you can suffer karmic setbacks, but once in an advanced life-form, you do not regress."

She shrugged and then lit another cigarette, forgetting that she already had one in her mouth. "Goddamned Atticus and his 'Grand Experiment.'"

"The Six," Indra whispered. "They were part of this... Grand Experiment?"

She narrowed her eyes at him. "Just how much do you know, then? Or are you just fishin'?"

He smiled at her, hoping their relationship had progressed beyond suspicion and into the realm of trust. "I confess, ma'am. Not enough."

"You're one of 'em, though? One of the Six?"

"I believe so."

"Can you see my face?"

Indra shook his head.

"Ah..." She put out the first cigarette, then the second, absent-mindedly. The windows shook and the cold seemed to press right through, reaching for them.

"Please, Darcy. We're running out of time. Can you tell me what you know? What did he do?"

She sighed. "I don't know it all, 'cause he was never one for sharing, but after Atticus drank down his cyanide-and-tonic cocktail, I was the one to deal with the shitstorm he left behind. I set poor Gabe, only seventeen at the time but with a good head on his shoulders, to working with the staff while I tried to hide my late husband's... I don't know what you call 'em—embarrassments. Stuff we'd all rather no one found out about. The past-life regressions, the blackmail, the wild theories on Egyptian mysticism."

"The Grand Experiment."

Darcy let out a laugh. "Yeah, that. I found a few notebooks, a journal or two Atticus had forgotten about, hadn't hidden away in his vault." She took a raspy breath, and coughed. "1976... You poor six bastards. One of you even a little boy. Atticus wanted people with birthmarks because, at least according to some of the research, birthmarks often stayed, life to life, in the same spot."

Indra nodded. "So, by searching for those with such marks, what did he hope to achieve? A confirmation of the theory of reincarnation?"

"Yep. The most important test ever, he thought, according to his notes. The Grand Experiment."

"But how? Of all the people born in the world... what was he going to do, go around checking everyone with a birthmark? The logistics of such an empirical test, such a scenario—it would be..." He stopped, suddenly feeling like someone had just swung a sack of bricks at his head. *Stupid. So obvious.*

Darcy blew smoke into his face. "I'm guessin' you finally worked it out."

He stared at the smoke, curling around in the air, blowing in the breeze. "Prosopagnosia."

She smiled. "As they say downstairs on Thursday nights, 'Bingo.' Now, listen up. You want to know who you are?"

"I do," Indra said. "But more than that, I want to hear you say I'm right. I want to know for sure how he did it. How he got the six of us to have Face Blindness in this life, how he left it that we could still see each other and only each other." Indra's breath was coming out in shallow gasps. Flickers of memories flew past his vision, pinprick images caught in the smoke rings. "I want to know everything."

Darcy snorted. "I'll tell you on the way there. After you bust me outta this shithole. I assume you've got a driver who can manage in this storm?"

"I do." Indra wheeled closer to her until their knees were almost touching. "But first, I want to hear you say just one thing."

"What?"

"I want to know for certain who he is. I know he managed the impossible—brought himself back in a new body, reincarnated and regained his memories. But tell me... who did Atticus come back as?"

Darcy let out a long breath. "I guess I've known for these past eight years. I've always known, deep down. A wife can't be deceived, 'specially not by someone like him. Con-man, my ass." She put out her cigarette and was silent for almost a half-minute before she spoke.

"From the moment she walked in, I knew there was a reason I hated that blind bitch."

BOOK THREE

THE GRAND EXPERIMENT

41

A single candle burned on the desk in Alexa's office. The curtains were drawn, and a crimson haze floated over the walls.

Monica knew she had been drugged. Some kind of injection. That nurse, Ursula–something, with the crystal blue eyes that never blinked—she had stabbed her shoulder with a needle the size of a dagger. But still, Monica's arms were bound behind her, ankles duct-taped. She sat in a desk chair, facing the rear wall, so she couldn't evade the giant portrait of Atticus Sterling smirking down at her.

"Magnificent, isn't it?" said a voice over her shoulder. Alexa entered after the nurse left, but Monica hadn't heard a thing, not even a breath competing with the raging storm. "I had it commissioned back in 1967 by an artist from Copenhagen, a fellow occultist specializing in persons of my... caliber."

"What? What... are you talking about?" Monica struggled to keep her head up. The face on the wall swam in and out of focus, the blurriness swirling into one ethereal leering smile with flickering red eyes. She had heard Alexa say something about 1967. More than forty years ago. What the hell was she talking about?

Alexa stepped to the desk and picked up a stack of files, then spread them out like playing cards.

Six files, Monica noticed, having difficulty focusing. Alexa ran her fingers over the top right corner of the first few, reading in Braille.

"Ah, here we go." Bringing one file with her, she walked back to Monica. "Ursula tells me you have a lovely almond-shaped birthmark on your back."

The room spun some more, and the man in the painting smiled. She could almost hear a low chuckling. *Why is he familiar?* That suit—the tuxedo, and the red bowtie. She had seen it before; it made her feel sick, nauseous, and cold. So cold. When had she seen him, and where?

"I remember the same birthmark on her. Elizabeth."

Monica gasped.

And Alexa leaned in excitedly. "You know that name? Elizabeth? Lisa Ellison?"

Alexa stepped back, raising a scolding finger. "What have you and Dr. Sterling been up to? Hiding in that closet? Did he put you under? Did he make you re-live your past?" She made a clicking noise with her tongue. "Didn't think he had it in him."

Monica mumbled something, a slurring sound. It sounded like bees were buzzing near her head, conducting a background orchestra to blend with Alexa's powerful voice.

"I should have known. You gave me the most trouble back then. Resisted the hardest, refused to relax and let me into the places I needed to go."

"I'm... glad," said Monica, finally raising her head. She struggled, tried to stand, and slumped back down, almost heaving as bile raced into her throat.

In the flickering candlelight, Alexa leaned forward, pressing her face inches from Monica's. Candlelight reflections burned on the surface of her glasses like jack-o'-lantern eyes.

"All right then, Monica... Or Lisa, if you prefer." Alexa

opened the file and flipped through the pages, her fingers sliding across and down the first couple of sheets, reading the Braille dots. "Yes, a lot of trouble. Thirty years old when you came here, answering the ad. Changed your mind, I recall. After the first month. Had doubts about the experiment. Too many questions. Money wasn't the issue; you wanted answers. Concerned about morality. Tried to call the authorities, then attempted to escape with a few of my subjects. I had to isolate you. Drugs. Food and water deprivation. Dull your mind to the point of acceptance."

Monica felt dizzy, so weak... Like she could just nod off for a day or two, maybe weeks. Travel into the sweet embrace of dreams and maybe become another person, someone like this Elizabeth Ellison, who apparently had the strength to resist. *God bless her*, she thought. *Not me. I'll just go on pretending this isn't real, that it's just a game, a stand-in rabbit for the real one.*

The file snapped shut and Alexa walked it back to the desk. "Anyway, I apologize that I don't have the time to give you the attention you deserve, since I assume you'll still be the same pain in the ass you were back then. I believe that, whatever else might be different, personalities don't change all that much." She patted Monica on the head like a dog. "So, I'll be quick."

"Gabriel..." Monica whispered.

"What's that? Oh, have you started to feel something for him? For that useless waste of a son?" Her hands sought out and found Monica's chin. Squeezed her cheeks, ran her fingers over her face, feeling, touching her skin, her hair. "Oh, I suppose you might have been pretty enough for him, but I think right now you'll find him just as he was in life—rather cold and stiff."

She headed around to her chair behind the desk, "I want you to listen closely to my voice."

Bees hummed, buzzing in unison, gradually dwindling in tone.

"Picture an hourglass."

"No..." Monica's head slumped forward as the candle blew out in a draft from the opening door. The shadows expanded, right up to the wall where the painting flickered, and then Atticus Sterling slid off the canvas, dropped to a crouch and crept toward her, a leering smile on his face.

"Yes. You *will* listen," Alexa whispered. "And we will finish this."

42

olding hands, Kaitlin and Jake ran headlong into the
pitch-black basement. Kaitlin dragged him ahead, and
Jake actually had to pull her back, stopping just before
they collided with a pillar. Using their free hands, they inched
forward, around the pillar and then backed against it.

Listening.

"They're coming," Jake whispered. "Don't move, they can't
see us."

She clenched his hand tighter, and it made his heart race.
"I'm not moving," she whispered back. "Jake…"

"Shhh." He didn't want to think about anything else now
except keeping her safe. Keeping them both safe. He held onto
her hand for dear life. *Don't let her go. Don't lose her like you lost
Mikey at Disney World. Stay together*, he could almost hear his
father's voice, echoing down through the years—the last thing he
ever told him.

Stay together.

The darkness was a tangible wall of shadow in front of them,
and somewhere in that direction—that door, the hourglass. The
vault.

If they could make it there. Maybe force the door…

Whispers from behind them. A light stabbed into the gloom. A piercing white beam trapping dust particles like moths in a tube.

"Shit," Kaitlin hissed, squeezing closer to him.

"Mr. Griffith?" a woman's voice. *That nurse.* The curvy one with the ice-cold attitude. "There's no way out down here."

Footsteps. The beam swinging back and forth, gliding over the other pillars, the boxes, the cabinets, the other doors.

Damn. Might have been better to get behind the boxes. The person holding the light moved closer, still sweeping the beam. Only one set of footsteps. The others must be waiting by the steps.

The nurse called again, her voice just as distant, back by the door. "Jake? And was that Miss Abrams with you? Looking oh-so different from her punk band days? What's the matter, Kaitlin, gone conservative in your old age?"

Kaitlin squeezed Jake's hand harder and whispered into his ear, "Tell you later, when we get out of this."

"It's a date."

The light shifted to their left, and Jake was about to breathe easier when it swung back around, sweeping the floor.

Were there footprints in the dust?

"Come out, come out…" said a man's voice.

Jake and Kaitlin inched around the pillar, trying to keep it as shelter, hoping to avoid the erratic motions of the light.

It came closer.

With his right hand, Jake dug into his jeans' front pocket. *Found it!* A quarter from one of yesterday's stops at a mini-mart.

He could hear the man's breathing. Closer, closer.

Jake held out his arm and, with a quick flick of his wrist, flung the quarter high and far away. It clapped against something—a cabinet or a metal locker—and the flashlight spun around. It tracked the sound, and the man ran towards it, the beam seeking, following the shadows.

"We've got to move," Jake whispered, and he was about to push off with her when he heard a series of high-pitched beeps.

"Shit!" Kaitlin hissed. "Indra's cell phone!"

"Stop it!"

The beam swung back around, caught Kaitlin peering around the side.

"There they are!" shouted Ursula from the stairs. Jake looked in that direction. Two other men were with her, their silhouettes outlined in the hazy stairwell light.

Damn it! Can't get out that way.

"Jake..." Kaitlin started, but then he pushed her out of the way of the rushing flashlight, hopefully into the concealing shadows. He ran around the pillar and caught the man from behind, jumping for his neck, taking him down and rolling.

The flashlight dropped and spun in circles on the floor, the light stabbing around in all directions. Jake landed hard on his shoulder, grunted and loosened his hold on the man's neck. He rolled to his knees and kicked free of a hand grabbing for his ankle.

And then he was up and running. Away from the stairs, toward the back, believing it was the way he had shoved Kaitlin. Heavy feet trampled after him. Someone had picked up the flashlight... Shouts, a woman's cry.

From somewhere far away: "Jake! Run, hide!"

He skidded and glanced over his shoulder, saw a group struggling as two big forms restrained Kaitlin, dragging her back to the stairs.

And the one with the flashlight, getting up and running toward him.

Jake stopped, preparing to turn and fight—to get past this one and then rush back to help Kaitlin—when a door opened right next to him. A grinding, grating sound—a sliver of blue light from within.

He had made it to the far end of the room.

The vault door scraped open. A woman, dark hair, heavy-set, poked her head out. Jake was framed in the light. His pursuer saw him, and Jake made his decision. He barreled into the woman, gripped her by the shoulders and flung her back the way he had come. She had time to cry out, and then she was flailing ahead, colliding with the bald man who was approaching at full speed.

Jake grabbed the edge of the door and swung it back, hard. It felt like a bank door, thick, with a wheel-lock on the back. When it shut, he spun the wheel, then put his back against it for good measure. He wasn't sure if it opened with a key or combination or some kind of sensor; he couldn't take a chance.

Then he noticed the contents of the room.

He stepped forward into the hazy, generator-powered light from the monitors. But what drew his eye were the relics hanging on the walls. The ancient bas-reliefs, the chipped sections of wall-carved hieroglyphics, the statues, the bowls and glass-encased papyri.

And there, in a clear case, with a single dim amber light set on its stand: an all-too familiar gold-trimmed hourglass. With red sand inside the lower bowl.

Someone beat against the other side of the door. Muffled shouts, but Jake was a world away.

43

The wind ripped through the splintered windshield and the snow blew in, hungrily smothering the roof of the upside-down Jeep, obscuring the blood, the debris, and Gabriel's crumpled form.

Another piece of glass, dislodged by a bitter gust, fell onto Gabriel's shoulder, and he stirred. *I think my legs are moving.* That was a good sign. His neck wasn't broken; his spine was still in one piece. He blinked away the blood, snow, and ice crystals that had formed over his eyelids. *How long have I been out?*

It couldn't have been too long, or else he would have frozen to death. He lifted his head, and the numbness followed him like a halo. His ribs were burning, his left shoulder throbbing in time with his heartbeat.

But he was alive. Fingers numb, ears tingling, he started to lift himself up, using the bent steering wheel as a lever, maneuvering around a jagged pine that must have just missed Nestor.

Nestor. Son of a bitch. What did he do? It had to be Alexa. She had got to him. Anger fueled his body, burned away the cold, the numbness in his muscles, and he slid out and crawled onto the base of a massive snowdrift obscuring the trees, the road, the sky.

Grunting, tasting ice-coated blood, fighting back the tempting promise of sleep, he started to dig.

⧗

SOMETIME LATER, **long** after he had given up on surviving, but still struggling anyway, still climbing and dragging himself out of the ditch, his hands drawn up into his sweater's sleeves, he saw a light in the storm's nearly impenetrable fury.

He stumbled and lurched forward and only then realized the land had leveled out and he must have made it back to the road. Snowflakes stung at his face as he stood unsteadily on burning legs. Hugging his shoulders, he blinked and squinted against the stinging flakes and the roaring wind.

At first, he thought the light, barely visible through the army of clouds and snow, was the sun. But then he realized he could also see the glow from the sun, higher up than the light coming toward him…

…the light that now seemed to be separating, forming twin orbs of gold, cutting through the snow and rolling through the blizzard. Then, finally, he made out the dull roar of a motor. And the crunching of wheels.

Grinning an ice-crusted, chapped smile, Gabriel dropped to his knees and held up his arms.

Please see me. He tried to wave his hands in the air, shaking off the snow from his black sweater.

The Hummer came to a skidding stop just a few feet away from colliding with him, and Gabriel had one clear thought: *I hope they're the good guys.*

⧗

STRONG HANDS LIFTED HIM, guided him to the rear seat, where he slid in next to a dark-skinned man with thin legs. A glance in the back gave him pause. An odder assortment of items he couldn't have imagined: a wheelchair resting on top of a plastic crate, and several ski-bags, open partway, offering the hint of rifles and other pistols.

A blanket settled over him and he breathed in air so warm it actually seemed too hot, stinging his raw lungs.

The dark-skinned man finished covering Gabriel, then directed a smile at someone turning around in the passenger seat.

Gabriel squinted. *That looks like… No way. Now I know I'm dreaming.*

"Boy," said Darcy Sterling, "what the hell are you doing out without your coat?"

44

ake backed away from the steel door, keeping an eye on the wheel-lock mechanism, expecting it to turn at any moment. He looked around for something to jam under it —a table, a bookcase, but even the chairs wouldn't line up right.

Maybe they don't have the access key?

He scanned the room again. Portable lights were linked to a tangled collection of wires running from the servers and equipment directly to a generator in the corner. *They aren't taking chances with this place. So what's so important?*

He would check that out in a minute, but first, he looked around for a weapon, hoping he might get lucky and find a gun lying on a table, or maybe a fire-ax. Even a letter opener?

Nothing. Nothing but manila folders, pens, coffee mugs and old McDonalds wrappers. The place smelled like an office break room, but not as musty as he'd expect for a basement, thanks to the air purifiers and de-humidifiers. *A lot of expensive stuff on the walls.*

A jackal-headed deity stood on the left side of one of the wall carvings, arms folded over his chest in apparent judgment of a line of crowned people on their knees before him. Other hieroglyphics were perfectly chiseled alongside these figures. Just looking at the scene made Jake break out in a sweat, like he was one of the souls being judged.

Tearing his eyes away, he looked around at all the monitors. His head swimming, he went from station to station, finally stopping at one that had a spreadsheet open on a split-screen view. To the left: an open folder, called *1976*, with six files inside, all with different file names. Jake frowned, then looked over the spreadsheet. The same names were recorded there across the top, in blue indicating a link to another file. There were six other names repeated in the columns below, familiar names most of them. Some were bolded and others were crossed out.

Elizabeth Ellison	*Tommy Sorrento*	*David Fritz*	*Carrie Colburn*	*Nick DeWolfe*	*Beatrice Kenway*
Monica Gilman		**Nestor Simms**	**Jake Griffith**		**Franklin Baynes**
~~Franklin~~	~~Franklin~~	~~Franklin~~	~~Franklin~~	~~Franklin~~	Franklin
Monica	~~Monica~~	~~Monica~~	~~Monica~~	~~Monica~~	~~Monica~~
~~Nestor~~	~~Nestor~~	Nestor	~~Nestor~~	~~Nestor~~	~~Nestor~~
Jake	~~Jake~~	~~Jake~~	Jake	~~Jake~~	~~Jake~~
~~Kaitlin~~	Kaitlin	~~Kaitlin~~	~~Kaitlin~~	Kaitlin	~~Kaitlin~~
~~Indra~~	Indra	~~Indra~~	~~Indra~~	Indra	~~Indra~~

WHAT THE HELL? Jake took a seat, momentarily forgetting about the threat outside, about Kaitlin's capture, about everything. He focused in on his own name, saw it bolded under another: Carrie Colburn.

Carrie Colburn... The name registered with him. A twinge, a dark shudder, the way he thought people must feel when they say someone just walked over their grave.

He clicked on her name, and the other side of the screen flickered, and a file opened. A Word document, twelve pages long, small print. On the top left of the first page was a scanned image, a somewhat blurry photograph of a youngish-woman, auburn hair and a cute smile. Freckles. Jake stared for several seconds before he realized what was wrong.

Not only could he see that face, but he recognized it as if he were a normal person looking into a mirror.

Breathlessly, Jake scanned the top section of data. She was born in 1954, current residence (as of 1976), Toronto. Admitted as a test subject in July, 1976. And there was a date of death: November 12, 1976. His heart gave a lurch. She was only twenty-two. He stared at the name for a long moment, feeling a sudden, inexplicable wave of sadness.

Tempted to read on, but feeling the pressure of time, the sense that everything, all of a sudden, now depended on him, he closed the file and was about to get up and check the other screens, which seemed to be showing various live feeds from around the institute. But first, just one more name.

He clicked on "Nick DeWolfe." A file opened. A picture of a young man, handsome despite the long unkempt hair. *I can see him too...*

And suddenly he had the strongest feeling, exactly the same as he felt with Kaitlin. Trembling, he was about to close the file and open up the one on Carrie again, when he saw the date of death. November 12, 1976.

Wait...

He clicked back on Carrie's file and scanned the data. *The same date of death?*

Back to the right side of the screen, he moved the pointer to another name at random: "David Fritz." Another picture, and by now Jake was hardly surprised he recognized this man as well— a balding sixty-ish man in a business suit. But he didn't react with the same intensity as he had experienced with Carrie or Nick.

He skipped over all the other information and went right to the date of death.

The same.

Closed the file, clicked on Elizabeth Ellison. Another familiar,

visible face. Date of Death: November 13, 1976. A day later...
okay. *What the hell? Did their bus go off the road? Or did they all
drink the same Kool Aid?*

Tommy Sorrento. Nine years old. Familiar face. Date of
Death: November 12, 1976.

Beatrice Kenway. Forty-seven. Died the same day.

Holy shit.

Jake sat back, blinking. Six people he somehow recognized,
dead now thirty-one years, and all of them here at one time... He
scanned a few files again. They had each arrived here during the
summer of 1976.

And they all died on or around November twelfth of the
same year. Did they all have Prosopagnosia too? Did they come
here seeking relief, only to find death? Or was it something else
entirely?

The answers were in those files, he was sure.

But time had run out.

In the corner of his eye, he saw movement on the next monitor, a screen that was split into eight sections. Each screen
showed black and white views of the institute, mostly in shadow
with faint lights punctuating the gloom. But in the second row
on the left, he could make out Kaitlin, her body limp, being
dragged into an office by the two men in black, with the slender
nurse behind her.

Jake rocked out of his chair. Scanned the table and lunged for
a cordless phone.

No dial tone.

He looked around for an intercom or something to communi-
cate to the front desk.

Nothing. *Shit.* And no cell phones anywhere. *What, was everything done with smoke signals?* Hoping to send an email out to the
authorities, he bent back to the computer, tried to open Google,
but immediately got a 'network unavailable' error.

Just my luck. Then he heard a sharp metallic sound and

glanced back to the door. The handle was turning first counter-clockwise, then spinning fast the other way.

Jake stood, hands in fists, looking around for a weapon, anything. Thoughts of Kaitlin, dead or dying, paralyzed him with fright.

The wheel stopped, and the door started to open.

Jake lifted the glass case, grabbed the handle of the hourglass and ran to the side of the door just as it opened. The taller of the goons—the bald man built like Fenrik back in prison—stepped inside.

Jake had a half-second to think of poor Fenrik, and how normal, how mundane an antagonist he seemed now. Shielding himself behind the door, Jake waited until the man's bald head came into view... then put everything he had into his best two-handed overhead, slamming the hourglass full-force down onto the man's skull.

The man crumpled without even a whimper, but the shattering of the hourglass echoed like a shotgun blast throughout the vault... and triggered the memory of his hypnosis session with Alexa. This destruction wasn't as dramatic, but it was liberating all the same, a great feeling to drop that bastard.

Jake stared at him, lying there in a crumpled heap. *Oh Jesus.* Jake held the ruined golden base of the hourglass another second, then let it drop on the man's body, amidst the broken metal and shattered glass. Blood was seeping from the back of the man's bald head, around the triangles of embedded glass and the clumps of red sand.

The body twitched once, then lay still.

Christ. One more murder...

Jake peeked out the door, into the cone of light until it was devoured by the darkness. No one there, at least no one that he could see.

Run!

45

abriel, still huddled in the blanket, sat shivering as his mother bandaged his cuts and scrapes while they were parked on the side of the road, making their final preparations and discussing strategy.

They were still about two hundred yards from the entrance to Daedalus, its outline barely visible up ahead in the blinding storm. The Hummer's side door opened, the wind and snow roared in, and the driver bent inside and started handing out guns and flashlights.

Gabriel stared at all the equipment and weaponry. "Are we going to war?"

Indra gave him a smile, matching the one on Darcy's face. "Yes, I believe we are. A war for our very souls."

☒

GABRIEL FELT EVEN DIZZIER as he contemplated the weaponry laid out before him. Indra helped himself to a gun and a flashlight. Cocked the hammer, pulled the magazine, and checked the ammunition.

The driver, Hank, was arming himself as he slid behind the

wheel again—two pistols in his belt, a shotgun in his lap.

Darcy reached back and snatched up the remaining .45 out of the bag, checked and then armed it, just as fast as Hank had done. "As long as we're at the buffet, I'm helping myself."

Indra gave a muffled laugh. "It's a wonder your husband managed to stay alive around you."

"I wish I had poisoned his coffee on our honeymoon. Damn him."

"He just may be damned," Indra whispered.

"Wait," Gabriel said slowly, holding his head and trying to catch up with what they had told him after his rescue. "I'm still not getting all this. Isn't it more likely that my father just befriended Alexa's parents, or—sorry, Mom, but maybe the girl was his, and he left her instructions? Like where to find the key to his vault, to the bank accounts…"

"Yes," Indra said. "It is far more likely. However, it does not account for us. The Six."

"Or his notes," said Darcy, "The ones I found and never showed you. 'His Grand Experiment.'"

"Hang on," Gabriel said, holding up his hands. "I don't mean to belittle your suffering, Indra, or your miraculous ability to see one another, but there has to be another explanation."

"There isn't," his mother said.

"You really believe it? That Dad's still alive?"

"Yes," she said.

"He's not," Indra countered. "Not in the sense you mean. Your father did not bathe in the Fountain of Youth or sip from the Holy Grail."

Gabriel shivered. "Egyptian Mysticism. Reincarnation. I don't… I can't believe any of that."

Indra shrugged. "You are free to believe what you will, but your father somehow implanted a message deep within his soul —his *Ba*, as the Egyptians called it; the part of a person that lives on after the body dies. He gave himself a command, most likely something simple. Perhaps that in his next life, he must seek out a place, something like a safe-deposit box or a time capsule buried underground. Somewhere he would have stashed journals, pictures, maybe a diary—a dossier, essentially, on himself... to himself. A way to reawaken his past life's memories."

Gabriel shook his head. "Alexa. But, I can't..." He looked at his mother. "So, what was this Grand Experiment? If he could prove that people could retain their memories, recapture their prior lives in the next one, then..."

"Then he'd damn well do it himself." Darcy waited until that settled. "Get it? For his test, he implanted a form of Prosopagnosia in all of 'em. All six. A kind of spiritual-level command that they would be blind to everybody except each other. You know, like those stage-show hypnotists who take a volunteer from the audience and then convince the poor sap that he can't see anyone else in the room? That he's really all alone... and then he's told to strip down to his underwear and dance around like a chicken."

She smiled to herself and then focused on Indra. "He ran the same trick in 1976. You volunteers... you were to be the true test: he was sure about reincarnation, but what he needed to confirm was whether, when we came back, we could maintain the ability to follow hypnotically-implanted suggestions—in this case, the command to recognize only the others in the experiment. He made these volunteers blind to everyone but each other in the next life, essentially mimicking Face Blindness. So then when they came back..."

Gabriel shifted, leaned forward. "...they might find their way here for treatment."

"Exactly. With this clinic specializing in Prosopagnosia, he was reasonably sure that at least one or two would show up here for care. And if they recognized each other—and also had the corroborating evidence of birthmarks or retrievable memories, it would confirm his theory. And then—even if he were an old man at that point—he'd try it on himself."

"But he didn't wait."

"No," Darcy said.

"He killed himself only a year later," Gabriel said, tensing. This was the big question, the million-dollar question he'd wrestled with all his adult life, living in the shadow of a cruel, distant father who had chosen to end his life without so much as a goodbye or word of explanation. "Why?"

His mother said, "The superficial reason: cancer. Diagnosed with it in 1976, just weeks after finishing with the six volunteers. At the time, I thought he was just a coward and didn't want to suffer, to go through the chemo and what have you. But now... now I can damn well guess the real reason."

"He did not have the luxury of time," Indra said quietly, his voice barely heard over the winds buffeting the Hummer. "He could not sit back and wait for the results of his experiment, for confirmation."

"Right," she said, impatience bleeding out in her voice. "He didn't want to miss their return, which he might have if he hung on, surviving only a few more years. So, he did it: repeated the psycho-gobbledygook, maybe in a tape recorder after he took himself under. Whatever. He told his *Ba*, or his soul or what have you, to come back at a certain age in the next life, go to some secret place only he knew about, and then find the stuff he left for himself. Take possession of the bank accounts and investments which had been earning interest for twenty years, take possession of..."

"Daedalus," Gabriel said. "Alexa. At twenty-one. The year she dropped out of school. But she's blind."

"Indra thinks it's Karma," Darcy voiced, a broad smile on her face. "Serves the bastard right to be struck with a birth defect even worse than what he forced on his poor subjects."

Gabriel held his head. "The secret to immortality. A seamless consciousness throughout every life. Born in a bad way, inferior social structure or with a physical impediment? End your life, hit the reset button, and start again. Your memories, your spirit, your very self will come along for the ride. If you do it right."

Darcy groaned. "As if one life isn't misery enough? You ask me, I prefer having nothin' to do at the end of this dance but shut off the music and kill the lights. But anyway, enough talk." She hefted the .45. "Let's get to work."

46

Through the basement without incident, Jake took the stairs, racing at full tilt, imagining the roar of a helicopter in pursuit, suddenly sure he could smell palm trees and the beach air. He sprinted up the steps, two at a time. At the fourth floor, in the soft flickering light, a nurse saw him.

Jake thrust himself at her, knocked her into a wall and was about to punch, when he held back. He turned her head both directions, looking for the tattoo.

"You're not one of them," he got out in a wheezing breath.

"One of–?"

"No time. Sorry if I hurt you!"

Jake pushed off and bounded back up the stairs. He wasn't sure if he could enlist any help from the staff, wasn't sure how powerful Alexa and her team were, but he wasn't going to let anything stop him from saving Kaitlin. He had to free her before Alexa did anything to her mind.

Like what she tried to do to me.

He had to do everything for her, although he wasn't sure why. He didn't understand all that business with the files and the six dead people from the past, or why he felt such a bond with this person named Carrie—or why he could see any of their faces. But it didn't matter now.

He had to get to her.

At the top floor, he slid to a halt, seeing the long corridor flickering in red tones, paintings hanging crooked and shaking with the gusting winds.

He turned right. She was on this floor somewhere, he knew that much from the monitor. *Time to go door by door.* He reached for the closest one, turned it—locked.

Break it down? He glanced around, into the shadows in both directions, then to the stairs to the other side. At least ten rooms on either side, twenty doors to break down. Plus, those two at either end of the hall... suites? Offices? She would be in one of those.

Suddenly, he heard a scream from that direction—the last door on the right.

He reached the door, barely slowing, then turned the handle and rushed in. A lone candle burned in a little dish on the desk. Curtains were drawn. So dark... A chair faced him, Kaitlin, tied up.

Alexa was bent over her, securing a gag in her mouth. As soon as the door opened, she spun, but Jake's momentum carried him in and knocked her over. He threw a punch for good measure, connecting with the side of Alexa's head as she slammed into the desk. She knocked the candle down, and her dark glasses fell off giving Jake a second to see the opaque white eyes, the mask of pain and fury, before the flame went out. He found Kaitlin in the dark, ripped out her gag and quickly freed her arms and feet.

She bolted to her feet, threw her arms around him in a quick hug. "We've got to go!"

A blur and Alexa appeared, aiming something that sizzled in the shadows behind the desk. An electric sparking light, and twin cords came shooting out, just missing Kaitlin and jabbing into Jake's chest.

He screamed as something jolted through him, rooting him to the spot. He'd been hit with Tasers a couple times back in prison, and he had hoped to never feel one again. No such luck.

He had an instant to whimper, "Run…" before the inevitable blackout.

47

Alexa jumped back to her feet. She'd hit one of them for sure, probably Jake. *That leaves...*

Something came rumbling across the floor at her. Alexa blocked it with her leg, feeling the pain up her calf. *Felt like a chair, Kaitlin kicked a damn chair at me.* She shoved it aside. *The candle's out. We're in the dark now, I have the advantage.* She felt along the ground, found her cane, and immediately jumped up, swinging at the place where she had heard a rustling sound.

The girl shrieked. *Gotcha!* Alexa stepped forward, swinging up and sideways. Nothing. She cocked her head, listening... heard a brush of motion, scuffling feet... the door slamming.

Alexa lunged but tripped on something...Jake's body. She got up, found the door, and flung it open. She heard the running feet, sensed they were turning now...onto the stairs.

Shit. She hadn't been able to even start deprogramming Kaitlin. Alexa dug out her walkie-talkie phone. "Critchwell!"

Nothing. "Critchwell!" She groaned. "Ursula?"

Where the hell were they?

The phone crackled. "Ursula here."

"Where are you?"

"On my way up."

"Stop Kaitlin! She's heading down the stairs now."

"Sorry... I'm in the elevator."

"What?" She almost shattered the phone in her grip.

"Just testing the elevator, in case you needed to bring Indra up."

Alexa fumed. How much longer until she could be rid of these incompetents? The hell with poison, she would strangle the girl herself.

"What does it matter where we handle Indra?"

"But the other patients, and the staff..."

"I don't care who sees us. Anyone who interferes, kill them. We're almost finished here, and I've waited too long. Where's Critchwell?"

"I don't know. I left him in the vault. He was going after Jake."

"Griffith got into the vault?"

"He knocked out Maria when she opened the door, and..."

"For God's sake! Jake's up here. I got him with the Taser, but he released Kaitlin first. We have to assume Critchwell is dead." *Hopefully. Save me the trouble.* Alexa slammed her cane against the floor in frustration.

And then she heard the elevator doors open. "I'm here," Ursula said. "Should I go after Kaitlin?"

"No. I need you to secure Jake. I don't have time now to deal with him—or to figure out why he didn't follow orders. Forget Kaitlin. I'll handle her personally, and Indra too, if he's coming."

"We think he's here," Ursula said. "Nestor saw a vehicle approaching, and sent me..."

"Fine." She dialed Nestor. He picked up at once. *Should have just used him from the beginning.* "Nestor. Hide yourself in the lobby somewhere. Kaitlin's coming down by the stairs."

"Already done," Nestor's voice came back. "And a Hummer just pulled into the garage. I'm guessing it's Indra."

"You know what to do."

"Yes."

Alexa clicked the phone off. "Ursula, hold the damn elevator for me."

48

Gabriel was the last to leave the Hummer after it came to a skidding stop inside the open garage, which fortunately was empty. With the snowstorm obscuring most of the view from inside Daedalus, if anyone had managed to see their approach, no one had appeared yet. Gabriel slung a backpack over his shoulders, containing two walkie-talkies, another pistol, and a pair of night-vision goggles.

Hank helped Indra into his wheelchair. As soon as he was settled, the blanket over his legs, Indra engaged the controls and wheeled around.

The light slanted in through the open garage door as the storm raged outside. It seemed more like twilight than noon as the blizzard, implacable and monstrous, pressed in from all sides.

Indra hefted his gun, sighted down the barrel, and then almost had it slip from his fingers as he tried to appear macho. He slid it under the blanket and reached for a flashlight. "Dr. Sterling, you say the power is out?"

Gabriel nodded. "Except for some auxiliary lights, but she will still have the advantage." He couldn't fully concentrate, still in pain and still thinking about the plan, which had them splitting up. He and his mother were going in through the alternate basement access door, to try to get in the vault and cut off any aid Alexa might receive from her Brotherhood, while Indra and Hank went to get the others and to deal with Alexa personally.

Darcy started heading to the access door, rubbing the .45 in both hands. "Come on."

"Wait," Gabriel said suddenly. "There's a problem. If everything you said is true, we can't just kill her."

Darcy frowned. "Why not?"

"The good doctor is right," said Indra quietly.

"Care to explain?" the gun in Darcy's hand trembled as another gust drove into the garage. "And do it quick, I'm freezin' my ass off."

Gabriel rubbed his bandaged head. "If you're right about all this, kill her, and she'll just come back twenty-one years from now. And unless she's not thought ahead…"

"Oh, we can be sure she has," Indra said. "Probably left new instructions in her secret place—in case of her premature death. No need for reprogramming herself. Die, and in the next life, the commands still hold. Whoever she is next time will find a way to go and retrieve those instructions, wherever she's hidden them. Driven by an uncontrollable need, no matter where he or she is."

Gabriel made his hands into fists, then opened them. "Then it's the same with you! With the six of you. That's why she's bringing you all here instead of just killing you."

Indra nodded, having reached the same conclusion earlier. "She has to deprogram us first. Eliminate the implants Atticus placed in us the last time. Otherwise, in every life, we'll be out there, potentially remembering, seeing each other, compelled to find out why, trying to solve the mystery."

Gabriel shook his head. "Then we have to find her safe location, remove the contents—"

"Or we turn the tables on her," said Indra, "Take her under

the way she's been doing to us. We wipe her mind, cleanse her *Ba*."

"And then," said Darcy, "we kill the bitch."

49

Monica awoke with a pounding headache, like that one Christmas morning after she and Paul had been drinking Merlot all night, watching a marathon showing of *It's a Wonderful Life*. Her head spun in one direction, the room in the other, twin forces tugging at her stomach, knotting her intestines.

She flexed her hands. Moved her fingers, then her arms. No more duct tape. She was free. She stood up slowly, wobbled and then made it to the oak desk, and leaned against its smooth, polished surface. A lone candle, burned almost to the base, sat in a pool of translucent liquid wax; it bathed the room in a calming, orange light, just enough to see by.

Enough to make out the huge painting on the wall. A giant, golden-framed portrait of a face from her nightmare. Here, finally, was someone she could see—the first face she could actually view with clarity—and it was one that filled her with unrelenting fear.

She had to get away from him. Get away from this room.

But she couldn't move yet. Still disconnected, trying to piece together the past hour. *Am I cured?*

Monica's memories were fuzzy... Images of that woman's

opaque eyes, unblinking, inches from her own... Impressions of an hourglass, crimson sands shifting, diminishing, bleeding out from one glass to another, one soul to the next.

Why did I just think that?

Layer after layer had been seared away, her soul laid bare. Pieces plucked from her spirit like feathers, leaving her defenseless. Then Alexa had gone deeper, tearing open her core and removing what had been planted there a lifetime ago.

But now, like after a diseased tooth had been pulled, it felt good. *To be free of it, to be pure again.*

Except for those cold eyes staring at her from the painting.

That artist should be killed. It was too real.

But I am real, she heard the painted man say, his booming voice echoing in her mind, fused with the lighter voice of Alexa Pearl. I am real. As really real as that beloved piece of shit rabbit of yours. I am real, more real than your mother's killer, the one you let off the hook.

Stop it! In a mounting rage, Monica picked up the candle.

More real than your poor husband, who couldn't even do something sweet for you without getting his head blown off.

She yelled and flung the candle at the painting.

The wax spattered, caught, clung, dripped.

Burned.

The painting flickered. The eyes, those terrible eyes. Twin drops of wax flared up and flames shot out from its eyes like some cackling demon.

Monica ran. She bumped into the chair, then staggered to the door as the whole painting suddenly burst into flames. The fire leapt maniacally to the curtains, to the tapestries... To the rug... The desk.

As soon as she bolted into the hall, the overhead sprinklers exploded, and a shrill alarm sounded. Suddenly she was getting drenched, looking back into Alexa's office where the fire raged against what felt like a late August thundershower.

Monica backed up, her face soaking wet, hair dripping into

her eyes. Doors opened. A few patients timidly popped their heads out. Then they were running, nearly tripping over each other, racing for the stairs, some of them with their suitcases or choice possessions. After the hall was empty, the water continued to fall from the ceiling, soaking the rug, collecting in puddles on the banisters, on the railing surrounding the open view all the way down to the lobby floor.

Monica turned away from Alexa's office, where smoke drifted out from the dwindling fire. The smooth, rounded balustrade called to her. The clear, empty space beyond. So empty, clear of anything. No guilt, no pain. Just... nothingness.

So, inviting...

It's time, said the voice from the painting. A voice now raspy, as if burnt, and then drowned in succession. She heard squishing footsteps behind her... Blackened feet sizzling with every step onto the wet carpet.

Impossible. Not real, not real. Just in your mind.

The alarm stopped, turned off somewhere or disconnected.

Monica reached for the railing.

Jump, said the seared voice behind her. Atticus Sterling.

Do it, Alexa said, her voice joining up with the other's, inside her mind. *Jump.*

Gripping the wooden railing, Monica risked a glance behind her. But no one was there. The landing, empty on all sides.

Good. No one to see me dive.

She lifted her leg, placing her knee on the top rail, and looked down. Five floors. A lot of empty, inviting space.

Just then, a door opened. Gabriel's office, at the other end of the main hall. For a fleeting second, she had a surge of hope. That he was there, that he would see her, stop her from doing this thing, this thing she couldn't resist. That he would stop her and hold her and talk to her. Take her under, plunge deep into her soul; he would root out the poison, excise the horrible thing Alexa had left in her mind. He would free her.

But it wasn't Gabriel.

A woman, that nurse with the snake tattoo. She came out, looking up at the sprinklers, shielding her eyes as the water sprayed her face. She looked back down, and her eyes met Monica's.

I can see her. I am cured.

Good for you, said the burning voice over her shoulder... in her mind. *Now jump.*

The nurse nodded to her, folded her arms. Back in the shadows of Gabriel's office, someone moved. Struggled.

It wasn't Monica's concern. Whoever was in there wasn't real. Nothing else was real. Nothing but the railing.

The drop. The jump.

Time to end it.

50

K aitlin stayed in the shadows, inching down the final bend of the stairs toward the lobby. The great expanse of marble looked like the tranquil surface of a moonlit pond, glimmering in the cold, shaded light from the windows. The area was empty except for one middle-aged woman behind the desk; she wore a thick black sweater and looked exhausted. The light on the wall over the door burned faintly, but enough to still illuminate the small tattoo on the receptionist's neck.

She's one of them.

Kaitlin took another step, directing her attention now to the silver elevator doors, suddenly convinced they would open at any moment. Another step, and she caught movement in the shadows behind a pillar. A man standing there, keeping an eye on the side door—the one to the garage.

She gasped. *Nestor?*

What is he doing back here? He should have left with Monica and Gabriel. *What–?*

An alarm rang out, a screeching series of sounds. Doors opened upstairs on every level and people rushed out... Running, heading to the stairs. Nestor burst out of the shadows, looking up. He caught her eye, and Kaitlin was about to call out when she saw his face twist into malice. He pulled something from behind his back.

She knew, even before she saw it—knew he had a gun. She backed up as Nestor pointed it at her. "No..."

Then the door to the garage opened, and a big, faceless man in a long trenchcoat burst in, followed by a familiar electronic wheelchair. Nestor swiveled to face the pair of newcomers, gun menacing, just as a crowd of patients and staff came thumping down the stairs.

"Indra! Watch out!"

Kaitlin struggled to stay on her feet as they stampeded around her. The receptionist and two orderlies ran out in front of the rush, into the lobby, waving their hands, trying to control the patients.

And then Kaitlin glimpsed the elevator doors opening. The darkened interior relinquished a wraithlike form, more shadow than substance.

THE MAN in the trenchcoat lifted a shotgun and pointed it at Nestor, but Indra yelled and yanked his arm down. "Stop! He's one of us..."

Kaitlin cringed as two gunshots erupted. The crowd froze in a moment of shared shock. Then came the screams, the lobby erupting into panic.

The big man in the trench coat crumpled to his knees; the shotgun fell to the floor and his hands clutched at his throat, trying to stop the dark gouts of blood streaming through his fingers. Another hole spilled blood, thick as red paint, down his chest. Indra wore a look of complete shock, turning to horror, as he turned from his dying companion to Nestor who now had the gun trained on him.

"STOP!" yelled Alexa, banging her cane on the ground. People continued screaming; some cowered, others started back up the stairs, away from Nestor, believing they had a terrorist in their midst.

Nestor spun, raised the gun, and fired into the wall above their heads.

Alexa shouted in the ensuing silence, "Get back to your rooms!" She tilted her head toward the front desk. "Maria! Shut off that damn alarm, now!"

Maria, her face blushed and splotchy, ran to the reception desk. She stopped before reaching the wall panel. "But what if—"

"Shut it off!"

"Ms. Pearl," Maria was shaking, staring hesitantly at Nestor now, then back to Alexa as if wrestling with something that hadn't been part of the plan. Kaitlin's heart surged. Maybe there was hope...

If Alexa's staff could turn against her...

Maria said, "What if there really is a fire?"

Nestor shot her. He simply swiveled around, kept his arm straight, and shot her once in the face. Then he stepped over her twitching body and pointed the gun at the next staff member, a smaller, cowering woman. "Shut it off."

The woman ran behind the desk and opened the panel, madly searching for the controls, as the rest of the patients surged back upstairs, fleeing in terror, preferring to face whatever natural elements raged upstairs instead of this gunman blocking the exit.

Kaitlin felt the heat from Alexa's blind gaze, sweeping back and forth, seeking her out. She retreated, blending in with the others. She caught Indra's eye. He gave a brief smile, and she opened her mouth...

But Indra shook his head. He had looked so utterly helpless in that chair but seeing her seemed to give him a burst of confidence. He signaled with his eyes, and she understood: *Go, get to the others. I'm fine.* And then he patted something under his blanket.

Kaitlin nodded, turned, and ran up with the residents, keeping her head down.

She would have to find another way to help Indra. But as she climbed, she realized she was headed in the right direction—to the one person she needed. If only she could revive him in time.

She had to get back to Jake...

51

After Indra and Hank headed for the lobby door, Gabriel led his mother through the supply entrance from the garage's south side, down the drafty stairwell into the basement. He held the flashlight since Darcy refused to relinquish her .45. Seeing her finger on the trigger, the gun trembling, terrified him.

"Mom—"

"Shut up, Gabe. You're lucky I don't shoot you now. Are you aware of how long it's been since you visited me?"

He hung his head. "I've been busy."

"I can see that. Playing little errand boy for that blind tramp."

"Mom, I—"

"Let's just go. We've got work to do."

They made it to the basement, emerging in near-darkness. "Stop. Turn off the light," Darcy whispered.

"Why?"

"Do it, boy. My eyesight's shit, but I think I see…"

He flicked it off and, as his eyes adjusted to the shadow-engorged interior, he thought about how he had spent so many frustrating hours down here, standing before that locked vault door, contemplating its mysteries, wrestling with the temptation to blast it down or blowtorch through it. All the while, that hourglass—his father's favorite tool, his symbol—mocked his impotency, chided his efforts.

"I don't believe it." He stared at the faint rectangle of light in the far wall, opposite the stairs up to the lobby. His stomach twisted, his feet and hands burning with renewed ferocity. The gash on his head throbbed and the swelling on his face felt like he had broken some cheekbones.

He needed medical attention, but all he could think to say was, "The vault door's open."

THEY CAREFULLY STEPPED INSIDE. The air smelled of death. Blood.

"The hourglass?" Gabriel whispered, carefully stepping over the body of Lance Critchwell.

"Damn thing." Darcy gave the grains of sand a kick and moved ahead, grimacing at the bloodied skull. She trod carefully, with awe, as if she had just discovered a tomb that had been hidden for thousands of years. Gabriel moved with similar caution, covering the other side, ignoring for now the set of tables, monitors, servers, binders, and loose papers. He switched off the flashlight and set it down on the nearest table along with the backpack. He kept moving to the closer wall where jagged carvings hung, depicting Egyptian rites with bold hieroglyphics.

The air was so clear, pristine, and he had the sudden notion that leaving the door open would cause all these artifacts to crumble into dust, the sacred words gone forever.

Good riddance. If all these pieces just dissolved in the dank basement air, disintegrating before his eyes, he wouldn't shed a tear, not after what this thing, this piece of ancient history, had done to his father. Whether or not all that mystic crap was true, his father believed it. And now, Alexa believed it and was acting on its implications, believing herself to be a god. *And us mere mortals are just dispensable obstacles in her path.*

He turned away from the walls, from the strange artifacts, the pottery, the clay jars, the jackal-headed statues, the pharaohs with arms crossed in death-like poses, decked out in their finest golden attire.

He headed for the tables, but his mother was already there. "Look at this," she whispered, her free hand pointing at a monitor. Gabriel came around and tried to make sense of the spreadsheet, the split screen and the six files grouped together with now-familiar names.

"What?"

"There's your experiment," Darcy said smugly. With the gun, she pointed to the spreadsheet. "Doesn't look finished, but she must have had her people trying to match who came back as whom." She peered closer, squinting. "Who's Monica Gilman? Says here she's that nice Elizabeth Ellison woman. Always liked that one. Stood up to Atticus, she did. Gave him a shitload of trouble."

Gabriel was shaking his head. "I still... can't..."

"Wake up, son!" She grabbed him by the collar. "Did the storm snap your brain? Give you frostbite of the noggin? I raised you smarter than this. Go with your gut, you know this ain't a joke. Your son of a bitch father went and did it."

Gabriel pulled away; sat at the desk and started pulling up the files. "Let me study this."

"We ain't got time. Didn't you hear the cripple upstairs? And hell, if you don't believe me, look at the TV sets here."

His head whipped around. *The cameras.* Alexa had them installed all over. So, this was where her people came to snoop on everybody. He immediately picked out the hallway on the top floor, the shared corridor between his and Alexa's offices. A lone nurse stood outside his office, like she was guarding it. *That bitch, Ursula.* Who was in there? Monica, still?

He pulled his eyes away, glancing back at the file he had opened. Only for a second, but it was enough. His eyes picked out the most important words on the screen, a skill he had called upon often trying to keep up with hundreds of psychological journals.

Two words: *apparent suicide*. He read on. November 13, 1976. Just after midnight, Elizabeth Ellison had slit her wrists in a bathtub while her husband watched TV downstairs.

A shudder ran through his bones, making his near-frostbite feel like blessed numbness by comparison. Suicide. He thought of Franklin Baynes jumping from the roof. Jake Griffith taking off into the snowstorm.

He got up, heat flowing through his veins. *Suicide...*

His mother tried to set him back down. "If you're on to something, keep at it. Indra figured we could find the answers down here... and a way to stop her. So let's not go jumping at shadows."

Gabriel sat back down, turning to the screen, calling up another file at random. "Carrie Coburn... died—November 12th. Cause of death: suicide. Hanging."

He slammed the keyboard, clicked on another file. "Tommy Sorrento. Nine-years old. Oh god..."

"I remember Tommy!" Darcy's eyes lit up. "Such a spitfire! Ate nothing but pancakes and ice cream. Figured if his parents saw fit to dump him here for some extra pocket change he was sure as shit going to eat what he wanted."

"Mom—he died two months after the study. The same date as the others. November 12th. Threw himself off a roof." His hands were shaking. "I'm going to find the same thing with all of them, aren't I?"

Darcy looked away.

"Mother. What did he do?"

She put a hand to her chest, as if blocking the words from reaching her heart. "I never knew for sure. But I heard about them, of course. From angry relatives accusing Atticus of doing something to their minds, warping them. Lawyers came to see us. Atticus paid a few of them off, I'm sure. Other times, he paid off the judges. Nothing stuck, and eventually the relatives moved on. And then of course, Atticus killed himself and left me to deal with the whole mess."

Gabriel closed his eyes, a whirl of faces and names spinning in his head. "All of them? All six?"

Darcy took a deep breath. "The damned experiment, and his usual lack of patience. He wanted results, couldn't wait for them."

"Christ. He had them all kill themselves." Gabriel's mouth went dry; the room spun.

"You have to appreciate his creativity."

"But it shouldn't be possible. Hypnosis isn't that strong, it—"

"It ain't supposed to be strong enough to leave yourself instructions in the next life neither, but damn Atticus learnt himself how to do it. Went in deep—real deep—as he'd say."

"All of them," Gabriel repeated. "All on the same day…"

"So, they'd hop right back into the rebirth line. Be born again together. And then he could use their ages as another flag to point out the potential returnees."

Gabriel held his head, waiting for the room to stop spinning, the dust to settle. "But Jake is younger, and I think I heard something about Kaitlin?"

"That just proves it. Since the original six were all killed on the same date, and they're not all the same age now…"

Nodding, Gabriel said, "Kaitlin and Jake must have only lived about nine years or so last time, then died and came back— so this is their second reincarnation since the experiment, and they still have the face blindness and everything else he placed in there."

Darcy nodded. "So now she has to take care of them for good, or else she'll have unfinished business." She smiled. "Potential competition. Always the chance someone could get regressed by a good hypnotist and remember, or the truth could come out in dreams or nightmares."

"Dad always hated unfinished business."

"His one dependable quality." She gave a raspy sigh. "Now

that he knows he's got this immortality thing figured out, he can do it again and again. The implanted memory will stick forever, through every lifetime, and he can always add stuff to his vault. Think of it now with technology. DVDs, video recordings, microchips. Billions of bits of data, entire lives for his new incarnation to review. Like catching up with old friends."

Gabriel's temples throbbed. "And that's why we have to find it... his vault or wherever he's programmed himself to go in the next life."

Scratching her chin, Darcy looked around the room again. "But it can't be this place, not down here. Alexa needed the key first, before she could get through the vault door. The key had to be somewhere else. Somewhere..."

Gabriel tracked his mother's gaze, scanning the room. "What are you looking for?"

She held up a shaking hand. "Just remembering something... If I'm right, he would've wanted it close, maybe kept it here in the vault as a reminder to reinforce the latent commands..."

"Wanted what close?"

"Look for a picture... you remember the one, I'm sure... of the cemetery? That tomb?"

Gabriel blinked, thinking. "Yes, I think I do. A really odd picture that used to hang in his office? A framed black and white photograph of a mausoleum."

"That's the one! So out of place with the rest of his psych awards, framed articles, and occult crap that it practically begged for an explanation."

"I remember... once, I asked Dad about it, and he just ignored me. As always."

"Believe me, you got off easy." She moved to the nearest bookshelf, rummaged around the shelves, then she knelt, moving along the bottom shelf, pushing things aside, until... "A-ha!"

She snatched up something from where it had been stuck

between two large leather-bound volumes. Spinning around, she held it up in front of Gabriel's face. "Look familiar?"

He stared at the black-and-white image of a cemetery at dusk. Gnarled trees with swollen branches cradling a tomb's ivy-covered walls. "The mausoleum…"

"I know this place," Darcy whispered, staring at it and tapping the glass with her finger. She spoke quietly, as if afraid she'd be overheard by the Egyptian deities. "A cemetery just outside of Boston. I know, I know—morbid as shit, but that was Atticus. This here's a huge mausoleum up on the highest hill."

"What was its significance?"

"I asked your father once, after he hung this picture in his office, oh—back in the '50s. He said that it belonged to a Silas-somebody. Berger, I think. Some renowned spiritualist and big-time landowner who died in the 1820's."

"Let me guess. Atticus believed he was this Silas man in another life?"

"Didn't say as much, not in so many words, but I think you're right. He was obsessed with the place. Went there a couple times a year, like a pilgrimage."

"Did he ever go inside?"

She shrugged. "I don't know, never went with him, but one time while snooping in his office, I found a bunch of Polaroids of the tomb's outer walls, especially the back. Don't know where those pictures are now, but I got a feeling he might have scoped out that tomb for a reason."

Gabriel closed his eyes and thought for a moment. "Trying to be like the pharaohs. Leaving the real treasure—the secret of who he was—in the tomb of his predecessor. But, if all this is true, he must have put something else in there too."

"The key to this damned vault." Darcy took a wheezing breath and clutched her chest. She held up a hand. "I'm okay…" She steadied herself. "Besides the key, I bet Atticus also had some secret offshore accounts and investments. Never did find all his money. Only left us enough to keep Daedalus running. Until..."

"...Until he got back," Gabriel finished. He wrung his hands together. "So, assuming we can even manage to incapacitate Alexa, then we still need to go up to that cemetery in Boston and find what she's hidden up there this time."

"Damn right."

Gabriel thought quietly, and his vision unfocused. "Mom?"

"Yeah?"

"I never really thanked you."

"For what?"

"For protecting me from him. For standing up to him. I can't even imagine what it was like for you."

"Had to be done. I loved you too much, too much to let you turn out like him."

"And... thanks for keeping the Institute running after he was gone..."

"I had help." She set down the picture. Squeezed Gabriel's shoulder, then pulled him close in a hug and spoke into his ear. "You did most of the work, Gabriel. Daedalus is yours, not mine. Never was. It's not your father's, and it's not Alexa's, no matter what the deed says."

Reluctantly breaking the embrace, he blinked at her, trembling again as his injuries throbbed and his head spun, and his mother smiled.

"Take it back, Gabriel. Take it back."

52

His hand concealed underneath the blanket, Indra silently released the heavy gun's safety. He kept an eye on Nestor, the man whose face he could see so clearly, so powerfully. He felt at once drawn to him and repulsed by him. *Traitor*, was all Indra could think, but at the same time, he understood.

"What did she promise you, Nestor?"

The big man spun around, leveling the gun at him. "What?"

Alexa glided up behind Nestor, facing Indra. They were alone again in the lobby. Her eyes swam in a sea of white-gray mist, devoid of any emotion, feeling or life. "Indra. I'd love to catch up, but we have to take a little trip first, deep into your soul."

Indra maneuvered the gun. Pointed it at her stomach. Maybe a gut shot? Had to wound her, not kill her. Funny, he thought. Ironic, maybe. They were both in the same predicament—desperate to do away with their enemies but restrained from using full force. They both had unfinished business to attend to first.

And then there was Nestor. Indra needed to take him out too, now, or he wouldn't get another chance. But there were ways other than gunfire.

"You didn't answer my question, Nestor."

Alexa touched Nestor's shoulder gently with her free hand. "Ignore the chatter of the dead." She stepped forward. "Don't make this difficult, Indra. The other four are taken care of. Let me cure you, give you back your sight, and then you can go on your way. No hard feelings. I'll forgive you for killing my colleague back in Jaipur. And…"

"…And will I forgive you for killing all of us back in 1976?"

In Indra's mind, Alexa's swirling features resolved, just for a moment, into a mask of pure fury, a shape topped with fiery red hair and steely blue eyes. Then her features fell back into confounded obscurity.

Nestor tensed his hold on the gun. "What's he talking about?"

"Nothing," Alexa hissed.

"Tell him," Indra said. "Tell your lapdog here what you did. Why you killed us off. Come on, Alexa. Tell him how you are far too selfish to share immortality with anyone."

"That's a lie!" Nestor hissed. "We will be together forever, and…"

Indra's laugh cut him off. "Seriously? Love? Is that it? You and her? My god, Nestor. She is blind, but not stupid. Playing you, just as she played the other…"

"Enough!" Alexa raised her cane, brought it to within inches of his face, and Indra saw something on the bottom—a slot, just the width of a blade tip.

Something else to consider, he thought, gripping his fingers around the gun's handle, raising it just a touch beneath the blanket. *Almost time.*

"Alexa?" Nestor turned toward her, lowering his gun. "He's lying, right? Let me kill him."

"No. I told you, it must wait."

"If he's lying, what does it matter? We have an eternity to kill him."

Indra made a mock laugh. "Where she is going, Nestor, you are not following."

"Shut up!" He aimed back at him. "I am her warrior. I—"

"You are deceived!" Indra sat up straight, eyes blazing. "Go ahead, ask her, ask about the others she has promised the same thing. Her 'Brotherhood'. Do you really believe she's going to reward all of them too?"

"Yes!" he shouted, veins popping on his head. "Yes…" he said again, weakly. He looked at her face, searching for confirmation.

"Yes!" Alexa answered, her voice trembling. "Don't let this cripple sow doubts in you. You know what I am."

"Nestor," Indra said, shaking his head with a little chuckle. "Alexa was a man in the past life. How does that grab you?"

"SHUT UP!"

He swung the gun around and fired—just as Alexa snapped her cane and knocked his arm out of the way. A piece of the wall behind Indra exploded, and Nestor reflexively struck back with his free hand—knocking Alexa to the floor.

Footsteps came pounding down the stairs.

Now! Indra told himself, just as two men in black turtlenecks came into the lobby, with guns drawn. They took one look at Nestor standing over Alexa—their leader, their redeemer—and fired.

⌛

NESTOR FIRED BACK, almost simultaneously. Something stung his hip, and another something slammed into his ribs. He fired again. *Bastards aren't taking me down. Not after I've come this far.*

He saw a satisfying gush of red burst out of the first man's skull. The second staggered with a shot in his shoulder, then kept coming. Firing wildly. Once, twice. Aimed again—

Nestor shot him in the throat.

Both men down, he stumbled back around, saw Alexa struggling to rise, then had a moment's calm. The fury was abating, replaced with guilt.

What have I done?

He hobbled, holding his side, feeling his blood pouring out, spilling on the floor, slick under his boots. But when he looked at Indra and saw a matching spot of bright red in the center of the cripple's chest and realized one of the Brotherhoods' errant shots had indeed found its mark, he smiled.

Until he heard Alexa's cry of frustration.

THE WINDOWS RATTLED, the lights flickered, and the winds roared along the turrets. Indra had an instant of shining clarity, a flashburst of insight, and a glimpse into a spider web made of golden thread, spinning and spinning, woven back into countless pasts, interconnecting and linking back in a seamless, perfectly integrated whole.

Shot, he mused with a giddy jolt of something like psychic adrenaline. His body was dying, that was certain. He started to laugh, and the webs turned to silver, then copper, rusting as they began to dissolve, releasing his vision of this life, this world. There was the shadowy lobby, the creaking walls... The big man with the gun.

It's over, he thought, or he said, he wasn't sure.

Someone answered, shouting, "NO!" A violent grunt, and the big shape crumpled as something long, metallic and shiny plunged in, then ripped out of Nestor's chest.

Indra blinked, an action that seemed to carry with it a note of finality.

When his vision focused again, all he could see were two eggshell-white eyes.

"STAY ALIVE!" Alexa spat, shaking Indra. She found his shoulders, shook him, then felt lower, touching the spreading warmth that drenched his shirt. A gun had fallen from his limp fingers, unfired. *Dammit, Nestor!* She heard him twitching now, dying behind her. The sword blade inside her cane had cleanly punctured its target, and Nestor was probably spending his last seconds wondering what had happened.

"Stay with me!" She slapped Indra's face. Again. She pounded his chest. "I can't let you go! Not yet. Listen to my voice, Indra. *Listen to my damn voice!*"

She heard nearly silent, bubbling laughter. Indra's chest heaved with great effort to make the sounds.

"I see the webs," he whispered. "So shiny..."

"Shut up and listen to my voice." She couldn't let him slip away. Had to get inside now, right now. Dive deep and strike. "You are drifting back, far back, beyond—"

Again, the laugher. Liquid, taunting.

"It's over," he said.

"NO!" She slammed his chest again. "You are falling back, so deep. Deeper and deeper. Listen to me, you are—"

"Free," came the whisper. "But... do not worry. I am not coming back."

"What?"

"Free," he said again. A cough. Giddy childish laughter. Then, weakly: "Free."

"No..." Could it be? Was he talking about what she thought? Was it possible? She had studied the theories to death, but never paid much heed to the parts about how to stop the wheel, to get off the cycle. Why would anyone want that? Besides, such speculation always involved mumbo-jumbo about selflessness and meditation and do-goodedness. None of that concerned her.

None of it. But still—was he saying he was done?

"Indra, if that's true, I'll take you at your word. As long as you're no longer my responsibility. No more unfinished business."

"...st... one," he whispered.

"What did you say?"

"Just... one."

She felt his heart, one beat, then an impossibly long wait for the next. *Beat*. Then he spoke: "Go... to your vault. See what I've brought you."

Beat...

And then nothing.

Alexa pushed away, and in her perpetual darkness, she gave the wheelchair a kick. She turned, bent down and found her cane. Pressed the button near the handle, and heard the blade whisk back inside.

She stepped over the bodies, then paused for a moment, listening to the wind raging outside, thumping and howling like a bloodthirsty crowd, cheering the imminent victor.

She headed for the basement.

53

The patients fled back up the stairs, faster than they had left only minutes earlier. Monica backed off the railing, watching as they nearly trampled each other, rushing to get back to their rooms. But she just marveled at the ability to see each one of them. Every face, every horrified expression. Such emotion, such a range of expressions and familiar looks. Such shared pain, horror, fear.

Something down there scared the shit out of them. Those gunshots she'd heard, the ones that had momentarily broken her resolve to jump. What was happening down there?

It doesn't matter. When the doors all slammed shut, and once again she was alone, she glanced down over the railing. Nothing down there but gloom, and a subtle, silvery sheen on the distant floor.

Nothing that's my concern. She felt the railing again. She just had to pull herself up and simply roll over the side. It would be easy.

Her heart was thundering, knees weak.

She heard a sound. It was that nurse. Outside the door to Gabriel's office; standing there, smiling patiently.

"Go on," she said. "Don't mind me. You have an important job to do."

She's right, Monica thought. This was important. This was *real*.

That's what it came down to. This task of hers, it was real—maybe the only thing that was real. Everything else was just a trick of her imagination.

So then, what's the point? It was a familiar voice, but still it took a moment to place it. Her mother's. Monica shut her eyes and pictured her childhood bedroom, an open book, and her mother's touch.

Why become real, if only to end like this...?

She started to climb.

Slipped backwards, but pulled herself up and slung her leg over. It was time.

A soft, smoky laughter obliterated her mother's voice. *Time*, it repeated, louder, and Monica heard what sounded like sand striking the bottom of a glass bowl, each grain booming, echoing in her soul.

TIME!

She got to one knee on the top, her weight shifting forward. Opened her eyes to the yawning chasm of welcoming space, wobbled forward, back, forward...

And heard thumping footsteps...

Another woman—a girl really, with short hair and pretty brown eyes—came dashing up the stairs.

Monica knew this girl, recognized her. Once more she dropped down and backed away from the railing.

Get back there! Do it—

Monica was about to call out when a gunshot exploded, the girl on the stairs crumpled and her scream tore through the air.

⧗

URSULA FIRED LOW, the bullet bursting through Kaitlin's thigh. Monica screamed and jumped farther from the railing while Kaitlin struggled to pull herself up the stairs.

"Stay out of this," Ursula said, turning the gun on Monica. "Don't you have something to do?"

Monica shook her head, trying to disperse the insistent humming that began as soon as she left the railing. It quickly became a chanting, rising in pitch and urgency. Ursula aimed at Kaitlin again. The girl had crumpled on the top stair, clutching her bloody leg.

They need her alive, Monica thought quickly as she inched closer to Ursula and Kaitlin.

"Stop," Ursula said, seeing her approach. "Or I kill her."

"You won't kill her," Monica whispered, barely hearing herself over the chanting that had now become a roar. "Not yet."

"True," Ursula said, steadying the weapon at Monica's face, "but I can kill you."

"Your master won't like that."

"Shut up." She took a step, closing the gap. "Why aren't you jumping?"

Monica shook her head again, dislodging chunks of sound, flinging away clinging whispers and urgent rumblings. The gun in Ursula's hand was only a foot away, aiming right at her. In the corner of her eye, Monica noticed motion... Kaitlin getting up, a look of pure determination on her face. Monica smiled, an action that caused Ursula to pause. Kaitlin tensed, and then jumped up with her good leg, launching herself into Ursula.

The gun went off, the shot sailing wide of Monica's head. Reflexively, she lunged, caught Ursula's wrist and held on, spinning with the momentum of Kaitlin's collision. Both women held on to the struggling nurse. Kaitlin tried to lift Ursula up, and then Monica tugged at her wrist, spun her around and helped Kaitlin slam the nurse back into the railing.

Screaming, Kaitlin still had Ursula's waist in a bear hug. She heaved up, lifting her feet off the wet floor. The gun went off again, and a section of the glass ceiling exploded. The winds roared inside, and Ursula howled as a jagged wedge of blue glass speared her shoulder and lodged there like a broken wing.

Monica struggled.

The voices urged, *jump, jump…*

She pushed against the words, batted them away and projected all that energy—all that fury and purpose—and helped Kaitlin shove the nurse up and over the side.

Ursula's long, trailing scream echoed grimly past each level. So did the ensuing thump on the lobby floor.

Kaitlin hoisted herself up on one leg, still leaning on Monica, taking deep gasps of air. "Thanks."

"Your leg…" Monica started to say.

"I might live," Kaitlin said with a grunt. She pushed off, limping toward Gabriel's office. "Come on, we've got to get to Jake."

Monica watched her go into the crimson-hued shadows. Then, she turned back to the railing.

Reality check time. No more delays. No reprieves.

The sands had run out. But she wasn't terribly sad. She had done something, made up for her crime, in a way. Given someone else a chance to make it. Another couple would have an opportunity because of her.

Maybe now, Paul would forgive her.

She hauled herself up and prepared to follow Ursula over the edge.

54

Reaching for the ornate brass handle of the basement door, the handle she knew was right in front of her, Alexa stopped suddenly as a sickeningly violent thud behind her rocked the lobby's marble floor, sending vibrations up her legs.

Alexa smiled.

Goodbye, Monica.

ALMOST DONE. Her business was nearly finished.

Good riddance to this life.

Alexa kicked off her shoes and walked in her bare feet, descending into the basement. The cold was exquisite, an intense tactile sensation, causing shivers on the soles of her feet, even her toes. Her cane in her left hand, finger on the blade release, and Indra's fully loaded pistol in her right, she moved soundlessly across the dusty basement floor.

Whatever or whoever Indra has in there, I'll be ready.

But would she? What if he had brought along a squad of marines with AK-47s? She wished Nestor was still around, that impatient fool, or Critchwell or one of the others; but when she actually thought about it, it was better this way. On her own. Going to meet her destiny alone, one shining, daring mortal who had managed to run off with the gods' secret. Taking a bite from the apple, scraping the bark off the Tree of Life.

She'd beaten them, slipped outside the game board, and stolen the prize.

But there was still unfinished business she had to take care of. Maybe she should go back up first, deal with Kaitlin, then come down here with Ursula as her eyes, and let the nurse spring any traps the head-case Indra had left for her.

But Atticus would not have waited. *And neither will I.* This was her institute. She had the home-field advantage.

She pressed on, striding unerringly toward the vault door, having committed this route to memory after so many daily visits throughout the years. She sensed a dim light probing around her occluded eyesight, growing slightly brighter as she approached. *The door's open,* she thought, and stopped, listening.

A voice inside.

A familiar voice, talking in shocked tones, stupidly broadcasting his position—and his defenselessness.

Just like a cockroach, she thought. Gabriel survived, after all. Alexa hefted the gun. *Oh Indra, this was the best you could do?*

🏺

SHE WAITED OUTSIDE THE VAULT, staying in the darkness, the shadows that had always been her ally, her lifetime associate. *Who was Gabriel talking to?*

He did have a habit of muttering to himself. *Annoying brat.* The way he would study as a teenager, reading aloud, quizzing himself. As if anyone wanted to hear him babbling all that textbook nonsense. Atticus had wanted to shake him silly and pry open his eyes, forcing him to see the truth, but... it wasn't worth the effort. Not after what Atticus had found out about himself.

About his true lineage. Tracing back to Silas, and before... long before that. He lamented all those lives wasted, the years spent wandering in the dark in the search of the same truths, over and over again.

She knew many of the pharaohs has done it, had come back again and again for centuries, maybe millennia, before either tiring of it all or just disappearing into the mountains some-where, enlightened beyond all the mortals below. Wherever they were now, it didn't matter. She was making her bid to follow in their footsteps.

People said it was the quest that mattered, not the prize. That was rubbish. How much stronger... how much better would we be, if born into complete possession of all our lives' previous labors? Then, we could truly advance. Evolve. Accomplish something! Anything we desired.

It was enough to make Alexa's blood seethe. She was so close; she would not be denied.

No more delays.

She burst into the room, aiming the gun toward the sound of Gabriel's voice. The cane in her left hand was held across her body, supporting her firing hand, and ready for a sideways slash if necessary.

"Finally made it in here, Gabriel? After how long?"

The room fell silent but for the humming of the emergency lights and the server equipment and the rumbling generator. "Doing any good reading?"

She didn't really care to hear a response. It was time to finish what Nestor should have done. She was about to squeeze the trigger when she smelled something odd. Something familiar. A moldy perfume smell and the toxic scent of old age. She cocked her head.

And heard Gabriel's whisper, ever so quietly: "Shoot."

Without thinking, completely by reflex, Alexa leapt back-ward, dropping at the same time and switching her aim.

Another gun went off and Alexa immediately zeroed in on the shot's origin. Crouching, she fired. Three times in succession.

She heard two high-pitched cries, then something slumped to the floor. The other gun clanked down after it. And Alexa crawled, crablike, to her left, swinging out with the cane until it contacted a soft body, then she reached out, felt for a thin, bony wrist. Searched for and found the weakening pulse.

"Son... of... a... bitch," came the choked, familiar voice.

Alexa stood up, training the gun now on the scrambling sounds from behind the desk. She heard Gabriel stop, and he made a gasping sound.

"Mom, no..."

"Unbelievable," Alexa said, fighting back the laughter. "Some things never change. Didn't you resort to taking mom to your senior prom, too, when no one else would go with you?"

Alexa heard his sharp intake of breath. "So... now you're sure. Before you only half-believed it. But how else would I know that disturbing little morsel?"

"Dad. You..."

"Yes, me." She had enough of this. No more unfinished business. She aimed at the sound of his voice and squeezed the trigger.

Alexa listened, but after the resounding echoes—no scream, no crumpling body. Nothing.

She narrowed her eyes, turned her head. He's holding his breath. Crouching, no doubt. Close to where he was. She aimed the gun a fraction lower. It didn't matter. She had eight bullets left.

About to fire, she heard something. Only, it came from beneath her.

No—that bitch...

A hand circled her left ankle, holding it fast and then—stabbing pain. Alexa screeched as teeth sunk into her flesh. A laughing sound, then a gnawing like a dog ravaging a rawhide bone.

"Damn you!" Alexa cried, kicking free finally, after two tries. Then she aimed down and fired. Again and again, left and right, strafing Darcy's body two more times. She followed up her shots with a kick into the now-immobile form.

And then something slammed into her. With a shout, Gabriel pounded her into the wall. Alexa dropped the gun, and it went flying somewhere, clattering against a far wall. *It didn't matter.* She got up, shook herself free. She flicked the button on her cane, switched it to her right hand, and swung out in a fierce arc, feeling it connect with something soft—and rip through.

Gabriel screamed.

Where did she hit him? She swung again—and missed. Too high. Stabbed lower, like a fencer, jabbing here, then there.

She heard him scrambling, kicking and rolling, grunting in pain. She had him. *Just push him to a wall and finish him off.*

Something metallic scraped along the ground. To her right. She swung—and missed again, then reflexively ducked just as a gunshot roared.

Bastard picked up Darcy's gun!

Alexa rolled, feigned one direction, then darted, head down, back toward the darker patch in her vision. The open door. Another shot whizzed after her, another miss.

He's still such a waste, she thought giddily, and then she burst through the door. Scrambled to the right now, plunging into the deeper darkness. Racing ahead, then making a right-angle turn. With her back against the big pillar she knew was there, she held the cane's blade up before her face, inhaling the scent of his blood. She held her breath and listened.

Listened for the tentative footsteps that came slowly, inching out into the gloom.

Into her element.

Come and get me, son.

55

Nothing to live for. That was it. The answer to the question she had been asking herself for almost two weeks now.

After Paul, there was nothing left.

Or was there? She did have this new family. Gabriel, and the others. Bound up together with a shared past, a terrible crime done to them. *But who was left?* For all she knew, those two in the next room were it, and Alexa Pearl was surely coming back to finish them off. And Gabriel... he was probably dead by now.

Nothing to live for.

She balanced once more on the railing. This, she promised the voices, would be the last time. She hefted herself up amid their thunderous clamoring, all of them encouraging her, urging her on, promising pleasures of all kinds at the end of her descent.

Just jump...

But mixed in with the voices were two others. Clearer, sharper. Laced with urgency, desperation. "Monica!" A woman's voice. Then a young man's: "Don't!"

In answer, the diabolic host of voices rose, rumbling over the interlopers. Monica wanted to tell them to relax, to reassure them of her steadfastness. She was going, damn it, she was going. Pulling herself up now to her knees.

I'm coming, Paul. She opened her eyes and looked up to the muted remnants of the stained glass overhead. What remained was still so beautiful, and what it revealed beyond—even more crystalline and kaleidoscopic. So heavenly, so Real. *I'm coming. I—*

Something jolted through her body, an electrical pulse thousands of volts strong. Two small barbs punched through the back of her sweater. . Her muscles seized up, her legs gave out, and she slid backwards.

Landing on the wet carpet, she looked up as the stained glass whirled around the faces of two angels bending over her.

And then everything went dark.

56

Gabriel slid on his knees in his mother's blood; felt for her pulse and choked back a cry. He closed her wide-open eyes. He couldn't help but stare at her face—at the huge, lingering grin and Alexa's blood still glistening on Darcy's teeth.

Forcing himself into action, he reached over her and grabbed the bag Indra had given him. Zipped it open, rummaged inside and found what he was looking for. He slipped the night-vision goggles over his head and flicked the switch. Raising the .45, he stood, kicked off his shoes, lowered his head and, with a burning in his heart, for the first time in his life truly wishing death upon someone, he strode out into the green-tinted darkness.

ALEXA HEARD HIM COMING. She gripped the cane with sweaty palms and tried to control her breathing. This was where her lifetime of practice would truly pay off. Every other sense was on high alert, acutely aware of every sound, touch, sensation. Every smell. Even the taste of the air betrayed its currents, the movements of someone scurrying about.

He was coming.

Coming right for this pillar.

How?

Flashlight? She doubted it. She had moved quick enough, weaving and blending into the shadows, sliding from pillar to pillar, having them all memorized.

Lucky guess? Probably. Although...

Her bare toes flexed on the floor, digging around in the grime and dust.

The dust...

Damn.

GABRIEL FOLLOWED THE FOOTPRINTS, so clear in the green-tinted haze. The little toes, the arches and small heel marks. A living roadmap pressed into the blurry dust. God bless her fanaticism for secrecy down here, limiting access to only her select few, excluding even the janitors.

Picking up his pace, he followed, looking ahead, watching the trail. Around this pillar, jogging to the next. Large strides here, baby-steps there. Weaving in and around and then...

He stopped. Studied the tracks below him. It seemed these were different somehow. Heavier, like two feet had been pressed into each print.

He looked up. Listened. Looked down again, staring at the marks.

Was she that smart, that precise? Thinking ahead, expecting him to be able to see with a flashlight? Could she have so precisely recreated her steps? And done it while walking backward? And blind?

Impossible. But...

He backed up suddenly, hearing a very slight sound, a low, barely audible breath.

Something flashed in his green-tinted lenses; it whistled

through the air, a swipe that would have slashed open his throat. But Gabriel had turned, spun and saw Alexa, crazed with those bulging white eyes, snarling face, her mouth open in a silent death-cry. She had come bursting out of the shadows. The cane above her head, bearing down on him again.

We can't kill her...

His own words came back at him. But he had no chance to think. He squeezed the trigger. The recoil knocked him back as he cringed, expecting Alexa's downward thrust to skewer him anyway. They would both die together; father and son, their blood filling one pool, their hands at each other's throats until their lives ebbed away.

But the impact knocked Alexa off her feet and sent her reeling back. She slammed into a pillar and slid down slowly, as if in slow motion. Finally, she just sat there, legs open, mouth wide. She said something Gabriel didn't catch in the echoing gun blast.

He crawled toward her, keeping the weapon pointed at her face.

The cane rolled away from her fingers, and her head tilted until he was sure she was looking right into his eyes.

She grunted, coughed up something dark, and felt along her breast for the neat hole above her heart. "Nice shot, boy." She coughed again. "But you haven't won."

Gabriel slid closer. He put down the gun. Reached for her. Could he try CPR? Close the wound...?

"Goodbye, son." Another cough. Voice getting weaker.

"Dad..." Gabriel leaned in close.

She spoke again, and it sounded like *him*. Like Atticus. His voice at last, ripping through Alexa's, asserting itself, mocking him. "You don't have a clue. You think it's over."

A grunting sound that passed for laughter. And then her head flopped back and lolled to the side. She toppled over and lay motionless.

Gabriel stood up, hanging his head but watching her still, as if expecting the night-vision sight to pick up the spirit leaving her body, to see it emerging, then coiling like a snake and fixing him with its red eyes before devouring itself.

57

The storm continued to rage for another five hours, dumping three more feet of snow over northern Vermont before finally, exhausted, and rightfully proud of its work, the clouds broke just in time for the sun to set over the slate blue dunes, the drifts blanketing the hills and frosting the mountains.

The plows began their work, and the roads gradually opened again. The cleanup crews worked all night on downed power lines and frozen generators. Daedalus operated, still in the dark, until the next morning when, finally, help began to arrive. Cell phone service came on again around three in the morning, and the calls started going out.

Daedalus operated, but just barely. Patients and staff alike were clamoring for answers to questions that went ignored.

In that time, the short time he had before the authorities arrived, Gabriel got a lot done.

Fortunately, he had very qualified help. Virisha Velanati, Indra's sister, had returned before dusk; and she brought friends. Men who cleared away the dead, including her poor brother, keeping the bodies in the garage, where it was cold like a morgue. Soon, there would be a flood of questions, investigations. Inquiries.

Monica was safe, other than suffering the trauma of being struck with a Taser; the same for Jake. Kaitlin's bullet was removed at the infirmary, and she was stitched up and resting.

After ascertaining the health of the three patients he was most concerned with, Gabriel assigned his most trusted aides to watch over them, to keep them in his office and tranquilize Monica only if necessary to prevent her from harming herself. Assured of their safety, he went back to the vault. He opened the files, then accessed the video and audio recordings, and found what he needed.

The words. The technique. The way Alexa did it. He watched and listened, over and over. Her session with Franklin in the infirmary had been caught on tape and, if he enhanced the volume, he could just make it out. And thanks to her paranoia, and the bugging of Gabriel's own office with a camera and recorder, he was able to listen in on Jake's regression.

Confident finally that he had it, he left the vault, looking ruefully first at the section from the *Books of the Dead*, the giant hieroglyphics poised in ancient defiance, unrepentant to the last.

Then he went upstairs and, fighting the vile taste at the back of his mouth, took his patients under. Dug deep, as Alexa would have said. He found and forced entry into that part of themselves his father had violated, trespassing into their sacred cores. For Monica, it wasn't too difficult to just remove the implanted suicidal suggestion that Alexa had left inside her mind. But for Kaitlin he struggled, having to stop and start several times, and eventually taking more than two hours. He wandered around the structures erected by his father, but in the end, he found the locked vault in her mind. The initial implant, the hourglass.

And he helped her destroy it. Freed her at last. Cured her.

But in Kaitlin he found something interesting and unexpected: that she and Jake shared some kind of past-life, built-in attraction toward each other. It hadn't been fostered there by his father as it had with the others—this compulsion to recognize and obsess about each other.

He had to conclude, in this case, it was something different, something more powerful than anything one could create by pure intention. And the look on their faces as they gazed at each other now was proof enough of something just as miraculous. When they had been brought here before, in 1976, they had been drawn to each other, had fallen in love... and it was something that crossed over two more lifetimes, still just as strong— perhaps because it was an unfulfilled, prematurely broken love the first time.

A different kind of unfinished business, Gabriel thought wistfully.

He sat now in his office, with three candles burning, one for each of his guests. Monica stood near the windows, looking out, marveling at the first sunrise she'd seen in two days. Jake and Kaitlin sat on the big leather couch, holding hands, looking into each other's eyes as if they thought the dream would abruptly end if they glanced away.

Gabriel picked up the walkie-talkie and held down the speaker button. "Virisha? Are you ready?"

"Yes. I'm in the vault. Tell me when."

He released the button and looked around the room. "It's up to you three. It's your lives we're talking about."

"Our *past* lives," Jake said with a loopy grin. "So... not really ours."

"And I say we let them rest," Kaitlin whispered. "I don't want to know any more."

Monica looked away from her reflection in the window. "What do you think, Doctor?"

Gabriel took a breath. He needed sleep, that's what he thought. But there was still so much to do. "I think this is too big a decision for me. The files are there, the links... indisputable, I believe. If you want to know about yourselves... I can't stand in the way."

"No," Monica said. "Screw it. This is the life we have. The people in those files... They had their shot. It's our turn now."

Jake raised a fist. "Right on, sister."

"Then we're in agreement?" Gabriel asked. After each one nodded, he pressed the button again. "Virisha? Burn it. Destroy everything down there. Including the artifacts."

Her voice crackled back to them.

"With pleasure."

⏳

WHEN VIRISHA CAME BACK UP to the office, nearly an hour later, Jake and Kaitlin turned to her enthusiastically.

"We need your help for one more thing," Kaitlin said.

Jake looked down at his boots. "But first—we're so sorry. Again. About your brother, about everything, and—"

She smiled. "Don't feel sad for him. He often told me how he knew, from an early age, that this was to be his last life. His last turn at the wheel. I always laughed, of course. So did my brothers. He was Indra. Always with his head in the stars. But... now I believe him."

"I do, too," said Kaitlin.

Jake coughed to break the mood. "But here's what we wanted to know. I saw the bang-up job you did for Kaitlin on her new passport and stuff, and I was wondering..."

"Ah."

Jake blushed. "I've got this little problem with the law. And, you know..."

"I do." Virisha smiled. "We'll take care of it. You'll have a new identity by noon."

"Sweet."

"No problem. But tell me, anywhere in particular you want to live? I'll create the driver's license for you that way, and—"

"No," Jake said. "Nowhere special. We..." he glanced back to

Kaitlin's eyes. "We were thinking of maybe moving to Central America. Get a nice place in Belize or something."

"Somewhere," Kaitlin added, "without a lot of faces to look at every day."

🕐

AFTER ANOTHER CUP OF COFFEE, Gabriel decided to head downstairs and prepare his staff for the arrival of the authorities. Time to test his leadership. Whether Daedalus would survive or not wasn't his biggest concern, and yet to lose it now would be like a final blow, the last laugh of Atticus Sterling.

No, he would fight for it. Alexa would take the fall, rightfully, for everything that happened here tonight. Only, the whole truth could never be known. He took a deep breath and prepared to leave the room, when someone took his hand in hers.

"I was thinking," Monica said quietly. "You might need some help around here. For a little while at least."

His smile broke free. "Technically, you're still a dangerous woman. Under the judge's ruling, you have to remain here in my care."

"I can accept that." Her eyes twinkled with a dull . "You know, the world doesn't have to know I'm cured."

"No, they don't. Although, with your history and what you've been through, you could be an invaluable asset to this facility. A sympathetic ear, someone who could help me connect with the patients and understand their suffering, and—"

"I accept," she said, squeezing his hand tighter.

Gabriel found himself responding, drawing strength from her touch.

"Good," he said. But before he closed the door behind them, Jake stuck his head through. "Uh, doc? You've still got some unfinished business, don't you?"

Wordlessly, Monica and Gabriel both nodded.

Jake smiled. "Then don't forget. Find a way to end it. Make sure it's over, that he, she—whatever—isn't coming back again."

Gabriel's palm started to sweat, and he knew Monica could feel his tension. She turned to him, looked into his eyes, and as the door closed and they were left alone in the hall, he found himself bending down to meet her lips.

When they broke away, Monica blinked and said, "Let's go. I've got some ideas on what we need to do."

"We have time," he responded.

"I don't think you want to wait."

"You're right," he said. "One thing, at least, that I share with my father. I don't like unfinished business."

EPILOGUE

Boston
Twenty-Two Years Later

M'buru Alfonsen made his way across the cemetery on a brisk October afternoon. He had on a threadbare hooded sweatshirt and a pair of ripped jeans he had owned for the past six years, bartering for them off a tourist back in Uganda.

He was a long, long way from home. But he couldn't help it. Last year, on his twenty-first birthday, something amazing had happened. A series of undeniably powerful dreams, accompanied by a compulsion: an urgent, uncontrollable need to come here. To Boston.

To this cemetery. To this mausoleum, the very one in his dreams.

He had done bad things, very bad things to get here. He had been a religious boy growing up, from a strict Catholic family. He had lost two brothers and a sister to malnutrition and disease. He had nothing, and his parents, old and weak themselves, needed him to beg the streets, to work where he could, doing whatever he could, to bring them food.

But after the dreams, he had no choice but to leave his parents to fend for themselves; he started on what he knew would be a long and desperate trip. He had stolen. Beaten and robbed people. He did things he would never think of again, but finally, he had made it here. All that effort to wind up at this place of death.

What could be calling him here?

To this single brick, this off-color brick in the tomb of this man—Silas Berger, dead for over a hundred years. This brick, set about waist-high. He knew from his dream that he needed to push the three bricks around it in succession, then push and pull back the brick itself.

He did so, and it released with a hiss, grinding slowly out from the others. He brought it back, looked down into the hollow space, and reached for the tiny thing lying inside.

An old business card, the paper browned and aged. With a cool breeze on his face and dry leaves crackling along the headstones, he read the words right next to the engraved image of an hourglass. Those words made no sense to him, but he recognized the second line as an address.

Someplace in Vermont.

MONICA WAITED with a pounding heart for the elevator doors to open. Five flights down from her office, she was finally at the lobby.

The doors opened and she came out into glimmering sunlight sparkling off the polished marble floors. She walked gingerly, favoring her left leg as her arthritis was acting up today. As far as pain went, though, this was nothing. She had suffered much worse.

"Mrs. Sterling," said the receptionist upon seeing her. "He's right over there, in the lounge."

Mrs. Sterling. She never got tired of hearing that. And after years of hearing it, years of living with the freedom of sight, years spent recapturing and reliving her lost life with a man who adored her, she finally felt like she had become Real.

There was a point to life, the everyday struggle to go on. To pick yourself up, lift your head, and to look to the future with hope.

"Thank you," she told the receptionist. "Go and find Dr. Sterling. He's probably in the library again. Find him and tell my husband that the person we've been expecting has arrived. Dr. Sterling will know what that means. Tell him to meet us up in my office."

Monica opened the door to the lounge and greeted her visitor. The young man with the scared, haunted eyes. She nearly wept at the sadness and confusion she saw in his face.

"Hello," she said. "I see you found our card."

"Yes," he answered, glancing around nervously. "But... I do not understand."

Monica smiled and shook her head. "You don't need to. Come." She put her arm around his shoulders and led him out into the hall. "Come up to my office. We'll talk for a bit. I want to hear about your life. And then, I want you to listen to me. To my voice."

"Why?"

"Believe me," Monica said, her eyes cold and determined. "You'll like what I have to say."

Printed in the USA
CPSIA information can be obtained
at www.ICGtesting.com
LVHW030926080824
787693LV00001B/17